GRAVES
IN THE
WILDERNESS

J.R. GORDON

AUTHOR BIOGRAPHY

Born in 1952, JR rushed through his school years, leaving for adventure at the age of fourteen. There was a vast and mysterious world out there to be explored. Before his twentieth birthday he had experienced the blast of fierce desert dust storms; the biting chill of blizzards; the steaming heat of jungles and the vastness of the great oceans during his quest to rediscover an already discovered world.

An adventurer, JR has experienced the shanty camps of the Australian outback, shared meals with natives in some of the most remote jungles of the world, prospected forbidding and remote wildernesses, experienced the turmoil of war and the calm of peace. His insatiable hunger for adventure, discovery and new experiences has taken him to the far-flung corners of the globe to little-known destinations.

As diverse as his adventures is JR's employment and recreation history. Once a professional horseman, miner, boxer, athlete, soldier, police officer, local government politician, businessman and now writer make up the mosaic that is JR Gordon.

Published in Australia by Temple House Pty Ltd,
T/A Sid Harta Publishers ACN 092 197 192
Hartwell, Victoria

Telephone: 61 3 9560 9920,
Facsimile: 61 3 9545 1742
E-mail: author@sidharta.com.au

First published in Australia 2005
Copyright © J.R. Gordon, 2005
Cover design, typesetting:
Chameleon Print Design

The right of J.R. Gordon to be identified as the Author
of the Work has been asserted in accordance with the
Copyright, Designs and Patents Act 1988.

Gordon, J.R.
Graves in the Wilderness
ISBN: 1-921030-43-7
pp374

Author's Note

Almost all of the characters in this book existed at the times and places in which I have written of them. Almost all of the events of the book are as historically accurate as I have been able to record them. In both cases I used the word 'almost' because I have invented some of the major characters, and assembled others from hints and pieces, historic activities,personalities and outcomes, in order to tell the story.

In the course of writing this book I examined many conflicting contemporary reports. If some details vary from generally accepted views, it is because that's how history has and will always be recorded, that is, by personal perception, belief and interpretation of those present during the time of the event. It is the modern day writer's prerogative to slightly edit such interpretations in an attempt to remove or adjust redundant material.

I have visited the lands of East Texas, the roads and battlefields of the civil war, the wilderness of the Australian Cape York region and it's now quiet gold fields and scrub-gullies that once echoed the cry of the marauding Merkins as they were felled by rifles.

Time and commentary has blurred the line where fact meets fiction, so much so that their intermingling often goes undetected. The enmeshing of the two is my preferred perspective in producing this fictional novel.

DEDICATION

*Dedicated to Chubby, the kookaburra, who
watched on patiently as this novel was written
without uttering one word.*

Also …
special thanks to Mike and Lyn Hay,
Rob & Desni Muller
and Glen & Shirley Parker.

CHAPTER **ONE**

Mac reined his horse in, cocked his head to one side and tried to catch the sound again. Rob, at eighteen years, the Campbell's second-oldest boy, stopped beside him, while Piper, the thirteen-year-old baby of the Campbell family, lagged peacefully behind, casually scanning the brush for fresh cattle tracks.

'What?' Rob asked, noticing his father move uneasily in the saddle.

'Probably nothing,' Mac replied, his dust encrusted eyes piercing the brush ahead on each side of the cattle pad. 'Thought I heard someone yelling.'

The words had barely been uttered when his horse tensed, jerked its head high and with ears pricked, focused on the country before them.

'Piper!' Mac called over his shoulder in his broad Scottish accent. 'Up here, lad.'

It was clearer this time. There was no mistaking the sound ahead of them of someone screaming. 'Stay close, boys. Be ready to turn,' Mac said as they cantered, three abreast towards the sound of the screams.

Ascending a small rise, they stopped abruptly. Not fifty yards in front of them down a sharp embankment near a stream, lay the bodies of six mutilated blacks, distorted in death, their blood soaking into the sandy soil. Past them, a woman shielded a young girl with her frail body. A naked young black sprang from side to side wielding a wooden club and knife in a futile attempt to beat off the six mounted Comanche aggressors who galloped around the hapless three, screaming as they closed in. Charging forward, a Comanche's pony caught the young black defender in the chest sending him spinning to the ground. A second horseman swung his tomahawk with such accuracy and force that the blade all but severed the head of the woman, while a third, dismounting on the run, ended the young girl's life with two swift strokes of his knife.

Back on his feet, the young black, now alone, stood

to face the dismounted Comanche killer as the horsemen continued to cover them with dust while circling and yelping their war cry.

Mac was well aware that Indian war parties constantly engaged their foe in mortal combat and accepted that it was their way. What he was witnessing went beyond all reasonable rules of combat. The wanton slaughter of unarmed women and children sickened even the hardy Scott, so much so that his decision to intervene was immediate and uncompromising.

'Pistols, boys,' Mac commanded. 'Rob, to my left, Piper, with me. At the gallop,' he yelled as all three spurred their mounts forward, cocked pistols held high, reins loose as they charged towards the carnage. Mac's pistol exploded into action first, sending the. 36 calibre ball whistling past a Comanche rider's head. Not wishing to engage the charging riders, the five mounted Comanche turned and galloped off, each taking a different course to confuse the pursuers.

Firing as they rode, Mac and Rob passed the riderless horse and Comanche warrior on foot. Piper, riding high in the saddle, levelled his Colt at the Comanche and squeezed the trigger as he sped past. Reining his horse to a sudden stop, almost unseating him, Piper turned, took more deliberate aim and ended the fight with a shot to the head of the luckless brave.

Piper's heaving chest threatened to burst his shirt as he stared at the dead Comanche before him. It was the first time he had ever shot a man. He'd always been there to load and scout while the rest of his family fought off attackers and he'd seen plenty die, but now, it was his pistol that had done the killing. Adrenalin coursed through his veins at breakneck speed. Totally absorbed with the situation he didn't hear the return of his father and brother.

'Right, are you lad?' his father asked, not waiting for an answer before dismounting and surveying the scene about him.

'I'll be damned,' he muttered, looking at the young, half-starved, naked black before him; defiance burned in his young eyes as he stood over the dead woman, knife in hand. 'Couldn't be much older than you Piper; and a Karankawa to boot.'

'Thought they'd been shot out,' Rob said.

'So did I,' returned Mac. 'By the look of these skinny devils they've been on the run for a long time.' Turning to the young Karankawa he asked, 'Speak any English, son?'

There was no reply.

Now all dismounted, the three ranchers made moves to gather up the dead for burial. The young Karankawa refused their help and by doing so indicated his ability to speak fairly good English. It was clear that the young Karankawa would accept no assistance in the burial of his family as he went about dragging the corpses

4

together without acknowledging that the ranchers were even there. Accepting his wishes, Mac bid his sons to mount for the ride home. Piper, the last to leave, took a calico sack from his saddle bag and rode to the side of the Karankawa. Handing it down, he said, 'There's some jerky and corn bake here. You can have it now. When you're done tending to your folks graving, follow our tracks for three miles or so and cross the stream. Another mile on and you'll come to Argyll – that's our ranch house, you'll be welcome there, I'll see to that,' he promised.

Cantering slowly towards Argyll, Mac Campbell again silently questioned the wisdom of his decision to raise a family on America's newest and bloodiest frontier. His family, of the Clan Campbell of Argyll, Scotland, had moved to Ireland some years prior. Subsequently, Mac had arrived in America as an Ulster-Scott, a label he didn't particularly care much for but accepted none-theless. It guaranteed title to land in Texas in the fast growing Irish settlements that had sprung up in the East-Texas coastal regions near the Nueces River, its val-leys, plains and beyond to the high country and San Antonio.

Arriving in Texas during the late 1830's, Mac obtained several thousand acres of land on the Nueces River, a few miles from the outpost of San Patricio. Together with his new bride, Christine, the daughter of a well-to-do Rich-mond family they entered an era of destabilisation and hardship. Revolutionary activity between Mexico and

Texas saw San Praticio become all but a ghost town with most Anglo settlers moving to Refugio or even further north to escape the turmoil of war. A fiercely determined man, Mac held his ground and recruited Mexicans and local Indians to work his land grant. During the revolution he remained openly neutral. If the Mexicans arrived, he would feed them. If the Americans arrived, they too, would be fed. On occasions when they both arrived at the same time he would feed and tend the survivors. His position of neutrality and willingness to help undoubtedly saved his life on many occasion as battle after battle raged within yelling distance of his ranch.

The time of the American/Mexican War during the mid 1840's was no different. Revolution seemed to follow revolution as Americans and Europeans pushed further south to open new settlements and build on those already existing, none wishing to accept that Texas ended at the Nueces. By the end of the American/Mexican War, Mac had increased his land holdings from San Patricio well into the interior and almost as far as San Antonio. His labour force included Mexicans, Germans, Irish, Indians and Africans. His farming diversification saw crops being sown on a large scale although cattle remained his major concern.

It was during the American/Mexican War when Mac and Christine welcomed the arrival of their third son, Piper, a brother for Hamish and Rob. The frontier family Campbell was now complete but existing in an environment of war and absolute uncertainty.

'Best you don't tell your mother any detail of today's action, boys,' Mac said, as they crossed the shallow creek near Argyll. 'In fact, mention of the Karankawa's return to these parts wouldn't be well received, so best we keep quiet on that as well.'

'What do you think he'll do?' asked Piper, the young Karankawa standing over the remains of his dead family fixed clearly in his mind.

'Who knows,' Mac replied. 'I doubt we'll see him again.'

Cantering onwards, Mac recalled aloud his first contact with the Karankawa soon after his arrival in Texas. 'Only time I've ever been scared, I mean, scared enough to believe that I would be killed, was when our camp was attacked by Karankawa on our way to Argyll,' he said. 'Hell, they were as fierce as I've seen. Had to be all of six and a half feet tall, painted up and coming at us in the night firing those damn four-foot arrows of theirs.'

'Obviously missed you,' Piper laughed.

'Tell you what, I saw one of them things go clear through a horse's belly,' Mac continued. 'And then, when their arrows ran out they'd charge with knives and clubs and would only accept defeat when the lead inside them became too heavy for them to keep running.'

All three smiled and exchanged glances, heads shaking as they did. 'Never seen a man smell so bad, either,' Mac said. 'More alligator fat and mud on them than an alligator's got; and clothes … just didn't bother wearin' any. Kind of unsettling when you've got a six and a half foot black creature, greased head to toe, screaming like a ship's whistle, charging down on you and all you can see is the creature's privates bouncin' about in front of you.'

Smiles grew to laughter before Rob asked, 'So why did they all get shot out?'

'Fear,' Mac replied. 'Rumour has it that they are cannibals and will eat their enemy, dead or alive. That, combined with the damned awful smell of them and their fighting skills makes even the Comanche give them a wide berth. I'll tell you, their strength has been their biggest weakness. Become a threat and you become a target. Become a good target and sooner or later everyone wants to shoot at you.'

'How come they're black?' quizzed Piper.

'Said to come from somewhere else,' Mac answered. 'Hell, how do I know? Why are you white?'

Unsaddling their horses, Piper yelled across the yard to his mother. 'Comanche, Ma, up on the low creek near the old stone hut. We gave them something to talk about round the campfire,' he said taking the Colt out of its saddle-mounted holster.

'That right?' Christine replied in her southern drawl as she took the pail of milk from the mulatto girl.

'Nothin' serious,' Mac added quickly. 'They went their way and we went ours, not to say we shouldn't load extra tonight and keep some hands local to the house, just in case.'

Piper strode towards the house. He felt taller, stronger

and more purposeful than the thirteen year old that had ridden out a day ago to scout for stray cattle up river. The pistol in his hand didn't feel as heavy as it usually did and perhaps now he would be allowed to wear it on his belt like Rob, or Hamish, his Texas Ranger brother who was out there with the best, rounding up desperados and Comancheros. As his foot trod the first plank of the front steps his mind flashed back to the mutilated and gutted Karankawa; the near beheading of the woman and the vivid recollection of his shot splitting the head of the Comanche brave, spraying his blood and features wildly into the air behind him. He suddenly felt ill and trotted around the side of the house to vomit.

After a sleepless night, Piper rose earlier than the rest of the household and walked to the horse trough to wash, as birds sang their morning songs. The sun would rise soon, bringing with it another hot day in the fields and on the range. He waved the early morning bugs from his face and propped himself against the hitching rail, gazing out towards the river at nothing in particular and seeing the same. A deep, soft voice, usually soothing, startled him back to focus. 'Master Piper,' steadied the voice of Black Abraham, a long time family friend and stable hand. 'Are you worried about the boy?' he asked, gesturing towards the shape squatted in the scrub.

'Well, I'll be damned,' Piper whispered.

'Your momma will have you eatin' cold dinners for a week if she hear you cussin' like that.'

'The boy, how long has he been here?'

"Bout an hour, he got to hummin' some tune aways back and woke me and Mary so I went and told him to git,' Black Abraham answered. 'Trouble is, he tells me he want to give the young master his sack back. Well, I let him stay Master Piper 'cos he got your sack sure enough.'

'Wait here,' Piper said as he walked quickly towards the now recognisable young Karankawa. 'Don't be telling anyone he's here, Okay?' he yelled back over his shoulder.

Black Abraham nodded. 'Best you put some breaches on the boy. Don't want no young buck runnin' about Argyll with his ass bare as my old head.'

Piper approached and cautiously squatted in front of him. 'Piper,' he said in the best adult voice he could muster. 'My name's Piper. What's yours?'

Staring through eyes as black as coal, the expressionless visitor sat taller before answering. 'Diego, my name is Diego but my father called me N'Kawa.'

'Okay,' Piper replied trying to disguise his excitement. 'I think Diego is fine?'

Diego nodded slowly and held out his hand that clutched the calico sack which Piper had given him the day before. 'I return your belongings,' he said.

Taking the loaded sack, Piper said, 'So you didn't eat the food, huh?'

'Yes, *gracias*,' he replied.

Confused, Piper eagerly put his hand into the sack

to clarify Diego's meaning. Not recognizing the shape or feel of the object hidden in the sack, Piper removed it for examination. 'Holy shit,' he yelled, leaping to his feet, instinctively throwing the object away. Wiping his hands on his shirt he shouted, 'That's a God-damn human hand you heathen bastard, a God-damn hand!'

'Not human, Comanche hand,' Diego corrected.

'It's a damn hand, a human hand,' a now quieter Piper scolded, still standing looking down at Diego. 'Hell, not only is it a hand, it's a cooked hand. Sheeeit, I can't believe it.'

'You killed the owner of that hand, it is rightfully yours. The other hand killed my mother and my sister so I have eaten that one … but because you acted bravely, this one I saved for you.'

'I don't want the damn hand, shit, Texans don't eat hands, cannibals eat hands,' Piper said.

Before they could continue the quietly heated discussion, the dog quickly grabbed the parched hand and ran off towards the barn, tail wagging. 'Oh shit,' Piper hissed in despair. 'If she doesn't eat that or bury it quick, you and me, Diego, are gonna be in more shit than a bogged Longhorn.'

Everyone stayed quite close to home for the next few days. It was agreed that Diego could stay with them for as long as he wanted. He was fed back to health quickly and being around the same age as Piper, he assimilated well and gave every indication that he would stay and become part of the Campbell family. A special room was

11

annexed to the barn and within a month, both Diego and Piper shared the room, always under the watchful eye of Black Abraham.

Each night, Diego would rid himself of clothes, smear his body with ash from the fires and disappear towards the creek for an hour or so, returning clean and refreshed. This continued for almost three months until Diego told Piper that the period of mourning had ended. Surprising Piper even further, Diego ran back to the site of his family's massacre and returned in the morning with a long-bow, two dozen arrows, a skin belt with knife and club and two leather-thonged necklaces threaded through stone and bone fragments. Giving one of the necklaces to Piper, he explained that it was from his dead brother, made by his grandmother. The other belonged to his father. By accepting the gift, Piper, in the eyes of Diego, became his half brother.

Winter passed quickly. Christine's long hours of expert tutoring saw Diego transforming into a young Texan with above average reading and writing skills. His halting Hispanic/Indian tongue had given way to the Texan drawl with an almost romantic hint of Span-ish. Although not overly concerned, Christine often commented to Mac that she sensed an internal rage smouldering beneath Diego's calm exterior.

The Campbell herd had grown and their crops expanded. The addition of a small but productive hog farm proved a winner with hog meat being sold to the nearby German camps and the townships of San Patricio,

Corpus Christi, and even Victoria. As the northern regions were colonized, Indian groups continued to harass travellers, outlying homesteads and ranches. The traditional landlords from the north mainly Kiowa and Comanche were driven south and into the area of the Nueces. Food was becoming scarce for the displaced Indians and so it came as no surprise that their attacks became more frequent.

Piper and Diego became inseparable. As their workload allowed, they would go off for days at a time hunting and scouting the countryside. Piper learned the way of the Karankawa-their beliefs, lifestyle, way of life and death. He became an expert tracker and could stalk prey, animal or human, as well as any plains hunter. On an expedition into the swampland Piper mastered the deadly Karankawa six foot longbow and killed his first alligator. Diego also taught him the art of wrestling, a favourite pastime of the Karankawa.

Diego had also learned well. Although preferring to walk, he soon became an expert horseman. Unable to adjust to the heavy cowboy boots worn by the ranchers, he had a pair of calf-high moccasins made up. His loin cloth was replaced by breaches and a fine buckskin shirt covered his upper body. The way he looked, sitting astride his horse, Comanche footwear, buffalo scout shirt and the wide brim of the Texan hat shading his finely featured black face, caused more than the occasional comment from passers by and neighbours.

One of the townsfolk asked when the Campbells had

visited for supplies, 'Mac, where'd you say that black boy was from again?'

'Washed up a way's back. Seems he comes from a land in the southern oceans. They apparently look like he does, talk like he does and, well, they're just like him, apparently. Poor little bugger, couldn't just leave him out there for the gators, so we fetched him home to Argyll,' Mac replied.

'So he ain't a nigra?' the questioner continued. 'Or is they nigras at that place he comes from?'

'Hell no,' Mac drawled as Piper and Diego listened and continued to go about loading the wagon. 'They speak Spanish and English, same as most of us. Said to live in fine mansions and take nigra slaves same as we do.'

Confused, the busybody nodded slowly before taking one last questioning look at Diego, who acknowledged with a tooth-flashing smile, followed by, 'Good day to you sir,' in his now perfect Texan drawl.

Word soon spread that Diego was the sole survivor of a shipwreck and hailed from a noble black race in a far-off land. It was a rumour worth the spreading. Had the townsfolk known that the Campbells were harbouring a Karankawa, a race that very few settlers had encountered, but learned about around the campfire, there would most certainly been some form of retribution. There was no doubt that sailors plying the coastal ports scoffed at the story offered by Mac, but nobody contested the story in earnest.

The summer of 1859 was drawing to a close. The eldest Campbell boy, Hamish had returned home with two of his Texas Ranger companions. The news they brought came as no surprise. 'I'll tell you all now,' he said, as the clan gathered around the fireplace. 'Before we see another winter through we'll be fighting the Yankees as well as the Indians.'

Later, calling Piper and Diego to one side he gave a more sombre parcel of news. 'Now this will sadden you, Diego,' he consoled. 'We heard only last week that a group of your people were gunned down crossing the Rio Grande into Texas, out towards the coast. I'm sorry.'

'Comanche?' queried Diego, staring at the floor boards.

'No, ranchers.'

'That was the other group, second to our group,' Diego muttered almost to himself. 'If they are all gone, then I am the only Karankawa left.'

A late supper was taken in silence as everyone dealt with the news about Diego's people and the impending conflict with the North. They all knew that their short years of prosperity would soon be over … replaced by chaos.

The following morning, after bidding Hamish farewell, a trip to town was planned. Ammunition and supplies needed to be restocked. It wouldn't be long before every saddle and every room in the homestead sported a Maynard carbine. Rising fifteen, Piper received his first holstered Colt to compliment the one holstered to his saddle. Diego refused to wear a holster but accepted the carbine and saddle-mounted Colt, both of which he had learned to use expertly.

With each passing day, war with the North became more and more inevitable. Politicians called on their respective electorates to prepare themselves while military commanders plotted and planned. Regiments were formed and moved to strategic locations. Ranches were depleted of their manpower as young cowboys opted for the excitement and adventure of possible conflict with the sassy Yankees up north.

Comanche, Kiowa and Comancheros constantly scouted the ranches and far-flung communities, watching with interest as the young cowboys headed off to enlist in various military organizations, leaving behind their vulnerable families. In small groups, they started to camp closer to the homesteads than they'd ever done before. By day they would approach the homesteads seeking food, only to be chased off. By night they returned, taking the food they had been refused. If discovered stealing the food, they were summarily executed by the ranchers.

As the rest of the family slept, Mac Campbell sat on the verandah rocker, alone with his thoughts. He knew what was coming, a war within a war. Without the protection of the cowboys and Texas Rangers, the Indians would seize the opportunity and commence all-out war on white settlers. While he had remained on Argyll during the war with Mexico, a dozen or so years ago, he

wasn't as confident now. His neutrality was being questioned, even from within his own family. As far as they
were concerned, Texas was a State that had the ability
to choose her own path and if that included the use of
slave labour, then so be it. If the Yankees in the north
took to meddling in Texas affairs, then they had better
be ready for an argument.

As the sun gave its first flicker of light to the morning sky, Mac, still alone with his thoughts, listened to
the birds as he tapped his pipe on his boot heel. He
wondered how long it would be before the quiet of
morning would be shattered by the blast of canons and
the screaming of shells overhead … how long?

CHAPTER **TWO**

Christmas dinner at the Argyll Ranch was a sombre affair in 1860. Try as she might, Christine could not coax the family into their usually festive spirit. At her insistence, the black labour had all been given two days off and an ample feast provided under the guidance of their trusted overseer, Black Abraham

'C'mon Campbells,' she urged in her best Southern-belle voice. 'The fiddler and the McCarthys will arrive soon, we're gonna have ourselves the best fandango ever. It ain't the end of the world, it's Christmas!'

'Christmas sure enough,' Mac said, 'but the end of the world bit, well, that may be open to question. Reckon it's ended now, least ways the world as we knew it. Lincoln as President and South Carolina seceding, you mark my words, there's big trouble ahead.'

He was right. With the election of Lincoln in the North came the promise of emancipation. Although an incorrect perception, emancipation to the Southerners meant the abolition of slavery and thus the end of their workforce.

'So what's Lincoln gonna do, Mac? Come down here and steal our workers? Huh?' Christine quizzed with raised brow.

'Already doing it, Ma,' entered Rob. 'Yankee do-gooders have been crossing into Southern States for months now, stealing slaves, taking them north and giving them their papers.'

'True enough, Chrissie,' Mac added with a slow nod of his head.

'Well, I'll tell you now, it's a fact for sure; our black workers won't have any of that. They're treated like our own and will do right by us,' said Christine firmly.

'I know that Chrissie, everyone in these parts does, but they may not be given the option. But let's not dwell on it, hey? Let's do as we're told and enjoy us a good ol' Texas ho-down!'

Cheered somewhat, the Campbell Clan set about concentrating on Christmas. What would be would be, and there was precious little they could do to halt the looming conflict.

Despite the civil unrest that prevailed, Mac continued to build Argyll. There were now several outposts on the ranch and the homestead had taken on an air of grandeur with the addition of more formalised entrance roads and gardens. He'd worked hard for what he had and was proud of it; proud too of his wife and sons who had stood by him, even when times were grim. Skirmishes with local Indian groups never came to much and became as much a part of range life as branding cattle. The Indians knew that they were outgunned and knew also that the Campbell Clan would never see a hungry woman or child pass by without offering some food. Their position with the Indians, even the warring Comanche, could be called a truce, albeit a flimsy one.

Mac had found a good market for his produce via a group of German settlers. It was agreed that treated pork and jerked beef could make up a quota the Germans couldn't meet for supplying ships that visited the coastal ports. It was not lucrative but a good steady income that was guaranteed cash money on supply, not from the ships, but from the Germans who held the contract. On the odd occasion, Mac would accompany the wagons into Corpus Christie. It was always a good break away from the daily ranch chores and a chance to buy hardware direct from the importers at the Port. The wagon line never complained about having another rifle riding with them as bandits often lay in wait along the trail.

After a couple of arduous months working the cattle, Mac decided that Rob, Piper and Diego deserved a trip with the wagons to the port. Piper and Diego, now almost sixteen, were under strict instructions to stay close to Rob and be respectful to his wishes. A new sewing box was to be picked up from the Eastern Traders, a present for Christine.

Piper and Diego joked about how they would spend their night in the city. There'd be dancing and drinking in the saloons, and women? Well, they'd be tripping over themselves to get at them, they laughed, mindful all the while of the shaking head of Rob. The trip ended soon enough without incident and the trio set about securing the order for their mother.

After settling the account, the three walked to the wharf store where the sewing box was to be collected. Entering the store, Rob handed a paper chit to the storeman. After some fussing and yelling out back, a wharfer, a burly man wearing the facial testimony of many a drunken brawl, appeared at the side door and yelled, 'Hey, nigger, get yer ass out here and tend to this box!'

The three Campbells, two white and one black, looked at each other with inquiring looks.

'You, nigger, c'mon, I ain't got all damn day. Get out here,' commanded the wharfer again, looking directly at Diego.

Silence fell over the men in the store. Diego, his black eyes burning into those of the wharfer, held his ground and said nothing.

'You insolent black son-of-a-bitch,' scolded the wharfer as he approached Diego. 'If these hayseeds ain't gonna straighten you out, I sure as hell will.'

Before he'd taken two paces forward Piper had released the thong on his Colt and had the pistol in his hand, levelled directly at the wharfer's forehead. 'The next step, sir,' he said calmly, 'will be the last you take on Gods earth.'

Not wishing to call the bluff of the young Texas roughneck with a pistol, the wharfer stopped. 'Nigger lover are you,' he chided. 'We got ways of dealing with your type.'

'Enough,' Rob interrupted. 'Put the gun away, Piper, and you sir,' looking towards the wharfer, 'you'll be good enough to have your men take the box out to the wagon. That way this wee misunderstanding is soon forgotten.'

'If it's all the same with everyone here,' Diego said, surprising the wharfer and the Campbells, 'I'd just as soon shake the gentleman's hand and assist with the box.'

'Hah,' yelled the wharfer with a sneer on his battered face. 'There ya go, done trained yer damn nigger for ya!'

Smiling, Diego thrust forward his hand and grasped the huge leathery paw of the wharfer. In an instant, Diego's right foot had levelled a solid kick to his groin. The second kick, an instant later connected with his dropping face, snapping his head backwards. Before his knees could buckle beneath him, Diego pulled him forward, turned to the right and hip threw him high into the air and then crashing to the floor with an almighty thud.

Pain burned like fire in the wharfer's brain as he tried

to right himself, only to be met by a calm and deadly serious Diego, crouching near his head, blade in hand.

'Sir,' Diego whispered. 'Although sore, your balls are still attached to your body. If your attitude towards me changes for the better you will remain a man with balls, otherwise, you will not,' he added, quickly re-sheathing his knife. Before rising, he clapped his open hands on either side of the wharfer's head, almost exploding his eardrums.

Hurriedly collecting the box themselves, the three departed the store, leaving the storeman with his mouth agape and the wharfer writhing in agony on the floor. 'Best we travel at night this time,' Rob commanded as they loaded the box aboard the wagon and headed quickly back towards their horses.

That night they camped on a dry creek bed on the outskirts of town waiting to rejoin the other wagons for the trip home. There was a deal of soul searching with no resolve. Diego, like it or not, even with the Campbell name, would always be a nigger in the eyes of those who chose to call it, especially in the South. There was no legitimate argument that could convince Diego otherwise. At Argyll he was a Texan; in his heart he was Karankawa but to the world, he was just plain nigger. Perhaps, he thought, it would be better to assume his true identity and continue his life in the tradition of his forefathers, but he knew that such a life would be very short-lived.

It was late February, 1861, when the Campbell's learned that Texas had seceded from the Union along with Florida, Alabama, Georgia, Louisiana, Mississippi and South Carolina. The smoulder had ignited a flame that rapidly turned into a roaring fire as Union Forts in the seceding states were seized by enforcers. Jefferson Davis was sworn in as provisional President for the Confederate States followed by President Lincoln's Inauguration in the North. Lincoln was quick to spell out that he held no intention to end slavery in those states where slavery existed, but the South did not believe him. Lincoln also trumpeted his intention not to accept secession from any state and believed that the secession movement could be halted, but it was too late.

Each rider passing Argyll brought fresh news of developments to the North. More Union forts were being seized or surrendered; the Union promised retribution and the Indians, bemused by the frenetic pace of events, sat quietly on the sideline watching and waiting. Some of the Mexican labour at Argyll took their families and left for Mexico after tearful goodbyes with Christine who treated her Mexican and Negro workers as extended family. Cowhands, loyal to the Campbells, also sought their leave and rode north up the Cotton Trail in an attempt to meet the Yankees at the border and show them what real men were made of.

Word of the taking of Fort Sumter by Confederate forces arrived at Argyll during the summer of 1861, hotly followed by the news that Virginia, Arkansas and North Carolina had joined the Confederate States. The States of Kentucky, Maryland, Delaware and Missouri, although not seceding from the Union, were slave states and could be counted on by the South to lend a hand if the going got rough … which it most certainly would.

Hamish Campbell had sent word back to Argyll that his Texas Ranger unit had been deployed further north. Christine sat on the verandah reading the crumpled piece of paper delivered by an army dispatch.

Dear Ma and family,

You will now know that the war between us and the North is well underway. Our Rangers are up here watching the border but as yet we haven't needed to do anything drastic. I've been made Captain and am sure proud of that. The country up this way is kinder in summer than East Texas and there is plenty of food to be had from the agreeable farmers. We had the true pleasure of meeting up with Colonel Benjamin Terry who is signing up volunteers for a Ranger Unit to join the war further north. Colonel Terry was lucky enough to see action at Manassas a few months back and is no doubt a fine leader of men. I am to meet up with him in Virginia next month to join the Eighth Texas Cavalry but we are assured that we will still be Texas Rangers. Tell Pa, Rob, Piper and that rascal Diego hello. Tell Black Abraham hello as well. I'll be home soon enough.

Your loving son,
Hamish Campbell

Tears coursed down Christine's cheeks as she folded the letter and tucked it into her shirt. Black Abraham shoo'd a couple of laughing kids as they played with a rope near the verandah. In the distance she saw the boys, her boys, riding in from a hard days work on the ranch. Their horses seemed to float through the shimmering haze that distorted their legs as they floated ghostlike towards her. An unwelcome cold shiver invaded her as she brushed the tears from her face.

That night as they lay in bed, Mac slowly caressed Christine's head, running his callused fingers gently through her hair. 'Y'know, Chrissie,' he said. 'There's talk that Davis will introduce conscription.'

'Oh, I don't think so. Hamish seems to think that it's all a lot of political posturing and this little war thing will be over before it starts.'

'Well that may be, but look at the logistics of it,' Mac replied. 'The North outnumbers us around three to one, they have the equipment and the factories and they don't really need to rely on foreign trade like we do.'

'I also hear that most sensible folk in the North don't want the war,' Christine said. 'They've already said that we can keep our black labour and that the money earned from our European exports will grow the North as well. I'd like to believe that the war will be no more than a skirmish in Virginia, or thereabouts.'

'Perhaps you're right,' Mac sighed. 'Perhaps you're right.'

In the bunkhouse, similar conversations were taking place. Was it to be a skirmish or a war? The barn annex that housed Piper and Diego emitted the cool glow of a lamp as they too pondered the fate of the North and South.

Black Abraham had already discussed the possibility of an all out war between North and South with the field hands. They were a generation of African slaves that had worked and lived at Argyll for most of their lives. Treated well and never flogged for misdemeanours, they enjoyed an existence far removed from that of their cousins in the Northernmost of the Southern States.

'Far as I can make out,' Black Abraham told his kin, 'You wants to leave, then you just up and leaves, and master Mac don't do no chasin' of you. Ain't no hounds gonna bother you nor whips cuttin' your back, but may-haps you tell ol' Black Abe where y'all be runnin' to?'

It was a point well made and one well taken. For as long as they stayed at Argyll, they would be treated well and could bring their children up with good food and work for them when they were old enough; not just work, but paid work. Mac had promised Black Abraham that any discipline was to be a matter for him and him alone. Black Abraham had dealt out plenty of discipline with the receiver protesting that it was better if master Mac dealt with them; but it was a system that worked and so a system that prevailed.

All of that was now threatened by uncertainty, from all quarters.

The Indian build-up near the homestead had reached a point where it had become alarming. Comanche camp-fires could be seen at night from Argyll homestead which unsettled Christine. Cattle were being stolen each day and herded inland to the hill country where Comanche and Comanchero groups camped. It was only safe to ride the ranch in company of four or more, and even then, armed so heavily that normal cattle farming could not be carried out effectively. Crops were being stripped in broad daylight by Comanche women and children who were sent into the crops, knowing that the Campbells had never waged war or fired a shot in anger against women or children.

'Piper,' yelled Mac one day as the Comanche women and children were cleaning out the melon patch. 'Get yourself up there on the barn with your Maynard and explode a few of those melons with hands on them. Just the melons, mind,' he added hastily.

Climbing the rails, an excited Piper positioned himself and dropped a .52 calibre slug into the breach. He smiled; he'd practiced on melons before and knew the mess a direct hit made. He for one wouldn't like to be standing anywhere near it, he thought, squeezing the trigger. The carbine bucked as it sent the projectile whistling into a melon, not two inches from an old squaw's moccasin, spraying the melon contents up her dress and onto her face.

Chuckling, Piper reloaded and took aim further to the left. Over the barrel his focus moved from the melon patch to the long, furrowed area beyond. There was movement there, lots of movement. Lowering the carbine he could make out four, no five, six, a dozen or more Comanche braves hidden in the contour out of sight of the homestead. His heart raced as he quickly searched the south bank towards the creek where even more Indians lay, partially concealed in the brush.

'Pa,' he yelled as loud as he could. 'Get everyone inside; Comanche raiders are all around us.'

Mac, tending to a leaky water trough by the stables, looked up towards Piper. Before he could question the call he saw the urgency etched on Piper's face and ran towards the homestead, yelling at Black Abraham to get his people into the barn. Diego had just finished shoeing his horse when the commotion started and walked casually around to the yard, scanning the near horizon as he went. His pace quickened as he saw the Indian women and children running as fast as they could toward the creek, dropping melons as they ran.

Inside the homestead, Mac raced from room to room, checking carbines and loads. Rob helped his mother to board up the windows while Diego pulled the barn doors shut and headed for the house. It was a drill they'd all been through before, only this time, Piper was out of place. He was still on the barn roof!

'Piper,' yelled Mac, his agitation clear. 'Get the hell off that roof and get yourself down here … NOW!'

'Dammit, Pa. Those crazy Germans are coming in. I can see a wagon approaching,' Piper yelled back.

'Shit,' Mac cussed under his breath. 'What a hell of a time to come calling.'

'Piper? Piper, can you hear me?' Mac called.

'Sure I can,' replied Piper.

'Okay, listen carefully now. Shoot one of them.'

'What, a German?'

'No you idiot, an Indian. Shoot a bloody Indian.'

Taking aim at a crouching Comanche five hundred yards off, Piper held his breath, steadied and fired. An instant later, the Comanche bounced up and fell backwards. The next instant saw the rise of two dozen or more Comanche warriors stampeding towards the homestead, screaming as they ran. Some fired their rifles wildly while others, tomahawk and knife in hand sped forward until a volley of shots from the homestead stopped them.

From the brush behind them Piper saw another dozen running towards the German wagon, which he could now see was loaded with women and children. Firing as fast as he could reload, Piper went about felling the Indians attacking the wagon.

'For Christ's sake Piper, get down here,' commanded Mac.

Comanche rifle fire kicked up the dust around Piper as he weaved his way across the yard and into the homestead. The second Comanche charge was only twenty yards away before Mac gave the order to fire. Each carbine round found its mark. The rapid fire continued as empty rifles were exchanged for loaded ones, Black

Abraham's girls working the reloading detail. The crash of carbine fire was interrupted occasionally by the deafening explosion of Christine's shotgun, taking at least one screaming Comanche out of the fight each time it did. The house was filled with the stench of cordite before the Comanche withdrew.

'Okay?' yelled Mac. 'Everyone okay?'

Adrenalin pumping, everyone called their 'Okay' back to Mac. Christine, probably one of the calmest under pressure suddenly gasped in horror as she looked through the haze, past the dead Comanche strewn about the front yard and beyond.

'The Germans,' she cried. 'The poor souls.'

Looking out, they could see that the wagonload of German women and children had been halted six hundred yards or so from the house. The wagon had been turned over as the Comanche busied themselves like ants, stripping the clothing off four women and tying them, spread eagled to the base of the wagon. Half a dozen young children stood crying, hands trussed in front of them.

Mac took careful aim, and fired, the slug ripping into one of the Comanche busying himself with one of the staked out German women. To his horror, the Comanche next to him retaliated immediately by grabbing one of the tethered children and severing his head completely with several blows of his wide bladed tomahawk. Holding the child's head aloft, the Comanche screamed towards the homestead.

Realising his error, Mac slumped against the door and cast a despairing gaze at those in the room.

As dusk approached, the Comanche built campfires all around the homestead and danced defiantly in full view and well within firing range. Fearful of a repeat consequence to the captive Germans, Mac ordered everyone to hold their fire.

'How many Diego?' he asked

'Maybe thirty … rifles, lances and tomahawks. Their horses must be back at the creek with another two, maybe three Comanche.'

'They'll wait until just before sun-up when we're at our weakest before attacking,' Mac said. 'An attack will give them the upper hand. Once they make the house they'll smoke out those of us unfortunate enough to have survived the attack.'

'Never sit back and wait to be attacked,' Diego said. 'Better to die attacking your enemy than be killed defending what cannot be defended.'

Everyone turned and looked at Diego but nobody spoke. Another bullet whacked into the outside wall. 'They will keep that up all night. They won't tire without sleep but we will,' Diego added with some authority.

He was right, and Mac knew it. Carefully they planned out their attack. It seemed their only avenue to survival.

Creeping silently, one by one, Diego brought six farm-hands from the barn and issued them with rifles. Then together, Mac, Piper, Rob and Diego made their way silently to the barn. After saddling and mounting their horses, shielded from view by the barn door, they went through the plan once more. Each of them carried a Colt in each hand, one in their hip holster and another tied to the saddle; a rapid firing arsenal of twenty four, .36 calibre slugs per rider. Their horses pranced nervously as they waited.

A thunderous roar left the house as eight carefully aimed carbines exploded In unison, startling the resting Comanche. Simultaneously the barn door swung open and four horsemen, galloping as if the devil himself was behind them, burst into the courtyard. Another explosion from the house saw more Comanche fall as the horsemen galloped onward, pistols blazing. As one pistol was emptied, it was discarded and another brought into commission. Eight carbines thundered again, this time to the rear of the house, and then again as the three horsemen closed on Comanche after Comanche at full gallop; each encounter leaving a dead or dying warrior in its wake.

Reaching the wagon, Piper leapt from his horse and quickly cut the women free, pushing them roughly under the sideboard for protection. With only one pistol remaining, he scouted the gloom trying to locate Rob and Diego. Two Indians screamed as they charged. Missing one, Piper used three rounds, cursing his mistake as another four Comanche materialised, tomahawks raised for the kill. Dispatching two of them before discarding his last empty pistol, Piper leapt across the wagon draw for cover, only to be met by another screaming warrior. Knife in hand, Piper faced the two, moving his blade in a slow arc as he crouched to fight. Hearing the galloping horses approach, the Comanche turned and ran, only to be gunned down by Rob who wheeled his horse to a skidding halt beside Piper.

'Back to the house,' he snapped. 'Take the women and children, Diego and I will ride cover.'

Later, safely inside the house and convinced that they'd at least bought time, the men rested as the German women and children were tended to. They told of their escape from their settlement further up the Nueces Valley. Comanche and Kiowa had attacked and killed everyone. They had managed to escape, only because they were returning from a visit and witnessed the attack on the settlement from a rise, unseen by the attackers.

'It's started,' Mac said. 'I told you all a year ago when this damn nonsense with the North was brewing. Once the Indians see our men folk leaving for another war they'll be all over us like a bloody rash. It's started.'

The only Comanche to be seen at daylight were the bodies of those that littered the courtyard and field beyond. The dead German child was retrieved for burial while the Comanche were dragged to a spot beyond the rise, laid beneath a pile of brush, soaked liberally with coal oil and set alight. The funeral pyre was refuelled each time it faltered until all that remained was a smoking pile of foul smelling charcoal.

Piper was given the freshest and fastest horse and

told to ride to town and not to return unless in company with armed Soldiers or Rangers who could best deal with the small Indian uprising. As he sped down the trail he saw tracks every few miles that evidenced a serious build-up of Indians. They had never ventured this close to town before. His father, the canny old Scott was right; they were in for a war within a war.

CHAPTER THREE

Mac had seen some successful plantings of sugar to the North East and arranged to experiment with a small crop along the creek not far from his now extensive corn fields. More fruit trees had been planted and were starting to bear good fruit. Mindful of the growing call for good quality wool, Argyll was low-fenced in areas that allowed the Campbells to diversify even further as a viable sheep holding. The scarcity of good lumber saw the erection of several mud-walled sheds around the homestead where grain, salt, skins and other commodities were stored. It was Macs intention to fortify Argyll homestead so as to be capable of withstanding the ever present and now more concentrated attacks by Indians. Food was already in high demand due to the war in the north and he knew that the time would soon arrive when food shortages would become commonplace.

Mac oversaw the construction of a substantial mudbrick wall around the perimeter of the homestead, complete with rifle slots and canon platforms. Intruders would find it difficult to enter from the outside, whereas those defending the wall would have a clear view of anyone approaching. Clay canons, built to exact dimensions, were made secretly in the barn and wheeled out to the canon platforms under cover of darkness. In the light of day, fresh paint shining in the sun, the clay muzzles of the cannons were trained threateningly on the approaches to the homestead.

The Cotton Trail from the north to Brownsville became increasingly busy as more and more ports were blockaded by the Union Navy. Wagons loaded impossibly high with cotton, grain and wool made their way south under the protection of the Texas Mounted Rifles and Confederate soldiers. Once at sea, many shipments of essential wool and food were intercepted by Union ships and redirected to the Northern war effort.

1862 saw the first conscription laws enacted. First in the South and then closely followed by the North. While some people in East Texas doubted the need for conscription, the bombardment of Corpus Christi that summer brought the reality of war closer to home. Argyll became a refuge for some of the wealthier residents of Corpus Christi who had the means to escape the coastal bombardment. Makeshift shelters were set up inside the 'fort' walls to house the refugees, mainly women, children and older men.

'Never thought Argyll would become this crowded,' Mac commented to Christine one afternoon as they sat surveying the tents. 'We're going to have to watch the supplies closely from here on.'

'There should be plenty for all,' Christine answered. 'This war will end as soon as it started. I have a feeling that once the dead are counted, these damn Generals of ours will come to their senses and call it off.'

'That's why I married you, Chrissie, always the optimist,' Mac smiled as he placed his arm around her shoulders and pulled her close to his side. 'Wonder where Hamish is now?'

'Lord knows, but I bet he'll be home soon as well,' Christine added confidently.

They couldn't know that Hamish was fast becoming a distinguished leader in battle after battle in Virginia. The Texas Rangers, commonly regarded as fierce fighters and smart tacticians, had become referred to simply as the Texans. To the uninformed, they presented as nothing more than a rag-tag bunch of well armed cowboys. They wore no specific uniform, took orders only from their own and thumbed their noses at all the pomp and ceremony that burdened regular force units.

'At least that damn conscription won't affect us, will it?' Christine asked, staring with raised brows straight into Mac's eyes.

'Not really,' he assured her. 'We'll lose a few more of our best cowboys but because of our ability to continue producing stock, food and wool, we'll be left pretty much alone to get on with it.'

'But you and Rob are conscription age.'

'That's true, but we'll do better for the South here on the farm than roaming around up there in the North someplace, and besides, who would keep these damn Comanche away if everyone was to run off and join the army, Huh?' he questioned.

'Riders approaching,' Piper yelled back towards the homestead.

A group of four grey-clothed figures entered the yard and dismounted in front of Mac and Christine.

'What brings you gentlemen out this way late in the afternoon,' Mac asked, walking to meet them, recognizing as he drew closer that the leader was an old friend from Refugio. 'Hart, good to see you. Fine new suit you have there!' he joked.

'Figured that seeing as we're late on the trail we'd stop by and take some supper with you good folk,' Hart smiled. 'A few extras sleeping in the barn shouldn't cause any fuss for y'all.'

'Be our pleasure,' Christine said. 'And how's Martha and the children?'

'Fine, just fine. Still not up to your cooking standards but fine all the same,' he replied with a grin.

After supper, Hart and his soldiers chatted with the Campbells about what was happening on the coast and further north. The war, it seemed, had spread to a dozen or more fronts and casualties were mounting at a horrendous rate. Both sides were losing men in frightful numbers to illness, gunshot and desertion. Hart reassured Christine that Hamish was well and was just too damn clever to get himself shot.

Before retiring for the night, Harts tone of voice took on a more serious and sombre note. 'It's no coincidence that I'm here,' he said. 'I came personally, rather than send a dispatch. Young Rob has to present for conscription.'

Before anyone could say anything he continued. 'Now, I know, I know, there's good argument to keep him here working the ranch but the orders are quite clear. Now, Mac,' he said, looking to a very concerned Mac, 'you ain't affected, being the owner of the farm but I'm afraid Rob has to present himself or join as a volunteer.'

It took a while before Christine choked out a trembled reply. 'I hear that conscripts of wars are not favourably treated, nor favourably thought of,' she said, consciously controlling her emotions.

'That's true; just as true as those failing to present themselves are hung. Please don't feel bad of me for saying that, but it's true,' Hart said.

'So what's to do,' Rob spoke for the first time. 'What now?'

'I'm by no means high up on the ladder here, Rob, but I reckon I can pull a few strings,' answered Hart.

'The Texas Mounted Rifles have a camp not half a days ride from here. Join us in the morning and I'll see that you are, as from tomorrow, one of the Mounted Rifles.'

'Sounds alright to me,' Rob replied, shrugging his shoulders. 'A few boys from the King Ranch ride with them. They reckon they've never laid eyes on a Yankee yet.'

'Probably never will,' Hart said, looking more comfortable now. 'Mainly deal with the renegades, Indians, deserters and conscription avoiders. Don't reckon they could teach you nothin' you don't already know and besides, you'll stay around these parts close to Argyll.'

Comforted by Harts words the gathering retired for the evening.

In the morning, after an emotional goodbye to Rob, the remaining Campbells went about their routine chores. Piper and Diego rode slowly along the cattle pad together. 'Just thinking, Diego,' Piper said. 'Remember that day in Christi when we whupped that ugly son of a bitch?'

'Yep,' replied Diego smiling.

'Where in hell did you think of that, I mean, the bit about cuttin' that ugly bastards balls out when you had him surrendered on the floor?'

'Just comes natural, I guess.'

'Yeehaaa,' Piper yelled. 'You sure is one crazy bastard and that's the truth. Damned if I didn't think you'd go right ahead and do it.'

'What about you?' returned Diego. 'Reckon you'd have shot him?'

'Hell yeah, wasn't for Rob interfering, that dumb, ugly bastard be dead as they come right now.'

Reaching the creek, the two dismounted to drink. 'Not too long now before we get into the action,' Piper said. 'That is if the war don't end before we make the age.'

'We?' Diego questioned, and without waiting for the answer, 'when was the last time you heard of a black joining the Confederate Army? Hell, the Yankees would rescue me and take me home with them!'

'I hear that the Tonkawa are used as scouts, so why not the Karankawa? Hell, you'd outride, outshoot and outsmart any white soldier in the Confederacy. You'd be made a General in short time, I know it, yes sir, Generalisimo Diego Campbell,' Piper joked.

'Put that on my headstone, then. Just after I'm shot in the back by a slaver,' Diego said, remounting.

It was ironic that Piper and Diego were joking about the war. They had both killed Comanche and Kiowa before they were old enough to shave. They had seen and been involved in more bloodshed than most grown men; as mere boys they had acted calmly under mortal conflict situations, but that was the way it was, that was life in the South East of Texas. Ironic also that their respective battles for survival had brought them together, as brothers, and now as brothers they contemplated another battle against a new-found foe.

Each passing month saw belts being pulled tighter

and tighter. The Union blockade, although only partially effective, meant that anything to trade had to be taken down the dangerous Cotton Trail to Mexico. Crops and animals continued to be stolen, not only by the starving Indians but by the army wagons that called regularly to re-supply the troops. It seemed to Mac that he was supplying the entire East Texas community as food stocks dipped lower and lower. Deserters and Union sympathizers were dealt with harshly as more and more appeared in the Nueces area. Those not shot were hanged. Knowing their fate, dozens of them crept west and south to join with others who had gone before them. Small bands of them employed desperate measures to secure food and clothing, often robbing travellers and attacking the outlying ranches. They became just another group of hostiles that required dealing with.

As the war in the north raged throughout 1863, the Campbells learned that Rob's unit had been disbanded. He had been sent further north where he had met up with his older brother, Hamish, now a veteran of the Texas Rangers. Christine wept silently each time she heard news of battles like Gettysburg where the South had suffered enormous losses, more than twenty-five thousand casualties in one battle. The number was just too high to comprehend. She dreaded the arrival of any dispatch riders, thinking this would be the news she feared. No news had arrived from the boys in months. It was said that the kinfolk of fallen soldiers were notified of their loss as soon as possible, so as far as Christine was concerned, no news was good news.

A Christmas present from the devil himself arrived just before Christmas of '83 in the form of Hart, their old friend from Refugio. Christine's blood ran cold as he mounted the weathered steps to the verandah, dusting off his pants as he walked.

'It's Hamish, isn't it?' she asked with a quiver in her voice.

'No, Christine, it's not Hamish. He and Rob are together and doing just fine, last I heard. Mind you, things are not going all that well up North, I hear that we have lost a few, which is what brings me here,' he said.

'Piper's still not quite of age yet, Hart. He stays here and so does Mac,' said Christine defiantly, anticipating Harts news.

'Where are Mac and the boys?' asked Hart.

'Out there doing their best to save what little food we have left after your soldiers cleaned us out last week. How long is this going to go on? Are we to all starve to death while you soldiers kill each other off to the last man?'

'Please, settle down ma'am. I don't like this war any more than you do but we do what we have to do to make sure we win it, otherwise …' Hart paused, rolling his hat brim nervously, 'otherwise everything we've worked for here in Texas will be gone. We will become a bankrupt state unable to feed ourselves.'

'Sir,' Christine replied with deliberate sarcasm, 'perhaps the sound of canon fire has deafened you somewhat. Didn't you just hear me? Hell, we are close to bankrupt and starving now. There is only so much we can give and only so much we can take. Can't you see, sir, we've had enough. Let the damn Yankees come, let them win this damn war, maybe then we can get on with our lives with full bellies and money in our poke.'

Taken aback by her outburst, Hart fought the urge to address her as he would anyone else espousing such a treasonous view; the noose awaited all who did. Considering his long relationship with the Campbells he checked his tongue and calmed.

'Christine, let's keep as civil as we can in these difficult times,' he said. 'My purpose today is to let you know that the conscription law has been adjusted somewhat. The adjustment means that both Mac and Piper either need to join up or present for conscription. I know they're sorry words to your ears but it's my duty to say them. I'm sorry.'

'Damn you Hart, not you or anyone else is going to take the rest of my family away, y'hear? You've told me your news, now hear mine,' she exploded angrily. 'I'm going inside and when I return I'll have a loaded Maynard. If you are still on Argyll, I'll shoot you just as sure as I'd shoot a heathen. Good day, sir!'

Hart knew that to stay and argue the point with Christine would be ill advised. She was a calm woman and he'd never seen her angry, but the stories of her courage and determination had become legendry. He decided that her advice was well worth the taking.

Once in the saddle, he turned and walked his mount slowly towards the gate. Behind him he heard Christine's footsteps on the wooden verandah, followed by the unmistakable sound of a rifle hammer being drawn back, cocking the weapon ready to fire. He stiffened in the saddle, urged his horse to a trot and then a canter as he headed for the gate that offered a ready exit to San Patricio.

Returning home, Mac, Piper and Diego were puzzled at the sight of Christine sitting on the verandah cradling her rifle. Her worried look told them that all was not as it should be. After handing their horses to Black Abraham, they all walked to where she sat.

'Some trouble?' asked Mac.

'Some,' she replied.

'Indians?' asked Piper.

'No, thieves, thieves in grey uniforms.'

'Thieves?' Mac asked. 'What did they take, Chrissie?'

'You,' she answered, looking to Mac. 'And you, Piper,' she added, fighting to hold back the tears as she moved her eyes to Piper.

'What in tarnation are you talking about?' Mac asked. 'You're not making much sense.'

Christine stood and embraced him before recounting through tears the purpose of Hart's visit.

Furious, Mac paced in circles shaking his head. Hands firmly on his hips, anger stamped across his weather-beaten face. He seemed totally lost for words, intelligent ones at least. 'The damn boys are not yet eighteen, that's a few months off,' he said finally. 'And who in God's name looks after Argyll if we're taken away? Who? Oh, I know, the black labour, shit, they'll probably call them into service as well,' shouted Mac angrily. 'Damn the man, I'm riding to Refugio.'

As much as they argued, nobody could talk him out of making the trip to settle the matter with Hart. The boys were instructed to remain at Argyll and stay close to their mother as Mac, astride a fresh mount, thundered through the gates and wheeled left in a cloud of dust.

'Ain't never seen Pa this way,' Piper said quietly.

'Hush now, boys. Come on inside, there's fresh corn bake,' Christine stammered, struggling to remain calm.

Four clear days passed before a tired and bedraggled Mac rode back into Argyll. There was a buzz of excitement as everyone ran to learn of his meeting with Hart.

'So, how'd you go, Pa?' yelled an anxious Piper. 'What did Hart have to say?'

'Had nothing to say,' was his dull reply. 'Seems he was caught by desperados on the way back to town and killed. Should have paid more attention to that road, he knew it to be dangerous.'

'Do they know who done it?' asked Piper.

'No, seems whoever done it got clean away. But I did get to talk to the Garrison Commander. He's so short

48

on men that he can't spare anyone to hunt down Harts killers. Told him we'd be glad to assist in the matter and if he swore us all in as Rangers we'd get the job done, no matter how long it takes.'

There was silence. Questioning eyes searched Mac's expressionless face as he unbuckled his gun belt and eased himself into the rocker. 'A shot of that rough old mash would go down well, Chrissie,' he said, smiling for the first time. 'Better fetch a glass for the lads as well, seeing as they're apparently all grow'd fightin' men now.'

'So, we're all Texas Rangers now?' Piper asked anxiously. 'All of us, including Diego?'

'Whole damn lot of us. Got a signed letter here to prove it. Told that Commander that if we used Argyll as our base we could raise a deputation and scout the valleys clear up to the high country if need be until we get those murderers to justice.'

'But you said that nobody knows who done Hart in,' Christine said as she arrived with whiskey and glasses enough for all.

'Well, that's true. Seems that if he stayed here much longer we'd only have to hunt as far as where you're standing,' Mac said with a wry grin.

'Now what makes you say that,' asked Christine.

'Texas Ranger guesswork, my dear,' he said, filling the shot glass and throwing its contents down his throat.

'Oh, so now we're celebrating the fact that you've got everyone 'cept me trotting off to war?' Christine asked, obviously annoyed.

'Seems to be the way it has to be. I'm getting a bit long in the tooth now though, hell, can't track like I used to and these lads here; well they're all but useless. Reckon it'll be well into next year before we get anywhere near the murderers. Now let's take some more of that liquor, barkeep,' he said, winking at the boys.

Christine turned to go inside. As she did, she glanced down at Macs revolver lying on floor beside him. She wondered how many of those chambers were empty. She guessed two at the most.

Diego's response to the news was one of cautious acceptance. Piper, clearly buoyed by the news that he was now a Ranger could barely hide his excitement as his mind overflowed with the expectation of high adventure, and the now real prospect of joining the war.

CHAPTER **FOUR**

Mac convinced his Mexican employees that the war would not come to much in East Texas. He persuaded some of them to fetch those who had departed already for Mexico when the hostilities commenced. It wasn't long before the old workers returned with the promise of higher wages and more diversified work. Although there were weekly skirmishes with the Comanche in and around Argyll and the region, at least now there were more troops patrolling the roads and moving about the countryside. Of all the problems, Comanche raids remained the biggest threat with their daring hit-and-run raids on ranches and travellers.

Times were indeed lean, but Mac managed to keep

enough food and to trade just enough produce to keep everyone comfortable. Argyll fared better than some of the smaller ranches where owners simply walked off and left for greener pastures, wherever they may be found. As clothing ran out, cotton garments were replaced by rough spun woollen ones. Boots, unable to be repaired, were replaced by calf-high moccasins in Indian fashion and rawhide jackets became commonplace. The signature wide-brimmed hat worn by Texans was, more often than not, the only way to distinguish between an Indian riding in and a rancher.

Together, the new Texas Rangers – Mac, Piper and Diego continued to oversee the running of the ranch, although they spent lengthy periods away from the homestead hunting for Hart's killers. Whilst on the case, they also branded cattle, repaired fences and drove what stock they could spare to the markets. Wool was baled and taken south to Brownsville down the Cotton Trail. Perhaps the Hart killers had ventured down that way and if so, the Campbells were sure to find them. Confederate money had become all but worthless and prices of even the basic necessities had risen several hundred percent. Payment for traded goods in Mexico was gold bullion which was spirited back to Argyll and hidden, appearing only when the purchase of hardware or other essential goods was required.

Returning from a trip to Mexico, Mac and the boys were met on the trail by a dispatch rider. Opening the dispatch, Mac learned that the Garrison Commander, although it pained him to do so, had decided to cease the operation to avenge Harts death. The three Campbells were to report to him in the first instance and following that, make their way north to link up with the Texas Ranger units that had been hit hard during recent skirmishes.

Back at Argyll, Mac gathered the family and Black Abraham around the table. 'We can't put it off any longer,' he explained. 'We've been given a lot of latitude and I'm sure that the Commander has been under some pressure. As I see it, if we don't do like the dispatch commands, we'll probably end up at the end of a noose as traitors. I don't like leaving Argyll and your mother any more than you do, but we have good loyal workers and this old rascal Black Abraham to take care of business while we're away,' he said, pushing Black Abraham on the shoulder. 'There are enough guns and ammunition here to hold out any Indian attack and it's as close as I can get to fact that the Yankees will never get this far south. Mother has the companionship of the other womenfolk from Corpus Christi who have all said that they will stay here until the Yankee blockade is lifted. This war has been long going now and from what I hear, it's not going to go much farther. I'm picking that we won't even get to Virginia before it's all over and in that case, well, we'll just have ourselves a holiday along the way. At least we'll be together,' he said.

Mac worked through the best part of the night to make sure that he had covered everything he thought important before leaving Christine alone. He knew that an order to strip the ranches of all available men folk meant one of two things. Either the war was going very poorly for them or it was going quite well but needed more men on the ground to finalise the issue once and for all. He chose to believe the latter.

After an agonizing farewell, the three men rode slowly away from the homestead. None looked back as they rode in silence. Christine couldn't help but notice that Piper and Diego had grown, so much so that they both sat higher in the saddle than Mac. Black Abraham nodded his approval as the tear-smudged face of Christine, his new master, smiled weakly as she strapped the pistol belt to her slim waist.

'Stay close to your rifle,' she ordered, 'and be sure to tell the others to do the same. We're in this damn war whether we like it or not.'

Mac's orders from the commander were clear in theory but vague in practical terms. He was to get himself and his two Rangers to Georgia where they would meet up with Captain Shannon. With any luck they should be there before winter. Others would join them along the way but if they failed to make contact they were to push ahead regardless. They were genuinely shocked to hear of the battles lost by the Confederates. The picture painted was a grim one indeed. According to the Commander, they should make all speed as reinforcements were gravely required on all fronts.

On the trail and headed North, Mac discussed the

briefing with Piper and Diego. 'It's grim, boys,' he confided. 'Seems that it hasn't all been going our way up north. Best I can make out, the only saving grace is that the damn Yankees want to recruit a few regiments of Texans,' he joked.

'Told you Hamish and Rob would be havin' a time,' Piper laughed. 'Hell, we'll probably arrive up there and join with them; there'll be Yankees throwin' down their guns all over the where, 'specially when Diego takes to talkin' about cuttin' their balls off.'

'Ease down on the cussin, lad,' Mac said. 'Plenty of time for that when we start digging splinters out of our arses up yonder.'

Making good time and only a day away from their expected rendezvous they camped alongside a wide river bed. The infantry units they passed along the way painted a graphic picture of what was going on up ahead. The sight of wounded men, sometimes in groups of a dozen or more had unsettled them a little. There seemed to be little if any direction of movement; some units were moving west, others east and some were just staying where they were, but not a great deal were making any northward movement. Piper took particular notice of a group of no less than thirty men, gaunt and bedraggled, all completely out of their minds and raving like lunatics. Some used sticks as make-believe guns while others jumped around giving orders to an imaginary army.

'Who are these men?' Piper questioned the only

apparent sane one in their midst, an old soldier who would probably die of age and not from a bullet.

'Shell struck, mostly,' the old man replied. 'Couple of years of hell will do this to a man. Some of these boys nearly suffocated under the mountains of dead on the battlefield, others had they's eardrums blowed to bits by canon. Even got one here someplace who was the only survivor of one hundred and fifty men. And that lad over yonder,' he continued, 'he's from the North but he believes he gots to get down south and return the canon ball stuck in his gut. Yes sir, this be the mad detail and you'll find many more where you're going.'

A light pre-dawn fog hung in the trees as the Campbells recommenced their journey. They would eat dry rations in the saddle. Making a fire was too risky; they had heard the sound of battle to the east the day before and were warned that they could just as well come across Yankees as Confederates in these parts.

They all froze as Diego mimicked a chirping bird, a signal they had long used when trouble was afoot. Piper and Mac looked to Diego who slowly pointed to a pile of busted trees forty yards away. They could all see a blue figure crouching, part hidden and looking the other way. Quietly they left their horses and crawled to a better vantage point, laying low behind another pile of busted timber. 'Be damned,' Mac whispered. 'Yankee's taking a crap. Probably from that small patrol we spotted yesterday.'

'Shall I shoot him?' Piper asked.

'Can't shoot a man taking a crap, not right somehow,' Mac replied.

'Reckon he'd shit if he was shot anyways, so it don't matter that much, all I'd be doin' is puttin' the shootin' before the shittin',' Piper giggled.

'Nah, let the poor boy crap in peace,' Mac whispered again.

'I know,' Piper said, as if struck by a brainwave. 'Diego could sneak up while he's got his pants down and introduce himself.'

Stifling laughter, the three lay watching as the soldier finished his business, returned up the opposite bank and disappeared through the brush.

'Let's go see how many more need a crap,' Mac said quietly as they mounted and rode across the river bed.

Hidden beneath the slight embankment, they checked their pistols.

'Alright,' Mac commanded, now deadly serious. 'On my word we scale the bank and ride like hell into their camp, and remember that Texan yodel, sure scares the hell right out of them, so use it.'

The horses were ready and with nods all round Mac had his queue. As one, they booted their horses up over the embankment, their screams piercing the crisp morning air. Atop the rise in full flight, the sight ahead made them choke mid scream. A Yankee column of at least a hundred soldiers, complete with artillery, was slumbering peacefully in every direction and as far as the trees beyond. The sentry, a man whom they had almost met moments before, bolted towards the main group.

'Holy shit!' Mac screamed. 'Forward, lads and ride like hell!'

Waking soldier's grabbed rifles and fired wildly as the three horsemen galloped full pelt through their ranks, hurdling canons and screaming like wild men. A bugler sounded the alarm as the three continued their race through the column heading for the safety of the trees and brush ahead. Swerving, jumping obstacles and firing at blurred shapes as they spurred their mounts on, riding as if their lives depended on nothing else.

Clearing the soldiers' ranks they eventually reached a thicket of trees and melted into their cover.

'Yeeehaaaa,' screamed Piper. 'How far's Georgia, Pa?'

'Shut up and ride,' Mac replied as bullets continued to buzz around them like a swarm of angry bees.

When enough ground had been put between them and what they considered to be the whole Yankee Army, they slowed and rested the horses.

Damn,' cursed Mac. 'How could Texans be so damn mule-stupid?'

'Must say,' offered Diego with a broad grin, 'I did kinda wonder about the tactics of charging an unseen enemy. Mind you, was that some excitement or was it not!'

'Damn, that was something to behold,' Piper concluded as they continued North.

It was in the fall of 1864 before Piper, Mac and Diego finally joined with Captain Shannon and the Tennesseeans in Georgia. They had become involved in a few skirmishes along the way but apart from their early morning raid on an entire Infantry column, they had more or less made the journey without serious incident. A Comanche attack on Argyll rated far worse than anything they'd encountered. That is not to say that they weren't shocked by the devastation they had encountered. It was even worse than they'd heard – mile, after inglorious mile of fresh graves along the roadside; discarded equipment; busted wagons and canons that littered the countryside. Half witted soldiers, Yankees and Confederates, minds distorted and twisted by the horrors of war aimlessly roamed the trails and roads, bodies without minds who would certainly perish in the winter, or perhaps before.

Residents, displaced from their once grand estates, huddled on the roadside begging food and doing their best to cover their shivering torsos with only the filthy rags they stood in. What greeted the Campbell trio daily was the pathetic damaged collateral of war. The scope and scale of the suffering was enormous, particularly among the civilian women who were now at the mercy of anyone who chose to defile them further; Yankee, Rebel or bandit.

Meeting with Shannon, Mac offered their credentials. To his liking was the stature and presence of the Captain. His formed opinion was that this was a good man to follow into battle. He asked about his other sons, Hamish and Rob and was told that they were further west and north on hit-and-run raids behind the advancing Yankees. He was also told, very bluntly, that their chances of survival in that theatre were very slim but that their job would be done. At least he had heard of them.

Calling the Rangers together, Shannon outlined their duties over the foreseeable future. They would be scouting for the Tenneesseans. They would be conducting hit-and-run raids on enemy camps and would be working well behind enemy lines. 'Above all,' Shannon spoke, 'we will avenge these poor displaced souls that beg our food and plead our assistance. We owe them that, they've lost everything, men folk included and now they face a bleak future. Feed them when you can, comfort them when you can but above all, let them know by your deeds that you are here to avenge their losses.'

Mac was pleased that they had been given a task that he knew they could handle well. At least now they could do what they'd been doing since arriving in Texas; practicing hit-and-run warfare, the only way to survive against the marauding Comanche and Kiowa seemed now to be the best way to disrupt order in Yankee columns.

Day after exhausting day they attacked Yankee columns of infantry. Their tactics saw surprisingly few casualties to their unit which always inflicted serious damage on the enemy. Piper had become the joker of the unit and was well liked for his quick wit and cavalier attitude. Diego, always at his side had become revered as a lethal fighter. Yankee captives passing through the Tennesseean camps soon started talking about the bullet-proof black Texan who could scalp a soldier as he rode by at full gallop, an exaggeration that was never corrected. A fearless horseman who would charge a dozen rifles, pistols blazing and finish the skirmish on foot, wading through the terrified soldiers, Indian blade in hand, carving as he went. Closer to fact was the ritual practised by Diego before every battle; the painting of circles beneath each eye, a splash of red ochre to the forehead and neck followed by the murmuring of a long Indian chant that called on the spirits of dead friend and foe to join him.

'Where'd you get the Kronk,' a Ranger asked Piper one day.

'Kronk?' Piper asked, genuinely confused.

'The Kronk, the Karankawa boy.'

'Didn't know they went by that name,' Piper replied.

'Sure they do, well, down Aransas way at least. Hell, if you got anymore, whistle 'em up and we might just turn this damn war around,' the Ranger said.

For years the Campbells had hidden Diego's true identity, now it was common knowledge and not only accepted but appreciated. Diego, too, was pleased that at last he would be seen for what he was; not a black, but a Karankawa warrior. It was of little consequence that he was fighting alongside those partly responsible for the death of his entire people and, truth be known, he felt little sympathy for their cause. What was important was that he was here with his new family and he would fight by their side for as long as they needed him to do so, the same as they had fought for him several years back.

Scouting a small Yankee encampment as winter set in, the Rangers prepared to attack. Quietly they moved to the best vantage point and counted the number of troops. It was obviously a mix of cavalry, infantry and artillery that had been left behind by a larger force they had encountered in a raid the previous week

'Can't make head nor tail of this group,' Captain Shannon confided. 'Seem to be either foot draggers or reinforcements waiting to be called up. Let's hit them anyway.'

After forming into two smaller groups, they positioned themselves to the south and to the west. When the southern charge engaged, the western position would move and strike their flank. Mac was delegated to lead the first charge from the south. Diego and Piper would ride with Shannon from the west.

As Shannon's group waited, Mac burst from the trees with his Rangers, yelling and firing as they rode.

'Wait for it,' Shannon cautioned his men as they watched, waiting to join the charge.

Impatiently standing their ground, they watched as Mac and his men closed to within thirty yards of the

Yankees before the canvas tent sides were dropped to reveal the waiting canons. Piper and Diego watched in horror as the canon muzzles exploded sending the deadly grape-shot into the charging Rangers. Ball, metal and chain ripped through the riders and horses, literally ripping them to pieces, their limbs and entrails spraying behind them. As the canons fell silent to reload, soldiers issued a volley of point-blank ball into the surviving Texans. Shannon's call to charge was drowned out by the second blast from the canons. Stunned, Piper hesitated, staring at the bloodied mess that was only a minute ago his father mounted atop a horse. All that remained was a scattered landscape of twitching body parts, some human and some animal. The screaming and gunfire snapped him back to the present as he booted his mount forward behind the others.

The battle ended quickly with Shannon withdrawing after inflicting heavy casualties. His losses were also unacceptably high and to stay and fight would only mean greater losses. Their tactics were hit-and-run and that's exactly what they did.

Clear of the battle they stopped and regrouped.

'The bastards were waiting for us,' Shannon told his men. 'Seems they've become accustomed to our tactics.'

'Captain,' a shocked Piper called, 'I'd like to go back and get Pa.'

'Can't let you do that, Piper,' came the reply. 'No such thing as returning to pick up the dead, those

Yankees would gun you down even under a white flag, believe me.'

'Can't just leave him there,' Piper protested.

'I know how you feel, son,' Shannon confided. 'Hell, I feel the same every time I lose a Ranger, and I've lost count of such occasions.'

Trying to understand, Piper was comforted by Diego. 'We can't go back, Piper,' he said in a soft voice. 'We can't go back.'

With light rain falling, they headed back to the secure encampment only to find that better than half of the army had moved further south. Returning from a briefing, Shannon took on the look of a worried, almost beaten man. 'The Carolinas are falling to the Yankees,' he told his weary group of Rangers. 'The only reason they haven't moved on us here is the weather. We're told that a force better than 60,000 is headed our way.'

'What are our orders?' asked a Ranger.

'Pray for more rain,' Shannon replied. 'At least that will delay them long enough for us to take the only sensible option and head south.'

For Piper, what little sense this war did make had now diminished. The wholesale death and utter slaughter of not only soldiers but civilians as well, protested loudly in his mind. The completely sacked towns and displaced people, the roaming madmen who once thought rational thoughts, all of this, and what lay ahead? More of the same? What of his brothers? He hadn't heard from either in over a year now, had they too been shredded by deadly grape shot in a lonely valley so far away from home by some young canoneer, also far from home, wondering what the hell he was doing there too. Futility overtook emotions of anger and grief.

Huddled beneath a leaking poncho, Piper grieved silently for his father. Vivid recollections of his death robbed him of sleep. Diego squatted at his side, awake but silent, for he too was dealing with emotions almost out of control. Neither men wept but both changed forever on that day. Nothing could ever be the same. The two kids from Texas on an adventure of a lifetime, now sat as two grieving men. Ahead lay a lifetime to reflect, heal and try during that lifetime, however long it may be, to make some sense of this day and those gone before.

The crisp, clear morning that followed could have been proclaimed idyllic were it not for the rancid smell of war that invaded and claimed it. The Ranger unit commenced their move southward as news arrived almost on the hour of defeat after defeat. It seemed that the Northern States of the Confederacy had either fallen or were about to fall. Union forces amassed on almost every front and pushed south, brutally crushing any opposition as it went. Confederate forces in the north were being cut off and either had to surrender or die. The situation was beginning to become hopeless.

Texans now focused on their homeland and quickened their pace. If nothing else, Texas would hold. It was one thing dying for the Confederacy but quite another dying for Texas, especially for a Texan.

The return trip was not a simple matter of riding off home. Battles were fought along the way and many Rangers died during the retreat. The speed with which they travelled often saw them ride into ambushes which would have been avoided under normal circumstances. This journey however, was anything but normal. They were returning home to defend their beloved Texas. If they made it back, they vowed to fight to the last in her defense. 'Remember the Alamo' was mouthed often around the evening campfires.

Once inside Texas, the weary riders thinned out as they each chose to return to their place of origin and link up with whatever army units had prevailed. Encouraged by the news that Texas was holding strong gave renewed vigour and resolve.

Passing a group of wagons, Piper and Diego, exhausted by travel and lack of food looked on helplessly as a body, heavily bloodied and bandaged fell from the rear of a wagon and onto the muddy track. The wagon continued to move forward, its cargo of dead and dying rolling limply against each other. A lunatic with only one leg and a hideously scarred face sat rocking back and forth on the buck board next to the reins-man, shivering as he mumbled incoherently. Piper looked at the pathetic creature and rode on.

'Piper,' Diego called. 'Piper, come back.'

Turning in the saddle, Piper looked back to see Diego riding beside the wagon. Reining his horse to a stop he waited for the wagon and Diego to catch up. 'What is it?' Piper asked wearily.

'That soldier,' he said, looking towards the wagon.

Quickly glancing at all of the soldiers in the wagon, a puzzled Piper finally asked again, 'What soldier?'

'The one on the board, there,' he said, pointing at the crazy creature with one leg and virtually no facial features. 'It's Hamish, your brother.'

'Stop the wagon,' yelled Piper. 'Stop the God-damn wagon!'

Dismounting, Piper clambered up onto the wagon and stared into the one good eye of the wounded soldier. 'God almighty,' Piper whispered, 'Can it be you, Hamish?'

The soldier's overcoat, covered in dried blood and mud, hung loosely off his shoulders and fell over the stinking, roughly bandaged stump that once was a leg. His horribly disfigured face, still encrusted with blood from the weeping wounds, stared blankly back at the enquiring face of Piper. Clutched to his chest was a worn saddle pouch bearing the cattle brand of Argyll … the letter A inside the Star of Texas.

'Diego,' Piper said. 'Diego; it's Hamish. By God it's Hamish!'

CHAPTER **FIVE**

The small convoy of wagons continued its slow journey southward. Piper and Diego commandeered the wagon with Hamish aboard and set out for Argyll. The other wounded soldiers were given what dry rations Piper and Diego could spare and were made more comfortable for the journey ahead.

'Don't know what's in that saddle pouch there,' the wagon driver said to Piper. 'What I do know is that he screams like a God-damn Comanche on the warpath if you make any attempt to wrestle it from him.'

'Could be anything,' Piper replied. 'Sure is something in there but if it suits him to hold it then that's fine, as long as it keeps him alive till we get back home.'

The next two days of slow travel saw another two of the wounded soldiers die. After burying them on the side of the track they pushed on into increasingly familiar country until striking the track south-east that would lead them to Argyll. Occasionally they saw Comanche riding at a safe distance but were not attacked.

It was late afternoon when the wagon lumbered across the creek, up a small rise and stopped. Before them was the familiar sight of Argyll homestead. Smoke curled from the kitchen chimney as coloured children played in front of the barn. A grey-bearded Black Abraham looked curiously towards them.

Piper's mind raced in confusion as he anticipated the long awaited reunion with his mother. How would he tell her all that had happened? Had she been told of Macs death? Had she heard from Rob? Question after question sped through his mind only to be interrupted by Diego. 'Best I take the wagon to the other side of the barn while you go see Ma,' he said.

'Yeah, yeah I reckon that's best. Ma shouldn't see Hamish like this. You go get him cleaned up and unload the others so Black Abraham can take care of them, I'll go see Ma.'

Piper rode slowly past the semi-permanent timber and canvas huts that still housed the refugees from the coast. Curious women stared while children retreated to their mothers as he rode silently on.

'Can we be of assistance, sir?' someone called, not knowing who they were.

'Nope,' Piper replied as he slowly dismounted and hitched his horse.

'That you Abraham?' his mother called from inside. 'If you children are playing in the horse trough your momma's likely to take a switch to you.'

Piper walked to the steps and stopped. Looking down, he quickly brushed off the dirt that encrusted his jacket and pants before removing the revolver from his shoulder holster and unbuckling the gun belt holding the other two pistols, quickly sliding them back towards the drinking trough.

He knew his mother would not like to greet him bristling with firearms. After removing his hat, he combed his fingers through his long unwashed hair and scruffy beard and cleared his throat. Before he could take another step he heard footsteps crossing the floor. He stopped, rooted to the spot as his mother appeared in the doorway, wiping her hands on her apron as she did.

'Piper,' she gasped, stopping as if she'd been hit by gunfire.

'Ma,' was all he could manage with a weak, nervous smile.

Christine's face lit up as she rushed down the steps and threw her arms around him. 'Piper, oh Piper you're back, thank God you're back,' she yelled as tears of joy and relief flowed down her cheeks.

'We're back sure enough, Ma,' Piper said, hugging her as he spoke.

'The others, Piper, where are the others?' Christine yelled excitedly.

'Oh, they'll be here in time, they just had to get a wagon around the barn and offload some wounded boys,' Piper replied.

Breaking loose from Pipers embrace, Christine started to run towards the barn.

'Ma!' Piper yelled. 'Wait on; don't go there, they'll be here soon. Ma!'

His words fell on deaf ears as Christine ran to the barn door only to be surrounded by the arms of Black Abraham. 'Missus,' he calmed, 'best you wait here Missus till Diego unload the wounded folk.'

'What's the matter with you, Abraham? Where's Mac?'

Piper's heart sank. He now knew that word had not been sent about his father's death. He walked quickly to his mother who was now silently searching for answers in his eyes; eyes that welled with tears as he reached her.

'Ma,' he said softly, searching for the right words. 'Ma, Diego and Hamish are here with me. I'm not rightly sure where Robbie has got to, but I'm sure he'll be along in time. Pa,' he hesitated, drew in his breath and looked deep into his mother's eyes, 'Pa ain't coming back. Pa ain't coming back, Ma.'

He watched as his mothers face drained. She suddenly looked as lonely and lost as he felt. They stood there gazing at each other for a moment before Piper added. 'I was with him Ma, me and Diego were with him. Ma' he didn't suffer any at all,' was all Piper could think of to tell her that may have some meaning.

Christine, stone faced, nodded, turned and walked slowly past a relenting Black Abraham and into the barn. Women were by now tending to the wounded soldiers while Diego knelt beside Hamish washing his face. As Christine approached, Diego rose and embraced her.

'Oh thank God you're safe, Diego,' she said as he hugged her.

Looking past Diego she could not control a stifled scream. The broken man that Piper had not recognised was instantly recognizable to his mother. 'Oh, Lord,' she sobbed, cupping her hands to her face as if in prayer. 'What have they done to you Hamish?'

Everyone stood their ground in silence as Christine walked to where Hamish sat, kneeled in front of him and gently embraced him. It was Black Abraham who moved first, kneeling beside Christine and comforting her the way he had done many times before. A Mexican woman arrived with a pail of warm water and rag to gently sponge Hamish's face as Christine rocked back, still holding his shoulders.

For one moment, the battered and scarred face of Hamish seemed to smile as his one seeing eye glazed over. His incoherent mumbling stopped as he slowly reached forward and handed the saddle pouch to his mother.

'This is for me?' she asked.

Hamish stared at her before again commencing his mumbling and rocking as the Mexican woman continued to sponge the dirt and dry blood from his face.

With trembling hands, Christine undid the pouch and peered inside. There were two small bundles of letters. Taking them from the pouch she could see that one bundle was in Robbie's hand while the other was in the hand of Hamish. 'These are letters from you and Robbie,' Christine stammered. 'You never posted them … can I read them?'

Piper replied for him, 'You go on and read them, Ma, we'll take care of Hamish and get him inside for a good bath and then into a clean bed.'

The old wooden bench beneath the apple tree was a place where Christine had often sat with Mac reminiscing and dreaming aloud about the future. Now, she sat there alone as she opened the first letter from Rob

Dear Ma, Pa and Diego, Christine dried her eyes, composed herself and continued to read –

Sure hope that you are receiving our mail down there. We've had word that Yankee patrols have sometimes intercepted mail riders to try and get information of what us Rangers are up to. Hamish said he's handed all mail to the mail riders so you will no doubt be reading this now.

Hamish is our Captain and there's talk that he could even get promoted. He's thought of highly by all and I

reckon the boys would follow him to hell if he gave the call. There have been times when I wondered about his orders but he's always there at the front so we follow and account for ourselves well. The Yankees sure know we've been in the camp after we've gone.

We don't go fighting all the time up here. Sometimes we just scout around and let the infantry and cavalry go out. There are times when life is quite lonesome and we just sit around talking about folks at home. We often catch young Yankees and because they're just kids we let them go on their way without their rifles. Some couldn't be any older than Piper and Diego and shouldn't have any part in this war.

Most of the country and civilians up here in the Carolinas are quite agreeable. The fresh peaches and berries are nicer than Texas ones and the kind folk don't mind that we take our needs. We saw a travelling minstrel show last week but had to cut it short and skedaddle on account of a troop of Yankees arriving for the same show.

Weather is agreeable at the moment and we still have a warm blanket each for the cooler nights. Say hello to everyone at Argyll and I'll write you again soon.

All my love, Rob

Christine clasped the letter to her bosom as the tears again flowed. She looked out over the orchard to the creek flowing peacefully beyond. The fresh, blossom scented breeze cleared her head as she placed Rob's letter back into the bundle and opened a letter written by Hamish.

Dear Ma, Pa, Piper, Diego and Black Abraham,

I will try and get this letter posted when we are further south and mail is not in danger of interception. Yankee squads have been intercepting mail and learning of our movements lately. For that reason I can only say that we are being very secretive about our plans and intentions.

I have some of Rob's mail for you but will hold it until I can safely post with mine. You should be proud of Rob. He has served with distinction and is well liked by all. We often talk about Argyll.

Tell the younger boys in Texas not to be in any hurry to get north. This war is not as kind or adventurous as they may believe. Death and destruction is on some grandiose scale never seen before and although it pains me to write it, the Yankees seem to be getting the upper hand. A recall to Texas in her defense soon would not surprise me.

In closing, we are all well and whichever way this war goes we intend riding into Argyll within the year.

Goodbye for now and love to you all,
Hamish

Christine carefully replaced the letter back into the envelope and slid it into the bundle. As she did, she noticed a scrap of paper in the bottom of the pouch. She was determined not to read the rest of the letters, not yet at least, but this one page without an envelope beat that determination. She unfolded it to again see Hamish's handwriting.

Dear Mr and Mrs Campbell,

As Captain of the Texas Rangers Unit in which your son, Robert Piper Campbell bravely served, it is my sad duty to inform you that he died in combat with the enemy while defending the great state of Texas and the Confederacy.

The official greeting had been roughly disregarded by a broad swipe of a pencil, inviting the reader to delete it. Christine cried openly as she fought for control. Beneath the formal notification of Robs death was a scribbled note.

That's what I'm supposed to say to the family of a lost son or father. There are to be no details, but I am his kin and you need to know the true story before you hear it wrong in years to come. Rob, and two others, disturbed a Yankee patrol four days ago. The skirmish ended with Rob and the two others coming away with a hefty payroll destined for some Yankee column to the east. They were surprised by a unit of Yankee Cavalry on their way back and taken to the small township only five miles down the river from where we are. One of our men escaped and led us to where Rob was being held. They accused him of armed robbery and by the time we got there, late in the night, we found that he'd been hanged in the street as a robber.

I don't have time enough to seek reinforcements, so as Captain of the unit I will lead our boys into the town tomorrow to avenge our loss.

My sadness is as deep as yours and the pain I suffer in telling you this news is indeed great. While we all mourn Robbie's death, we can all take comfort in the revenge that we will deliver tomorrow to the Yankees responsible for the wrong they have done us.

All my love,
Hamish

Folding the paper, Christine walked slowly to the creek. Her steps counted back the days to their arrival at Argyll. The good times; the dreams; the joys and the happy occasions filled her mind and forced the tragedies aside. She felt empty, beaten and desperately alone as she sat on the sandy bank of the creek. Hugging her knees to her chest like a child, she closed her eyes, desperately trying to erase the hurt she felt.

The light touch of a warm hand on her arm startled her. Looking down she saw one of Black Abrahams grandchildren cuddling up beside her. She had been watching Christine with interest and although could not comprehend the situation fully, had followed her to the creek knowing that she was sad. Without a word the little girl handed Christine her wooden doll, placed her head on her side and consoled her by wrapping her small arms around Christine's waist.

The weeks that followed gave rise to long days of hard work by everyone at Argyll. The wounds were deep, but in each other they found the strength to carry on as a family and claw back the dreams and determination that once was the mainstay of the Campbells of Argyll. The wounded soldiers were nursed back to health and stayed on to help. If the shoulder was to be put to the wheel, everyone would lend their weight. A monument was erected at the entrance to the homestead in honour Mac and Rob Campbell. Regardless of the emancipation proclamation, Mexican and Negro labour stayed on. As far as they were concerned, Argyll was their home; they had always been free, as were their families, a pledge and promise made by Mac Campbell, in what now seemed an eternity ago.

Texas, like the rest of the Confederate States was being starved into submission by the North. Confederate money was not worth the paper it was written on and goods of any description from the South were traded with financial contempt. Argyll remained self sufficient but could only produce for its own and those who worked or sought refuge there.

A visiting patrol of Union soldiers brought news that the Civil War had come to an end with the surrender of General Smith in May, 1865. The patrol, led by a young Cavalry Officer arrived ahead of a troop of black Cavalry flying the pennant of a buffalo head. Everyone at Argyll had known for some time that all was lost and expected a visit from Northern Troops sooner than later. It was agreed that to take up arms would only lead to more dead Campbells, so the patrol was allowed to enter Argyll unopposed.

'Something we can do for you gentlemen?' a tanned and lean Piper asked as the young officer rode into the yard.

'Captain Slater,' the mounted soldier stated formally. 'We'll be operating out of the area west of here and into the Indian Territories. We'll need grain for the horses and fresh rations for the troops. We'll pay good money for good supplies.'

'Well now, Captain Slater,' Piper said sarcastically, 'if you get your boys to harvest the grain and crush it, why you can have all you need. And of course, if the boys are up to it, perhaps they could go out and chase a few longhorns down and butcher them, hell, seems everyone else does.'

'Piper!' Christine scolded. 'Time to let bygones be what they are; let these soldiers get what they need and be on their way.'

'Thank you Ma'am,' said the Captain, tipping his hat. 'The war is over; we're here now to make sure you people are safe from the Indians. Once we sort that issue out I'm sure that we can all commence the task of rebuilding the United States of America.'

Diego, barefoot and with shaved head, wearing only breaches, his muscular back glistening in the sunlight, trotted from the barn with a handful of grain. Subserviently lowering his head as he approached the mounted Captain he said, in his best Southern slave manner, 'Ah's got's some grain for y'all, Massa ... y'sar, massa, got's the grain. Y'all slip yo ass offa that there leather cradle an' ol' Diego poke all the grain yo needs rart down yo' gizzard ... yassar.'

'Ma'am,' the Captain said, addressing Christine. 'Tell your man here that the grain is for the horses, all of the horses, not just mine.'

'No sar, Massa,' replied Diego before Christine could interject, 'Y'all gots t'eat grain like Massa 'n Missy here. Hell, us nigras gots to wait some 'til y'all done with its goodness and shits it out. Then we all boils it up with creek grass and eats it, and by the look of the number of nigras y'all gots followin', y'all needs to eat a bellyful so y'all can crap enough to feed everybody ... yes sar!'

'Enough, Diego,' Christine smiled as she looked at the nervous Captain. 'Captain, you can set camp anywhere near the fence and Black Abraham here will take care of the grain and food. Perhaps you'd like to join us for supper?'

Piper looked at his mother in amazement. Yankees

81

for supper? He couldn't believe it, nor could Diego. Perhaps, they thought, their mother had finally come to grips with what had happened to their father and brother, perhaps she had tired of hatred, in her mind at least, and was starting afresh. Perhaps … just perhaps, she may be right.

That night at the supper table, Christine chatted away continuously trying to get the boys to at least acknowledge their invited guest. Finally, Piper addressed the young Captain. 'See any action during the war?'

'No, I didn't,' came the candid reply. 'I was conscripted, but because I was running the family business I was advised to remain in Boston and continue the business.'

'Oh,' said Piper, feigning surprise. 'I was conscripted along with brother Diego here and Pa, and we left our family business to answer the call. Pa got….' He stopped and continued eating.

'Please, I don't wish to open recent wounds,' replied the Captain. 'Can we all accept that the war is over and we are now as one? My being here is to ensure that you people are rid of the dangers from the Indians. Once that's done I will return to Boston and we'll all get on with life.'

Piper looked across the dining room where Hamish sat, rocking in his special chair as Magdalen, the house maid, helped spoon feed him some mashed corn and potato. 'Careful Maggie,' he called, 'be sure not to get any of that corn on Captain Campbell's shirt.'

Captain Slater turned to look at Hamish. 'Captain Campbell, you say?'

'Uhuh, best damn Captain the Texas Rangers ever saw,' Piper answered, glaring menacingly into Slater's eyes.

'Heard a lot about the Rangers,' Captain Slater said. 'Fact I heard that if we had a thousand of them the war would have lasted only a year or so,' he added spooning another load of corn.

'Yep, if we had a thousand more, same result would have been had, but in our favour,' Piper said, maintaining his eye contact.

'Sorry about....'

'My brother, he's my brother,' Piper said.

'Of course. Sorry about your brother.'

'And the other one?' Piper asked.

'Sorry, I'm not with you,' Slater replied.

'The other Texas Ranger brother who was killed,' said Piper. 'And then there was another Ranger, my father as I recall.'

Christine let the conversation run. Captain Slater paused for a while, picked up the napkin and wiped his mouth as Piper and Diego now continued to eat.

'You boys were Rangers, weren't you?' Slater asked.

'Sure as hell were,' Piper replied.

'Cussing at the table?' Christine questioned.

'Sorry Ma,' Piper said before addressing Slater again. 'Yes, we were rangers, still are as far as I know. Seen more action here on Argyll and up there in the Carolinas and all damn stretches in between to last any man a lifetime.'

'Join me as scouts out in the Indian Territory and I'll personally guarantee that Argyll gets top dollar for all supplies from here-on-in,' came the unexpected offer.

'Sir,' Christine said finally. 'About you are the remnants of my family ... my life. The ones that are not here have been taken from me because of war. What I still have will not be taken by another war. When you ride out of here it will be without a Campbell.'

The supper table continued in silence for a short while, broken finally by Captain Slater. 'Ma'am, gentlemen, I thank you for a fine meal. I appreciate that you have suffered and I give you my word that I will do all in my power to ensure that only prosperity comes to your household from this point on. Mind you, I'd sure like you two boys to ride with me; I'd certainly feel safer for it.'

In the morning, grain and food enough for the trail, Captain Slater rode up to the homestead and handed Christine payment. Two soldiers carried a long box from a wagon and placed it on the verandah.

'What's in that?' Christine enquired.

'Something for the boys,' answered Slater. 'Slightly illegal under the circumstances but tell them just because we're from the north, doesn't mean that we're enemies.'

As they rode off, Christine slid the top of the case back to reveal two repeating rifles and four new Peacemaker pistols complete with boxes of ammunition. 'Oh, that's nice,' she said under her breath, 'just in case they find another war to go off to.'

She left the box where it was and went inside to bring Hamish out onto his seat on the verandah. She was worried about the shrapnel that still lay embedded in his thigh. Field surgeons, retreating in the face of the enemy, had precious little time to conduct effective surgery on the wounded. Although the raw leg-stump had healed, pieces of metal that lay embedded within his thigh, continuously festered causing him immense pain. Christine wondered, now that the refugees had left Argyll and returned to Corpus Christie to reopen shops and warehouses, perhaps there was a doctor there whom she could call on to have Hamish's shrapnel removed.

CHAPTER SIX

1867 saw Argyll starting to reap the rewards of hard work and perseverance. Beef prices had started to rise and demand in the North was increasing. Wool prices were good and seasonal crops added much needed cash. Attacks from Indians were rare due to the constant patrols by the Army which allowed Argyll to function as it had never functioned before, without war. Lawless elements were still present but were dealt with swiftly by ranchers and townsfolk from the ever increasing population. Texas was becoming a destination for those willing to work hard and become Texans.

'I'm taking Hamish to a surgeon in Corpus Christie,' Christine announced to Piper and Diego one night. 'If we can get them damn pieces out of his leg and buttocks he may heal up totally. Who knows, once that happens his mind might even return.'

The wagon was loaded and ready to roll. 'Hang on,' Christine yelled. 'Won't be a minute,' as she rushed inside and grabbed the old saddle-pouch Hamish had given her.

'Ever read all the letters, Ma?' Diego asked.

'No, not yet. But I might get a chance in Corpus Christie,' she replied.

Diego rode ahead while Piper brought up the rear as they journeyed to the coast. The road was much safer now but it was still unwise to travel alone. At the end of the war, the Union had forbidden all but Officers of the Confederacy to keep their side-arms, however, because of the Indian problem, they seemed to turn a blind eye to this in Texas. Whatever the rule, both Diego and Piper carried revolvers and a saddle rifle wherever they went.

Once in Corpus Christie, Piper and Diego made sure Hamish and their mother were safely in accommodation before returning to Argyll. The doctor had said that they would probably be best staying there for a week or two, even three, so that any possible complications after the operation could be dealt with swiftly.

Back at Argyll there were horses to be broken, fences to be mended, cattle branded and stock moved. It was an exceptionally hot summer but Piper was pleased with the progress on Argyll. They had returned to freighting their goods the relatively short distance from Argyll to

Corpus Christie rather than down the Cotton Road to the Rio Grande. They had boosted their hide tanning sheds and were smoking more pork now, a commodity returning handsome dividends from the North. Pulled beef was also now packed at Argyll and freighted to the coast for distribution.

The time soon came to pick up Hamish and Christine. Wagons would follow with produce but Piper and Diego rode ahead. Five miles out from Corpus Christie they were stopped by two shotgun-toting guards behind a wooden barricade.

'What's the problem?' called Piper.

'Quarantine area,' one of the guards replied. 'Nobody allowed past this point, we got the black vomit in town, some swamp fever they say.'

'Well, how bad?' asked Piper.

'Some say two, maybe three hundred dead. Who knows? Could wipe out Christie entirely, some say.'

'Is the hospital safe?'

'Shit,' came the reply from one of the guards as he spat tobacco waste. 'Hospital's where they went first. Reckon the only thing alive in the hospital at the moment is skeeters.'

'Move aside, I'm going to the hospital,' Piper said.

Both guards drew the hammers back on their shotguns and levelled them at Piper. 'No you ain't,' one of them said. 'Nobody goes in and sure as hell, there ain't nobody comin' out. They is the rules and I intend stayin' alive, so, my friend, you ain't goin' in.'

'Okay, 'Piper said, calming down. 'We'll just camp out here with you and wait.

Little did they know how fast their camp would expand. Arrivals, some that had travelled a week or more, simply refused to leave and camped at the quarantine border. Within three days more than fifty people were camped on the roadside waiting. Finally, on the fourth day a horse and buggy arrived from the township. The driver, a mask covering his face, yelled advice that everyone should return home. He also advised that half of the town had died from the black vomit and those still surviving were burying the dead in mass graves or burning them in sulphur fires to stop the plague.

Some at the checkpoint left but Piper and Diego stayed on, waiting for news of their mother and Hamish. The all clear was finally given. Those who wanted to risk the plague were allowed to enter town on the understanding that if there was another outbreak they would not be allowed to leave. On that understanding Piper and Diego entered and rode to the hospital, bandanas over their mouths as if riding into a dust storm.

They learned from the nurse who had admitted Hamish that the fever had claimed him early. Christine, unwilling to leave Hamish had at least arranged a proper burial before the fever took hold in earnest. She had then stayed on to take care of the sick children but had succumbed soon after. She was buried in a mass grave along with dozens of other victims, her belongings burnt.

Piper and Diego were now hardened to death, but this was different. They had seen both their fathers die violently; they had joined a war that had taken a brother and now, all that they had left had been taken by an act of God. The only true Campbell survivor, Piper, stood on the street with his adopted brother, Diego. Whether they were too accustomed to it, or just too tired, neither shed a tear although their hearts were overburdened with indescribable grief. They felt robbed and cheated, not by war this time, but by cruel circumstances.

Returning to Argyll they spread the word of the tragedy. The grief of the long serving employees was as great as their own. Soldiers, whom they had saved on the track and had become part of Argyll, broke down when they heard the news. Argyll was back in mourning.

'Argyll is ours now,' Piper said to Diego as they rode slowly along the cattle pad to an out-station.

'No, Argyll is yours, my friend,' he replied.

'Wrong,' Piper said. 'Argyll is as much you as it is me. Your first family died here and we've grown up together here. We're brothers, and the Clan Campbell looks after its own, and you, Diego, are now part of the Clan.'

For a full day they rode and talked. Talking seemed to put issues at rest and tragedies behind them. They were bonded more than ever and searched for direction from each other. Their return to the homestead was via the site of Diego's family's graves. Standing over his father's grave, Diego fingered the necklace of beads, bone and shell around his neck.

'This is where you became a Campbell,' Piper said quietly.

'This is where the Karankawa people were supposed to end,' Diego replied. 'And yes, this is where I became a Campbell. Whatever the future, I ask only one thing of you, Piper, and that is, know me now by the name given to me by my Indian father.'

'Don't want to be a Campbell?' Piper quizzed.

'Yes, and a proud one, but the name Diego was given so that I might be recognized as Spanish and not Karankawa. A Spanish name would keep me alive whereas a Karankawa name would certainly have seen me dead. Death is something that holds no fear for me anymore, so while I am a Campbell, my name is N'kawa.'

After straightening the stones around the graves, the two friends mounted and headed up the small rise past the rocks where a young Piper had galloped years before into a group of Comanche intent on murder. They stopped and looked back. 'N'kawa, brother, let's get off home and figure out what's to be,' Piper said.

Almost four years passed before Piper and N'kawa had worked the tragic past from their systems. They watched as some of the larger land holdings, due to sub division, were reduced in size and productivity while Argyll continued to grow. They had become successful ranchers in their own right. Each day was dedicated to ranching and rarely did they venture from Argyll. The Indian Wars still raged in the Central Badlands and to the Central North but that was of little consequence to Argyll. As long as the Soldiers were out there keeping the Indians busy they could get on with their work knowing that the cattle-drives would be safer.

It was on a trip to Brownsville that Piper and N'kawa met Señor Montoya, a Mexican cattle and land baron, who had made it clear that he would like to secure breeding ranches in the Nueces Valley region. After a long and convivial evening with the Montoyas, Piper and N'kawa retired to sleep off the tequila.

'You asleep, N'kawa?' Piper asked.

'No.'

'Ever thought about selling Argyll?

'Why?'

'So we can go do something else. See the world. Go to some place that isn't bounding from war to war and when it's resting, dreaming up some other way to start a God-damn new war,' Piper answered.

'Lot of our history buried back there. Can't take the bones with us,' N'kawa said, almost asleep.

'We stay there and pretty soon our bones will be planted there as well. Hell, neither of us has a family now … nobody, we're it!'

'Dream about it tonight and talk to Montoya in the morning. I'm going to sleep.'

When morning arrived, Piper rolled over and pulled the blanket up to shield his eyes from the morning sun. 'Ah shit, is it morning already?' he muttered.

'Sunrise was good,' replied N'Kawa, standing beside the bed looking down at Piper before yanking his blanket off.

'Bugger off,' yelled Piper, as he looked through squinted eyes at N'kawa. 'Jesus!' he yelled, sitting bolt upright, eyes wide open. 'What have you done?'

N'kawa stood there smiling; head smooth-shaved except for a tuft on top from which a feather hung down across his left ear. Circles were painted beneath each eye and his bare chest displayed broad stripes of yellow ochre. His neck was painted a hideous red.

'Y'look like a bloody turkey,' Piper yelled.

'I look like a Karankawa about to have coffee with someone who wants to buy my land. Over the past few generations they simply shot us and took it. Let's see how they bargain with a ghost.'

'I'm confused now,' Piper said cautiously. 'Are you saying that I have no title to Argyll?'

'You saved the Karankawa from total extinction … that gives you title,' N'kawa grinned. 'Well, some at least.'

'Okay, okay, but you ain't going down to the dining hall dressed like that.'

'Watch me.'

The crowd in the dining hall had started to thin a little as Piper and N'kawa walked in and strode to the Montoya table.

'Excuse me sir,' a waiter called to Piper. 'Your friend will need a shirt on to eat in the dining hall.'

'Damn lucky I talked him into wearing pants,' Piper called back. 'And don't worry, he ain't eatin', just sittin'. Perhaps you could go fetch a comb so he can tidy himself up a bit.'

A bewildered Montoya stood as they approached, motioning for them to join him at his table.

'Señor Montoya,' Piper said, exhaling as he spoke. 'You said yesterday that you needed land up in the Nueces. No doubt you'd like to get your hands on Argyll.'

'Of course,' Montoya replied, still staring at N'kawa.

'We've got several thousand acres fully stocked at the moment,' N'kawa said, glancing at Piper as he spoke. 'It's for sale until five p.m. today as a going concern, less one hundred acres on either side of the creek including the homestead, barn and other buildings at the homestead. Four cattle breeders, sheep breeding stock, six horses and pig breeders will be held from any sale. If we have your answer by five we'll have the survey drawn and stock inventory made up ready for transfer within the month.'

Piper could barely believe what he had just heard, nor could a very confused Montoya who sat, mouth agape staring at the painted black person with a feathered tuft of hair seated opposite him, who had just offered to sell him a large slab of Texas, an offer made with the authority of a city businessman.

'Five o'clock then,' N'kawa confirmed as he stood. 'Come on, Piper, things to be done, ranches to sell. No time to be sitting around sipping coffee.'

Piper stood up, nodded dumbly at Montoya and followed N'kawa out of the food hall and upstairs to the room.

'Way I see it, Piper, is that if Montoya wants it, he'll

buy it, but the more time we give him the harder the bargain he'll drive,' N'kawa said over his shoulder as they climbed the stairs. 'If he's not here at five then we leave for Argyll at sun-up.'

'Mmm,' Piper managed. 'Price. I don't remember discussing a price.'

'We take whatever he offers for the land, and sell all stock for the same price we get at the sales. Improvements can be easily calculated and shouldn't present a problem. Montoya is a rancher; he knows the value of stock and improvements just as we do.'

Piper was still shaking his head in disbelief when Montoya walked to their table at five o'clock that evening. It was almost ten p.m. before the group was shaking hands and signing agreements. A generous land value was agreed upon in lieu of improvements. The annexation of one hundred acres of land either side of the creek leading to the homestead was also settled in favour of the Campbells.

They didn't celebrate that night; instead they sat together in their room discussing possibilities again, a discussion that continued from the saddle all the way back to Argyll, at which time it was settled. They would depart Argyll within the month, as arranged with Montoya. The homestead, out-buildings and one hundred acres either side of the creek, plus breeding stock would be gifted to Black Abraham and his extended family. Those who wished to stay on and work the land could do so under the guardianship of Black Abraham.

Piper and N'kawa pledged that they would take no more than a horse, pack-horse each and all of their personal belongings. Their plan was to ride north; back over the trail of sorrow they'd ridden some years before, back through the battlefields of the Civil War and on to New York. Once there, everything behind them would remain there. They would board a Pacific-bound clipper and start a new life somewhere down in the South Seas, free from war and all that accompanied it. They had enough money to buy land and stock, and enough desire and ambition to match their considerable bank balance. There would be a new Argyll; a peaceful Argyll, an Argyll where they could settle without constantly digging and filling graves.

They agreed that they would wait no longer than two weeks in New York before deciding upon a destination. Whatever was available, they would take. And so it was, late in 1872, after a sobering ride through the battlefields of the Civil War that Piper and N'kawa remembered so vividly, they stood together at the stern of the clipper Rain Cloud as she cast off and filled her sails, bound for the Pacific Ocean and Hawaii. Neither had been aboard a sailing ship whilst under sail and both spent the first few days wishing they were still on dry land as the clipper rolled and groaned, smashing into wave after inglorious wave, each one sending salt spray onto the faces of passengers too ill to go below. Sailors went cheerfully about their duties and taunted passengers jovially about their lack of sea legs.

Once accustomed to the movement of the ocean beneath them, Piper and N'kawa adjusted well to ship life and assisted the seamen during the long days at sea. It eased the monotony and they learnt skills once foreign to them. By the time they reached the Islands of Hawaii they were considered good hands to have aboard.

The months that followed saw Piper and N'kawa jump from ship to ship, working on board to pay their passage. From clippers to old barques and sloops, some barely seaworthy with crews to match, on they travelled to exotic ports rarely heard of in the civilized world. From the silk and spice runs of the Indias to the steaming jungle ports of the Pacific and Java they roamed, like latter day explorers, all the while learning of new opportunities in the Pacific Islands and further beyond in Australia and New Zealand.

Sailing south down the east coast of Australia gave them their first glimpses of the great Southern Land. The pinnacles of the Glasshouse Mountains and Ranges beyond lay off the starboard bow as they sailed into the narrow channel leading to the Brisbane River. 'Civilization at last,' Piper said to N'kawa.

'That's what they tell us,' N'Kawa replied.

'So, how long are we here for?' Piper asked, almost with mischief in his voice.

N'kawa grinned across his shoulder at Piper. 'Let's get ashore, pay off and let the good folk of Brisbane know that we've arrived. Keep our options open, I'd say.'

CHAPTER SEVEN

T he weeks that followed were very agreeable to Piper and N'kawa, who had taken lodgings near the wharves closest to the city. Brisbane was a bustling, thriving city that boasted all the commercial atmosphere and entertainment a visitor could want. The spring air was clear and the weather comfortably warm, unlike some of the destinations they had recently visited.

The two visited the Commercial Trading Bank to arrange for the proceeds from the sale of Argyll to be secured in a cash custody account. They later joked about the raised eyebrows of the bank manager when he had learned of the sizable deposit offered by the two buckskin clad cowboys, one black and one white, both bearing the name Campbell and registering joint ownership of the impressive account.

Most evenings were spent in the saloon bar of the hotel where they met sailors, townsfolk, gold prospectors who had made good and graziers who had taken up land for cattle farming in the hinterland regions. They quickly learned that their decision to remain in Australia, for the while at least, was a good one. Opportunities for cattlemen were abundant, especially further north and into the interior where explorers were constantly opening up new gold fields and farms. It seemed that gold was being found just about everywhere in the north, causing the birth of some sizeable towns. Some would turn into ghost towns when the gold ran out but others would flourish with industry. From experience, they knew that cattle and land held the key to long term prosperity, not gold.

It was a fresh evening as they sat in the saloon listening to a pianist smoothly rehearsing his routine. 'Reckon the holiday's about over,' N'kawa said.

'Yep,' Piper replied, lowering the shot glass to the table. 'Shame, I was just starting to like this old lad on the piano; kind of relaxing.'

'If he was half as good again he would be travelling with us,' an educated voice sounded, causing them both to turn and take in the well dressed young man standing behind them. 'My apologies, I couldn't help but overhear your conversation,' he added.

'Well I thought he was pretty good,' Piper said.

'Oh, please,' the stranger offered. 'I meant no offence. I'm with a travelling opera and musical show. We travel a lot and just recently performed in the United States. Today, we gave a show in the Brisbane Theatre.'

'Shame we missed it,' Piper said genuinely. 'Don't mind a bit of music.'

'Perhaps you can hear us at some later date. We leave on the first tide tomorrow for the Northern goldfields. No doubt you gentlemen are headed that way,' the stranger said.

A woman approached and cut their conversation short. 'Cristoforo,' she said with friendly smile, placing her hand on the stranger's arm. 'Has all of the gear been transferred to the steamer ready for tomorrow?'

'Yes, it's all taken care of,' he replied.

Piper watched her as she departed the lounge. 'Lovely lady,' he nodded slowly.

'And the best opera singer in the country,' the stranger said. 'Gentlemen, you have just been in the company of the great Countess Marie Carandini. To hear her sing is to enter the parlour of heaven itself.'

'You work with her?' Piper queried.

'Yes, and I live with her. She's my mother. Still thinks of me as a child and still addresses me by my childhood name, regardless of my protests,' he said feigning a look of despair.

'Mothers do that,' Piper agreed as he stood to offer his handshake. 'Piper Campbell, and this here's N'kawa Campbell,' he added motioning to a now standing N'kawa.

'Christie,' the stranger replied with a broad smile of his handsome face, 'Christie Palmerston Carandini. Perhaps you'll enjoy our theatre when next we meet in the North?'

'Be our pleasure, Christie,' Piper confirmed.

Christie turned to leave, stopped, then turned back to Piper and N'kawa. 'Both Campbells?' he asked with a confused look on his face.

'That's right,' Piper answered. 'My brother here doesn't like wearing hats and gets sunburned some. It's taken him years to raise that tan.'

The smiling trio parted company in good spirits as the lounge pianist continued his happy melody.

Piper and N'kawa were starting to get restless as the days passed without any decision being made as to checking land and stock prices. They had ventured into the hinterland and further to the Southern Plains where the good grazing land had already been taken up. On more than one occasion they had commented to each other how similar the land was to that of land in Texas, poorer in places and better in others. Stock was more of the English variety and not as hardy as the Texas longhorn but it seemed easier to handle and fattened quickly.

A chance meeting with a cattle farmer from the Gympie diggings gave them some direction and further whet their appetites. He told of the difficulty facing diggers on the far northern fields around Charters Towers and even further afield on the Hodgkinson. Going for gold was one thing, finding food was another. It was a known fact that diggers had starved to death while working their claims. The farmer also told them that there was good grazing land in the Townsville district that could be opened up and used as a breeding holding while supplying the northern fields. There were good horses and some breeding stock already at Townsville, all they had to do was ship more up to get things rolling. They were also cautioned that the North was rough country and the natives unfriendly.

Later, the two sat behind a bottle of fine whiskey and gazed out over the masts of the ships tied up along the wharf. 'What do you think?' Piper asked N'kawa.

'Well, old Mac told us that fortunes were made following the gold diggers with food, but that was in kinder country by the sound of it,' replied N'kawa.

'Not really. Sacramento was no more than a shanty town in the wilderness before Sutter and his boys found gold, and look what happened there,' Piper said.

'Mmmm. I guess so,' N'kawa said past a mouthful of German sausage and bread-biscuit.

'We're agreed then,' Piper said with enthusiasm. 'Tomorrow we load a wagon with supplies, arrange for cattle and horses to follow and catch the first steamer north to Townsville.'

'Who's going to arrange the cattle and horses?'

'We'll leave that in the capable hands of our new friend from Gympie.'

'Very trusting of you,' N'kawa said, 'but I agree, we leave when we can.

Two days later, they boarded a steamer destined for the northern ports. A wagonload of supplies was loaded aboard while Piper and N'kawa said their goodbyes to those they'd befriended in Brisbane.

Although the steamer was small, she was fast and cut through the water at a far more agreeable pace and pitch than the old sailing ships they were accustomed to. In a little more than a week, stopping only once at Bowen, the small ship steamed into Townsville harbour and unloaded its cargo and passengers.

'Shit,' Piper muttered to N'Kawa. 'Doesn't look too much like cattle country to me. Kind of scrub country like you get west of Argyll, too damn dusty and too damn hot.'

'What's beyond those hills, I wonder?' N'kawa asked.

'More scrub and more dust, I'd say,' Piper replied slapping his face, squashing a dozen sticky, black flies.

Beyond the shanties they could see cattle standing in a long yard. A few horses were corralled next to them, swishing their tails at the pesky flies that swarmed the area. The atmosphere and character of the place projected anything but prosperity.

'I think our time here will be limited, N'kawa,' Piper said. 'Best we can do is scout around and see what the country is like to the north and south of here.'

'Didn't know you liked walking all that much,' came N'kawa's reply.

'We'll buy more horses, we can always take them

with us when we leave, which probably won't be all that far in the future,' Piper said.

With the wagon ashore and their camp made, the two set out to select four good horses; two for riding and two as packs. The horses they chose were in surprisingly good condition and displayed enough spirit to warrant their purchase. A government contingent cautioned them against riding too far from town as the natives were sometimes hostile and would kill their horses for food, given the chance. Again, there was silent confusion about N'kawa, the black horseman who was clearly not a mayall of any description and spoke with a Texan drawl. The tuft of hair to the back of his scalp appeared hideous to some, though nobody dared question a man of his size, athletic build and commanding gait. Although both men wore buckskin, only Piper carried a revolver and saddle rifle, a repeating Winchester given to him by the visiting 'protector' of Argyll some years ago. N'kawa chose to carry only a knife, for medical emergencies he insisted.

Riding south, away from the settlement of Townsville they met a Native Mounted Police patrol led by an English Officer. After a brief discussion with the Sub-Inspector leading the patrol, they continued on. 'That fellow would have made a damn good Yankee officer,' Piper laughed. 'I reckon he takes his job too seriously. And did you see the soldiers?'

'Thought I'd laugh,' N'kawa said. 'Hell, even a well-to-do Apache couldn't get that much gear on him. Those jackets and hats must be as hot as hell itself.'

Neither meant any offence by their comments, but the sight of Native Troopers dressed in heavy woollen breeches and jackets, heavy knee-high boots, flared leather gloves, peaked caps and neckerchiefs struck a comical chord with Piper and N'kawa, who laboured under the same forty degree heat without the discomfort of such an extensive wardrobe.

Amused by their meeting they rode on and scouted the land to the South. The plains area was vast, stretching as far as the eye could see but it was their bet that it held little long term cattle value due to the probability of flooding.

'Damned if I want a few thousand head drowning in this place,' Piper said as they turned back for their camp.

'Must be better land to the north,' N'kawa said. 'Maybe we'll ride there tomorrow and see what's on offer.'

Reining in their horses they looked in amazement as a mob a kangaroos bounded away from them towards the hills. 'I'll be damned,' N'kawa said. 'That's the kangaroo we've been hearing about. Sure is a strange critter.'

'Sizeable rat,' Piper said. 'Hate to try and catch one. They've got to be covering more ground than a horse at full gallop.'

'Maybe we could farm them,' said N'kawa with a chuckle.

'Damned uncomfortable to ride by the looks,' Piper laughed as they rode on.

Returning to Townsville by late evening, the two tended their horses and strolled to the buildings closest the waterfront. The number of people in this frontier town surprised them. They guessed that these few thousand people were here for one reason or another associated with gold. Sailors, soldiers, police and government people mixed cordially with a host of other trades, the largest in number being diggers. Trade stores, bars and food stalls were plentiful and the large Chinese contingent was quite obvious.

'Remember that food we near crippled ourselves on in the Orient?' N'kawa asked as they strolled along the dusty street.

'Sure do, wasn't that something?' Piper replied.

'Well, unless my Indian nose is broken, I smell much of the same coming from those buildings there,' he said, pointing towards the end of the town.

'We're about to eat, my friend,' Piper said, rubbing his hands together.

Walking to the end of the buildings they entered the food house that was the origin of the exotic aromas. Inside, Chinese men and women sat on benches beside long tables laden with steaming bowls of food. Seeing the two tall men enter they all stopped eating and stared. Piper, remembering his manners, quickly removed his hat, smiled and walked towards a vacant spot on the nearest bench.

'Ah, gentlemen,' an old man said as he shuffled from the servery area. 'You in wrong house. This Chinese

107

food house, you must go down street for food, Chinese eat here.' He continued in broken English, smiling as he did.

'Hell no,' Piper beamed. 'This smells like just the place me and N'kawa here should be eating in. You go on now and bring out the supper, and plenty of it.'

'No, no,' the old Chinese man persisted, his smile now replaced by a frown. 'Food only for Chinese, no white people eat here, only Chinese.'

Surprised, Piper stopped, looked at N'kawa and replied, 'He ain't white, he's black. I don't mind if y'all dish him up a large helping and I'll help him eat it.'

The gathering suddenly broke into Chinese, all seemingly speaking at once. It was impossible to tell whether they were agreeing or disagreeing as they shook their heads, nodded and raised their voices at one another.

'Best we move on, Piper,' N'kawa said wisely.

'Hell no,' came the reply as Piper stepped forward, sat astride the bench and ordered. 'Chinese food, please,' he said towards the old man, smiling as he did.

Again, everyone stopped eating. An old lady jumped up and shuffled quickly to the kitchen, probably in protest. Piper looked slowly around, all the while smiling his best smile.

'Boots,' N'kawa said. 'Come back out and take your boots off. Ain't nobody here wearing boots of any kind.'

'Oh right,' Piper replied as he slowly stood, turned and walked towards the door. 'I take these things off and I hope they got some real sweet smelling food on the cook to mask the smell.'

At the door they both removed their boots and re-entered the room. There were a few nods from Chinese heads, but there, like one of them sticky black flies, was the old man again, only this time more agitated. 'Chinese food shop, not Chinese, no eat here. You go down street to white and black eating shop.'

It was clear to N'kawa that Piper's persistence and carefree attitude had, in the eyes of the Chinese, surpassed ignorance and entered the realm of arrogance.

'So what now?' Piper enquired of N'kawa. 'Shirts off too?'

Before N'kawa could answer, a girl of nineteen or so appeared from the cooking area and hurried towards them. 'Come on, please sit at the end of the table, I'll get food for you,' she said in perfect English. 'They are not accustomed to eating with foreigners. You must be new here so we can feed you this time.'

The old man cackled in Chinese as he stormed off to the other end of the table to continue his meal.

'If it's any problem, Ma'am, we'd just as soon leave,' N'kawa said politely.

'No,' the girl replied cheerfully, 'besides, you have your shoes off now. Come, sit here.'

They both sat down as the girl hurried out to the cooking area to fill their plates. N'kawa felt uncomfortable as he glanced warily towards the eating Chinese, all of whom fired glances back that were other than complimentary. Piper sat there quietly, watching the girl in the kitchen.

While N'kawa saw a young Chinese lady carrying two bowls of steaming food towards them, Piper saw a creature of beauty like no-one he'd seen before. Her smile seemed to light the room. Her coal black hair, tied tightly back, glistened as she approached, while her eyes sparkled the reflection of the red wall and candles.

'There you are, Chinese food for you,' she said with her radiant smile as she placed the bowls on the table before them.

Fumbling awkwardly, Piper dug into his jacket, almost knocking the bowl from the table. 'We'll pay, it's not that we want free food, no, nothing like that, we'll pay,' he said, sounding more than a little stupid.

'You can pay the owner of the house when you've finished your meal,' she replied. 'Enjoy your food first.'

'Well, can't I pay you?' Piper said.

'Piper!' N'kawa said abruptly. 'Pay the man later, eat food now, *comprendé?*'

The girl smiled over her shoulder, sensing the difficulty of the situation as the two ate their meal. The Chinese gathering had apparently accepted that they were here for a meal and that was that.

When they had finished, the two thanked the old man, paid him and left, totally contented. They had barely exited the door before it was slammed and boarded shut.

On the street, Piper encouraged N'kawa to join

him at the rough-walled bar nearby. Once inside, they ordered a drink and stood with a group of diggers and sailors. Upon recounting their evening, the group roared with laughter, belting their legs and hopping around as they did. 'Bloody new chums,' an old digger roared, 'bloody amazing.'

'Well, we didn't think it was that funny,' Piper said defensively.

'Let me tell you,' the old Irish digger said, after he'd composed himself. 'The Chinese keep to themselves on the diggings, and anywhere else they go. You boys busted into their grazing ground. That must have really pissed them off. But the best of it, and you'll have to excuse me N'kawa, I mean no offence, but the best of it was taking a black man into their camp. Shit, a black man entering a Chinese camp looking for food 'round these parts means that there'll be one less Chinaman on the fields tomorrow!'

This was followed by more roars of laughter.

'You'll have to complete the joke,' Piper said with a frown.

'You don't know?' replied the old digger. 'Hell, Chinese foolish enough to venture into the northern fields have become flavour of the month for the Merkins. They'd rather eat Chinese than kangaroo now. Tasty little buggers, apparently. And there you go, bold as brass, sitting one down to eat food with them.'

'Merkins?' N'kawa enquired.

'Yeah, Merkins … blackfellas, not that I'm associating

your good self with Merkins, of course,' the old digger said.

'In any case,' another digger yelled from the bar, 'we don't much associate with Chinkies. Bastards will take over a good claim while you take a shit down the bank. Can't trust 'em and its best we keep the thieving sons-of-bitches off the fields altogether. Remember the trouble they give us in Victoria and New South Wales?'

The diggers all mumbled their agreement, nodding their heads in unison. 'No place for them here in Queensland,' an anonymous voice added from the rear of the group.

'Well, lads,' Piper announced cheerfully. 'When one of you sun-struck scratchers can cook me up a meal better than the one I've just had, I'll consider agreeing with you.'

The situation had the potential to erupt into something ugly, but it didn't. Bidding them farewell, Piper and N'kawa left the bar and headed back to camp. They both agreed that they had a lot to learn about life in the Australian Wilderness, particularly about its inhabitants.

Detouring, at Pipers insistence, they walked the street past the front of the Chinese food house. Passing a shack opposite the rear of the food house, they stopped. The young Chinese woman who had served them earlier stood watering a vegetable garden in the dim light. She was about to turn and walk back to the hut when Piper called in a quiet voice. 'Excuse me, Ma'am.'

She stopped, turned and smiled. 'Oh, it's you again. You want more food?' she asked with raised eyebrows.

'Why no,' Piper replied excitedly. 'No, we just thought we'd come by and check on y'all. Make sure you're safe, and everything. Me and N'kawa here, that is.'

'Oh, thank you, but there's no need,' came her reply.

'Well yeah, but you never can tell…'

'Piper,' N'kawa cut him short. 'Camp would be a good place to be right now.'

'Your friend is very protective of you,' the Chinese girl smiled. 'It's good to have a protector.'

'Why no, not at all,' came Pipers defensive reply. 'Old N'kawa here ain't my protector, he's my brother. You can go on back to camp now, brother,' Piper said, looking at N'kawa. 'Go on, off you go,' he added quickly.

'Now that would be silly,' the Chinese girl said. 'You out here on the street alone. I'm going to bed now, goodbye.'

She flashed Piper one last smile before turning and walking inside. The curtain flapped shut as someone inside withdrew from it. Turning, Piper yelled, 'Wait on there, N'kawa; wait on.'

Back at camp, they unrolled their bedding and settled onto the warm earth. Crickets and frogs had long ago started their nightly sing-along as the two drifted towards sleep. Piper's voice interrupted what would have been a smooth passage to sleep for N'kawa.

'What did you think of her?' he asked

'Good cook,' came the sleepy reply.

'No, I mean, what did you think of her?' Piper insisted. 'She's a goddess.'

'I agree, she's a goddess,' N'kawa said. 'Perhaps you could marry her. We could invite the town to the wedding; she could cook for the white folk while I could eat her parents. That way everyone would be happy and you'd get your dowry back.'

'You are one deranged blackfella, N'kawa, you know that?' Piper said.

'You keep looking at Chinese girls and you'll be one whitefella minus some essential body parts. Go to sleep, brother.'

He couldn't sleep. His mind kept filling with visions of the Chinese girl until it overflowed. Throughout his recent travels, he had enjoyed the good time girls at ports around the world but they were exactly that, good time girls, there for the taking as long as you had a few dollars to part with. But this, this was different. He was sure that there must have been more beautiful girls along the way; it's just that he couldn't recall them now; his mind was full of only her.

Exhaustion finally took over and Piper drifted off to sleep. N'kawa opened his eyes slowly and looked across the tent at him. He recounted the words from the diggers at the bar. The Australian blacks ate Chinese, they had said. He wondered; did they eat the flesh for food or for some other reason? His first family, the

Karankawa had eaten flesh for revenge or to ingest the spirits of a brave warrior, usually a Comanche. He had once shared the flesh of a Comanche Chief, killed by his father and had watched as the men of his group carved up other screaming Comanche, roasted their flesh and ate it while they watched. They were always careful to let one Comanche go after witnessing the feast; that ensured that other Comanche would think twice about attacking Karankawa. With these thoughts circling his mind, N'kawa eventually dozed off.

CHAPTER EIGHT

As the months passed, the Campbells secured a small holding, built a rough slab-and-canvas shack and concentrated on establishing good shorthorn breeders. Townsville was growing by the day. Ships came and went, leaving behind a mixture of souls keen to stake a claim in the new territory. Substantial houses and warehouses sprang up along the waterfront and beyond. Townsville was rapidly taking on the appearance of a vibrant settlement.

Sugar, wool and even cotton industries were quickly established along with fresh food production and, of course, beef. Word was filtering through almost daily about the desperate conditions on the central gold fields where food was becoming more expensive than gold itself. The Campbells had decided that once their stocks were substantial they would drive a herd inland and north to the goldfields. They could take up grazing land and continue to supply for as long as the gold lasted.

As the fierce Townsville sun continued to parch the throats and hides of all who settled there, word arrived that about four hundred diggers had followed Mulligans track into the inhospitable country of the Palmer Basin. Their trek had taken them through hundreds of miles of rough country. Once at the Palmer, although excellent gold was being won, the supply line for food was simply too long and arrived late, if ever at all. Diggers were literally dying from exhaustion and hunger as they battled the elements on the river of gold. As more arrived from the southern fields, malaria and dysentery added to their woes and many would die trying to make their fortune.

Meeting with the Mining Warden and Magistrate one evening, Piper and N'kawa were invited to join a steamer that was soon to arrive, bound for Cooks Town on the Endeavour River. The Hann expedition had crossed from the Palmer to the Endeavour a couple of years earlier and had indicated that supplies to the Palmer fields would be better and faster served by blazing a trail from Cooks Town to the Palmer.

This was the invitation the Campbells had been waiting for. 'As far as I'm concerned,' the Magistrate said, 'if it were my decision I would close the field down. Too dangerous, and our ports and supply lines are not yet ready for a rush into a wilderness of such morbid disposition. Mark my words, the amount of alluvial gold being won there means that half of Australia will soon be on the diggings, and that worries me.'

'Why not close it down before it gets too established?' Piper asked, clearly displaying his ignorance.

'Not possible,' the Magistrate smiled. 'We've all seen gold fever before. Diggers will walk all the way from Gympie to the Palmer if they hear that payable gold is being won. The consequences are merely an after-thought until it's too late. No, we'll just have to push on and manage it as best we can.'

'So, what part do you see us playing?' Piper asked.

'It's no secret that you boys are good cattlemen. Seems you can put your hand to most things. Then of course, there's your experience dealing with Indians and again, it's no secret that you were both Texas Rangers during the American Civil War,' the Magistrate explained. 'Our Native Troopers and Mounted Police have seen a few skirmishes here and there but nothing like what you boys have encountered. A couple with your experience, not to mention the extra firepower, might just come in handy up there.'

'Well, we're cattlemen, that's a fact and that's what we'll be going north to do, raise cattle,' Piper answered. 'That's new territory up there and I think it's best to address any possible conflict once we get there. Seems to me that the natives can't be all that much of a threat – I hear that their weapons are no more than spears and clubs, hardly a match for rifles.'

'Perhaps,' the Magistrate said, 'but they are not to be underestimated.'

'Of course not, but I think that a good old fashioned parley at the outset could avoid conflict,' Piper offered. 'Let's get around the gettin' there business first, huh?'

'Fine,' replied the Magistrate. 'The steamer Leichhardt should be here within the week. I'll arrange for adequate passage for you two plus stock and horses.'

Pleased at the outcome of the meeting, Piper and N'kawa made their way to the Chinese eating house. They had now become friends with the Chinese merchants although the old Chinese man kept a wary eye on the two, especially Piper who was obviously fond of the young Chinese lady, much to the old man's disappointment and disapproval.

They had learned that the Chinese group was from the Victorian goldfields and rather than fossick for gold, had remained merchants, butchers, carpenters and general traders. Originally from Hong Kong, they knew only too well that wherever the diggers went, the need for food, clothing and equipment followed. Their objectives were not unlike those held by Piper and N'kawa. The young lady that had caught Piper's eye, Mei Ling Siu, was born in Victoria and educated as circumstances permitted, which accounted for her fine grasp of the English language. Although most of the group spoke English, few ever did, preferring to chatter away in their Chinese tongue which didn't endear them to the diggers.

'Well, my Chinese friends,' Piper announced as

he pulled a bowl of steaming fish-broth towards him, 'within the week we move north to Cooks Town.'

The Chinese nodded in agreement before the old man said, 'We also go north.'

Surprised, Piper glanced towards Mei before asking. 'You know about the steamer?'

'Ah, yes,' came the old man's reply. 'We know before you know about steamer. We go to build shop and butcher your cows for miners,' he added with a little mischief in his voice.

'I'll be damned,' Piper grinned, looking at N'kawa who sat eating quietly.

'We hear very bad news from Palmer,' the old man continued. 'Many Chinese go there and many Chinese die. Blackfella no like Chinese. Digger no like Chinese. Chinese no like Chinese, but we go anyway. You protect us.'

'Now hold on a minute, old fella,' Piper argued. 'If you stay at Cooks Town we'll take care of you, but if you go running off into the wilderness, then you're on your own. Me and N'kawa here haven't agreed to head north to ride shotgun for anyone.'

'But Palmer is where shop needed,' the old man protested. 'No good at Cooks Town if needed at Palmer, make no money!'

'Okay, okay, the Mounted Troopers will look after you on the way to the Palmer. Don't worry,' Piper said, unconvincingly.

Muttering under his breath in Chinese, the old man shuffled out of the room. Mei sat beside Piper.

'You won't convince the old man that we should stay in Cooks Town,' she said. 'Maybe later on when we have shops set up at the Palmer we can return and set some up at Cooks Town.'

'Let me get this right,' Piper asked. 'You are going as well?'

'Of course,' came her reply.

'You are going with the troopers to blaze a trail to the Palmer?'

'Yes, of course,' she repeated.

'That is the silliest thing I've ever heard. That's wild country up there; full of critters, disease and heat enough to fry a man's brain, not to mention natives apparently on the warpath. No, you can't go,' Piper said shaking his head.

Her face lit up as she smiled at him. 'We'll be alright. You and N'kawa will be there.'

'But we won't.' he replied, anger almost creeping into his voice. 'Didn't you just hear me, we are staying at Cooks Town to set up a ranch and build a few houses. We're going to rebuild what we once had in Texas, only bigger and better. We are not going there to ride around playing soldiers.'

Mei patted Piper's hand as she got up from the table and flashed one last flirtatious smile before returning to the kitchen, leaving a frustrated Piper silently seeking answers in N'kawa's expressionless face.

'Worries me a bit,' N'kawa said on the short ride back to their holding.

'Chinese?' asked Piper.

'No, where this seems to be leading. From what I can gather, soon we will be landed at some deserted river in the wilderness with a bunch of government people and soldiers who are hell bent on blazing a trail through native territory. Does that sound familiar to you?' asked N'kawa.

'You mean Argyll?'

'I mean America, Texas, Mexico and yes, Argyll. Have you forgotten what happened to the American trail-blazers back in the sixties and even now?' N'kawa continued. 'I thought that we left all that behind us when we boarded that ship in New York.'

'Hardly think that there will be the slaughter and carnage here that we had with the Indians, hell, they don't even ride horses and only carry spears,' Piper scoffed.

'Karankawa didn't ride horses and only had spears, clubs, bows and arrows and yet we fought off the invaders for hundreds of years before being hunted down and slaughtered like animals by the white men, Mexicans, Comanche and anyone else who felt like killing someone at the time,' N'kawa said in a calm voice.

'So you think that could happen to the natives up north?' queried Piper.

'Maybe, maybe not. Let's just say that it has potential.'

Both men knew that when miners entered a new field they cared little about environmental balance. If gold was there to be had, they would get it and to hell with balances and woe betide anyone, black, white or yellow who stood between them and their precious gold. The wilderness had become an existence down the barrel of a gun, both knew that and both knew also that what N'kawa had said was true, the potential to ride smack bang into another war was very high indeed.

By the time the Leichhardt arrived, Townsville was abuzz with excitement and anticipation. Taking on nearly a hundred diggers, troopers, mounted police, the small contingent of Chinese, government officials, cattle and horses, she steamed away and headed North, black smoke billowing from her stack as she lumbered under the weight. Aboard, Piper and N'kawa settled their cattle and horses down before joining Mei and the other Chinese who had been allocated deck cargo positions. Fortunately, the weather northward was fine with calm seas. The Campbells met an engineer, Macmillan who was to lead the expedition and blaze the trail from the Port to the Palmer. Howard St George, the Gold Commissioner, would accompany Macmillan while the Mounted Troopers and Police would come under the control of Naval Lieutenant Connor. In all, Piper estimated that around one hundred people would land at Cooks Town, including the Chinese; the only group to include women in it's midst.

The closer we get, the more concerned I become,' N'kawa said to Piper.

'I'm starting to agree with you now,' Piper replied. 'From what I can make out, there will be about eighty diggers and twenty Chinese walking behind a troop of Mounted Police, led by a Naval Officer, and all under the command of an Engineer.'

'They're talking about a hundred and fifty miles through mountains, scrub and rivers, not to mention the possibility of hostile natives,' N'kawa frowned, 'and all in heat that would sap a rattler.'

'Sure doesn't look good,' Piper sighed.

The two were still pondering the shortcomings of the planned expedition when the Leichhardt steamed into the Endeavour River and anchored. Two survey schooners were already there, their crew ashore busily hacking the mangroves away to allow the Leichhardt to draw closer to unload. All hands aboard made short work of the unloading and it wasn't long before rough tents were being erected along the river bank. The sweltering weather, flies and mosquitoes bid them welcome. A digger, keen to cast a line into the river for fresh fish was confronted by the snapping of a crocodile, causing his hasty retreat to the campsite. Kookaburras sounded their chorus, as if laughing wildly at the newcomers to their wilderness home.

Of their own choosing, the Chinese camped well away from the diggers and government officials. Piper and N'kawa were even further afield near a makeshift rope and sapling corral for their horses and cattle. They would set about building something more substantial at first light. Campfires were lit along the river bank as Macmillan addressed the diggers. 'Men, we will camp here and rest the horses for a day before heading west,' he yelled.

'Not on your Nelly,' came a concerted reply from diggers, already well into their rum supplies. 'We're out of here at first light, make no mistake Macmillan,' they yelled.

Macmillan, unable to reason with the unruly mob, decided to see what the morning would bring and retired to plan the trip with St George, Connor and Sub-Inspector Dyas of the Native Mounted Police. They guessed that the diggers would see good sense in the morning and use the day to prepare and rest before the expedition ahead.

N'kawa and Piper instinctively took in their surrounds. The quiet Chinese, rowdy diggers and nervous Native Troopers as they patrolled the camp, rifles at the ready as if expecting an attack at any minute. The Leichhardt lazed against the bank but they all knew, with her departure would come the reality that they were alone in the wilderness, the nearest European camp somewhere over the mountain ranges, well over a hundred miles away. All they had to do was find it.

'Ever see this many rifles in one camp?' Piper asked N'kawa as they sat by their fire. 'Damn place is bristling with them.'

'I guess we'll see in the morning, but I'm damned if I can see how they are going to carry all of that gear with them,' N'kawa said.

'Ain't no way they're all going to be on that trail

tomorrow,' Piper said, shaking his head. 'Let's go see Macmillan for an update.'

Joining the official group, Piper and N'kawa knelt and took a tin of hot tea each. 'How many men are staying to set up this base here?' Piper asked Macmillan.

'None, as far as I'm aware,' came the reply.

'Can't just desert the camp,' Piper said sarcastically.

'Be another ship along in due course,' Macmillan replied, 'I'm told that steamers are already on their way with more diggers and traders who will secure Cooks Town. Then, once we've blazed the trail, wagons can start hauling from here.'

'Fine,' Piper said. 'We'll meet them when they arrive.'

'So you're not travelling with us then?' Macmillan asked, surprise in his voice.

'We didn't come here for gold, we came to farm,' Piper replied. 'What about the Chinese, are they going with you on the trail?'

'They've indicated that they will be following us,' said Macmillan. 'If they keep up, that's fine. If not, well, they'll get there in due course if the Merkins don't take them first.'

'You won't be protecting them? Seems you got more firepower here than the Yankees at Bull Run,' Piper said, looking around at the abundance of rifles and ammunition cases.

'We didn't invite them, they wanted to come. They

can tag along but I'll not be splitting the group to look after a bunch of Chinese scratchers,' Macmillan added.

'Then the group will need to ride only as fast as the slowest walker,' Piper offered. 'In case you haven't noticed, the Chinese are unarmed and have two or three women in their group.'

'Listen to me, Piper,' Macmillan said with authority. 'I didn't invite pedestrians on this expedition, diggers or Chinese. My job is to blaze the trail, and that's what I'll be doing. If you wish to consider military tactics then my suggestion to you sir, is to return to America and join the cavalry.'

Clearly angered by the remark, Piper stood and glared at Macmillan. 'Like it or not, this will turn into a military expedition. You will probably meet hostile natives, and you will probably engage them. It would seem to me that you simply don't have the sense not to ... Sir!' he added sarcastically. 'And when that happens, a refusal to retreat to the pedestrian lines and protect them will see their blood on your hands. Goodnight ...Sir!'

Leaving the official camp, Piper and N'kawa headed to the Chinese camp and squatted with them. 'Mei,' Piper pleaded, 'You must talk the group into staying here until the trail has been blazed and more ships arrive. Please.'

'They won't listen,' she replied softly. 'They need to get to the Palmer before other Chinese arrive from the south and set their shops up. You must try to understand them.'

'Then you must stay here, with us,' he said.

The old Chinese man, hearing what Piper had said, yelled his disapproval. 'No stay here, no stay here. Mei Ling Siu come, you stay, Mei Ling Siu come,' he shouted, waving his arms about wildly.

'Old man,' Piper confided. 'The troops on horse-back won't wait for you. You'll be left behind and could get lost.'

'Or eaten,' N'kawa added, smiling and gnashing his teeth.

'We keep up, no worry, we keep up,' the old man insisted.

Although the night was warm, Piper draped his jacket around Mei's shoulders, an act of fondness seen as unacceptable by the old man who ran to her, pulled the jacket away and threw it back to Piper.

'Mei,' Piper pleaded again. 'Please, please convince them not to go.'

Her eyes told him that she already accepted that he was right, but he knew she would not be able to con-vince them. 'Alright,' Piper said with a raised voice. 'If I go with the column will you leave Mei here with N'Kawa?'

Once again the old man protested at Piper's interfer-ence and demanded he leave their camp. All Chinese would go to the Palmer and that was final!

It was a furious Piper that sat talking to N'kawa later. 'Pig-headed damn Chinese. Can't they see what's going to happen?'

'May not happen,' calmed N'kawa. 'The Troopers may not even encounter any natives, in which case they'll all get there safe and sound as long as they can find the Palmer River.'

'That's a pail of longhorn crap and you know it, N'kawa. That country out there belongs to the natives – of course they'll be there. I'll tell you now, the first native they see, friendly or not, will be a dead one. Just look at the armoury those diggers are totin'.'

'You're telling me a lot of problems but givin' me no solutions,' N'kawa said.

'Damn it, N'kawa, I don't have any solutions, short of walking back there and whuppin' that pompous engineer who thinks he's a soldier.'

'Might be the answer.'

'Y'think so?'

'No, but you'll feel better for it,' N'kawa chuckled.

The sudden screaming from the digger's camp ended their conversation. Men yelled and screamed as they jumped around in apparent panic. The thunderous boom of a shotgun, then another had Piper reaching for his revolver and crouching for cover as rifle slugs ricochet wildly through the trees like hornets.

'Snake, snake,' a rum-primed digger yelled as he loaded another cartridge into the breach, scattering the other diggers until finally one of them held up the remains of a large, headless tree python. Piper and N'kawa looked at each other in disbelief.

'Don't worry, Piper,' said N'kawa, 'I read you like a

book. We have no choice; we have to go with them. If nothing else, we'll save them from themselves. The Chinese will feel safer and who knows, maybe we can head off a bloodbath.'

'Do we tell the Chinese?' Piper asked.

'Not yet, we tell nobody until they're ready to move out,' replied N'kawa. 'Better that only we know our plans, that way Macmillan can't play soldier boy with us.'

CHAPTER NINE

P iper and N'kawa were awake when the first birdsong pierced the morning air, thick with smoke from the smouldering campfires and the furnaces of the Leichhardt. Their skin was clammy from the humid conditions and as as they left their tents and made their way to the campsite, bracing themselves against the onslaught of mosquitoes. While the diggers slumbered, the clink of tin could be heard from the Chinese camp. A light burned aboard the Leichhardt casting eerie shadows into the mangroves.

The Campbells walked quietly to the corral and took the hobbles from the horse's legs before lowering the makeshift fence rail, allowing the cattle to venture into new grass. The animals would graze no further than the grass that lay within view. Piper and N'kawa, wearing buckskin boots, made no sound as they walked through the digger's camp. The smell of liquor rudely invaded their senses as they passed canvas after canvas. Tripods of rifles, muzzles left open to the night air provided an obstacle course to be carefully negotiated. Cockroaches scurried through the unwashed tin plates while lazy morning flies buzzed between rodent droppings. Piper and N'kawa's eyes spoke their silent language to each other as they passed, heading for the light aboard the Leichhardt.

Once aboard, they were met by the hushed voice of the Master, Captain Saunders. 'Bright and early, lads,' he bid them as they entered the Captain's room.

'Thought you'd have the breakfast done by now, you old salt,' N'kawa replied.

'Just about to. What'll it be? Duck eggs, bacon and bread?'

'Uhuh, and plenty of it,' N'kawa beamed as he and Piper sat at the chart desk.

Gone for a moment to rustle up the ships cook, Saunders pondered the reason for their early morning visit. Upon returning, he grabbed steel mugs from the cupboard and filled them from the warm coffee pot near the wheel. 'Had a visit from Macmillan late last night,' he said. 'Seems you two and he had a slight disagreement.'

'Not at all,' Piper replied. 'Our idea of leadership differs slightly, that's all. And besides, we've just walked through his camp unchallenged by man or animal; rifles out in the open with muzzles to the air and at a rough guess, I'd say half of the diggers will be down with dysentery before they make a week on the trail, judging by the critters feasting off their dinner plates.'

Saunders stifled a hearty laugh in deference to the early hour. 'Macmillan tells me that they will not be leaving before tomorrow morning, that gives you time to get yourselves back in his good books, lads,' Saunders said.

'If it's all the same to you, skipper,' Piper replied, 'I'd just as soon give the man a wide berth.'

N'kawa added, 'Everyone tells us that the Merkins are fierce and attack at every opportunity. If that's the case, and this is what they're up against,' pointing towards the tents, 'then God help these poor souls.'

'You need to cut Macmillan and his boys a bit of slack,' Saunders said, now quite seriously. 'He didn't ask to have diggers along and certainly not the Chinkies; but he's stuck with 'em. He'll do what he has to do but he's told me that he won't be waiting behind for stragglers.'

'Well, those Chinkies are every bit as important to us as the diggers,' Piper said. 'We'll defend them with equal vigour if it comes to it.'

'So you're going with them,' a surprised Saunders blurted.

'No choice under the circumstances,' Piper replied.

'Well then, you boys need to be aware that the Merkins in these parts can be savage. All I'm saying is watch your arses, and closely. They're partial to sneaking in during the night and getting real nasty, so you just be careful,' Saunders advised.

'You see,' N'kawa said, 'the problem we have is that all of the diggers and troopers believe the same thing. They won't be waiting to see what the Merkins want to do or say; as soon as they see them, they'll shoot first and ask questions later. Believe me, I know how it happens.

'Well, the stories I often hear from travellers paints a grim picture, that's all I can say,' Saunders said as he pushed his chair back for the ships cook to serve breakfast.

Breakfast done, Piper and N'kawa again walked past the sleeping diggers and on to the Chinese camp where everyone was preparing food and washing. N'kawa continued on to the horses, while Piper ventured into the Chinese camp and approached Mei.

'Good morning,' he said quietly.

'Oh, and good morning to you,' Mei replied with her characteristic radiant smile.

'Have any luck persuading your people not to follow Macmillan?'

'No,' Mei replied. 'It really is better if we don't talk about it.'

'Okay, sorry,' Piper corrected himself. 'Hey, want to come over and see how the yearlings are coming along?' he asked, like a schoolboy asking a girlfriend if she wanted to share his fresh lemonade.

Looking quickly around the camp, Mei giggled her reply and took Piper's hand as they strode towards the cattle.

'Now they're nothing special just yet, but these little fellas here are the future of Queensland's cattle industry, I promise,' he boasted.

After a quick inspection of the yearlings, Piper turned to Mei and took both her hands in his. The first rays of sunlight on the horizon glittered across the water behind her, silhouetting her against the peaceful backdrop. 'Mei,' he said. 'I know that you have to go where the Chinese group goes. It's not wise, but I know what you have to do. The column will be pulling out tomorrow at first light and we have decided to go as well, just to make sure that you will be safe.'

Mei didn't answer for a while, preferring to stare into the handsome face before her rather than speak. 'My father would hit you with his butcher's knife if he saw you here holding my hands,' she replied seriously, before bursting into girlish laughter, turning, and running back to the Chinese camp.

Piper smiled as an inner warmth enveloped him. 'Think I like that girl,' he said to one of the yearlings as he scratched its head. 'Yep, reckon I do,' he added, as he walked back towards his tent.

His momentary delight was shattered by the sound of a canvass tent being ripped apart, followed by insidious laughter from the diggers. The ripping sound erupted again as the digger cocked his leg and forced another several pounds of pent-up gas from his nether region, again howling with laughter as others stirred and protested the sound and smell.

The camp slowly bundled out and shuffled around preparing breakfast. Soon after, five diggers, all with impossibly heavy packs set out on foot towards the west. Defying Macmillan's orders, they had decided that now was the time to get moving, not tomorrow, so off they trudged through the scrub, rifles over their already burdened shoulders. They would never be seen again.

'Before they even start, Macmillan has already lost control of his men,' Piper muttered to himself. 'No plan, no tactical considerations, no control, no respect – do we really need to go with this group tomorrow?'

For the rest of the day everyone went about the business of packing supplies and making ready for the arduous trek ahead. Captain Saunders told Piper and N'kawa that their cattle, pack horses and supplies would be safe at the river as there would now be a ship at anchor until the next load of diggers arrived, probably within the week. A police contingent would remain at Cooks Town and there were some carpenters who had arrived on the Sandfly who would also be staying at the camp.

N'kawa and Piper agreed upon taking only the barest of essentials. Saddle bags would carry enough dry food for a week and they were expert at living off the land, even a foreign one. They had gone days without food before, during the Civil War and during their expeditions deep into the hill country of Texas in pursuit of renegades and Comanche. In their youth, N'kawa had taught Piper how to survive by eating frogs, crickets, snakes and anything else that represented even mild sustenance. If anyone could survive this trek into the unknown, they could.

In the late afternoon, they saddled their horses and rode through the scrub for a mile or so. It was military habit, learned from scouting with the Texas Rangers. Before embarking on any long range patrol – check everything as though your life depended on it. The horses were in fine condition, and although the saddles were different to those used in Texas, they were comfortable all the same. Saddle bags were set and balanced. Leather strapping was tested and oiled. Piper managed to thong a pistol holster to the pommel of the saddle and arranged his repeating rifle-boot to the rear of the saddle pad. Across the rear of the saddle he thonged his ground roll and oiled poncho, over which he draped a large water skin. His belt carried another cross draw revolver, spare ammunition and a bowie knife, sharp enough to split a cigarette paper.

N'kawa's horse carried much the same except for a rifle. Piper was concerned when he learned that N'kawa would be carrying only a belt knife and saddle thonged pistol. Instead of the rifle, N'kawa carried the tasselled bow-boot of the Apache. Inside, were his longbow and a dozen arrows. He still wore no hat, defying the scorching sun that beat down upon his shaven head. But it was his choice and a respected one at that. Nobody questioned this large, rather unorthodox human who usually spoke only when spoken to and only then if the speaker deserved a reply.

A mile or two from camp they stopped at a small stream, dismounted and squatted as their horses drank their fill. Piper dipped his hat into the cool water and scooped it full before placing back onto his head. 'Bloody hot,' he sighed.

'Thought I taught you better,' N'kawa said quietly.

'What's that?' asked a confused Piper looking to N'Kawa.

'You should have seen them as well.'

'Seen what?'

'About six natives. Been shadowing us for half a mile or so now,' N'kawa said quietly. 'High ground to your left.'

Feeling a little nervous, Piper turned as if to get more water and scanned the left bank. 'Nothin' there,' he said, exhaling as he blew water droplets from his nose.

'Oh, they're there all right,' N'kawa persisted. 'At least six, all naked as the day they were born and carrying spears longer than any I'd care to come into contact with. Hate to say it, but they looked as fit as any Karankawa I've ever seen, and damn near as tall.'

Piper climbed back into the saddle, adjusted his seat and jerked the reins to get the mare's attention. 'Wake up, old girl, may have to grab some distance very quickly,' he muttered.

'They won't attack,' N'kawa said as he slowly mounted. 'If they wanted to spear us they would have done it half a mile back. They're just watching for the moment.'

'Reckon you could have told me half a mile back?' Piper asked lazily.

'You've gone soft, my friend. Too much Chinese ... food and thought! Better sharpen up real quick,' N'kawa said, 'hate to think all I taught you was wasted.'

'No chance of that,' Piper answered as he urged his horse forward, glancing all the time towards the embankment, trying to catch a glimpse of the elusive natives.

N'kawa looked past Piper and gestured in a lazy Ranger salute as they rode on. Following the direction of the salute, Piper stiffened in the saddle as he saw the tall Merkin, painted face and body, standing not twenty paces from him. The two spears towered above him as he stood motionless and unafraid.

'Jesus,' Piper cursed under his breath, 'he's one ugly son-of-a-bitch, ain't he?'

'Uhuh, him and the other dozen. Must learn up on my counting again,' N'kawa replied. 'Best we ride at the trot to test the girth straps now.'

Breaking into a comfortable trot and then canter, the two headed back to camp, knowing that at least a dozen pair of eyes watched their every move as they went. Piper stole one last, nervous look over his shoulder. He did not doubt N'kawa, but still only saw the lone, proud native watching them depart.

When they arrived at the camp there was industry everywhere. Packs had been rolled and tools secured.

Diggers with wheelbarrows loaded to overbalance and others with small carts and harnesses, to be pulled, not by horses but humans. The Chinese had their convoy set out. Basket after basket lined the track, ready to be balanced on the long bamboo poles for carriage. Everyone would sleep on the ground in the open tonight for fear of being left behind when the horses moved out in the early morning light.

'This is just plain insane,' Piper said to N'kawa.

'It is that,' N'kawa replied. 'How far do you think those barrows and carts will go?'

'About the same distance as those heavy packs with tools,' Piper answered.

'At least the Chinese seem to be travelling a little lighter,' N'kawa said as he surveyed the baskets.

'Sure hope so, they'll have to keep up.'

Riding up to the diggers camp the two stopped and looked at Macmillan, who was seated with the other government officials.

'Just crossed some natives a mile out,' Piper said. 'Might be a good idea to go on out there and introduce yourselves before tomorrow.'

'Now why would I do that?' Macmillan questioned.

'Just thought it would be neighbourly of y'all,' Piper answered.

'They keep out of our way and we'll keep out of theirs,' Macmillan said, with an attitude that failed to impress.

'And if they don't?' came Pipers next question.

'Then we'll persuade them, won't we,' Macmillan said.

'You'll be crossing their land,' N'kawa chimed in. 'Wouldn't hurt to get permission first.'

Macmillan walked towards the two. 'Remember one thing, lads. I'm in charge of this expeditionary force and I will decide what I should and should not do. You would do well to remember that. Get in my way or countermand my orders and I'll treat you as I would an unfaithful dog.'

Piper could feel the anger inside him building. Glaring at Macmillan he thought of retaliating, but held his tongue. Turning his horse he deliberately pulled back on the reins causing the horse to move backwards in the same movement, almost knocking Macmillan to the ground. No more words were spoken as they rode towards the Chinese camp.

Mei sat beside some baskets adjusting the cane loops that would secure the baskets to the pole. For the first time she wore a coolies hat, baggy jacket and trousers.

'Hello, Mei,' Piper called as he approached.

'Oh, hello Piper,' she replied with her usual smile. 'Just getting ready for tomorrow.'

'Those baskets look a little heavy for the old man; do you reckon he'll manage?' Piper asked.

'Much too heavy for any old man,' she replied. 'These are my baskets.'

'Well, absolutely not!' Piper protested. 'Ain't no way I'll see you carry those baskets.'

'Please, Piper,' Mei said frowning. 'This is our way, please accept it. If you don't, there will be trouble. Please?'

Piper again had to check his desire to speak. Nodding, he rode past and on towards his camp. This night will be as long as any, he thought. It was impossible to accurately map out what might happen during the next week or so. His mind kept returning him to the native they had seen that day. How proud he looked, standing there, chest out defiantly as he stood his ground. How must he have felt? What must he have been thinking? Strangers on his land, sitting astride animals that he had only heard about from other tribes.

Were these the same strangers that could kill with thunder in their spears, or a different, friendlier, stranger seeking safe passage to the mountains in the north and west?

As if reading his mind, N'kawa hobbled the horses in silence before recommending a good nights sleep. Their campfire lay quiet as they both retreated to the shadows of the wagon, all the while scanning the brush around them for movement.

CHAPTER **TEN**

The late October sky was dark and heavy when Macmillan, St George and black-tracker, Jerry left Cooks Town to find a suitable first camp. Through heavy clouds, the humidity, although early, was oppressive and unrelenting. Every movement required more effort than usual and any activity, however slight, brought on profuse perspiration. It was a thirsty place and ahead of them lay the vast regions of scrub, mountains and waterless plains that had to be crossed.

Black-tracker Jerry finally arrived back at Cooks Town to show the expedition the way to the first camp. Sub-Inspector Dyas positioned his Mounted Police at the front of the column, then led the expedition away from the river into the bushland. Diggers walked behind with enormous back packs of food, clothing, tents and tools. The Chinese contingent was instructed to remain at the rear. It was made quite clear that they were not, under any circumstances, to join the main group of diggers.

Piper and N'kawa rode together at the rear of the Chinese group. If there was trouble up ahead they could deal with it best from their position to the rear. Occasionally one of them would ride past the Chinese and on to the digger's column before returning.

Within four hours the column had stretched out over more than five hundred yards as it weaved through the bush and broken country. Within six hours it had extended to a mile, as the merciless heat and humidity took its toll on the pedestrians.

Piper looked ahead at the bunch of Chinese as they shuffled onwards in single file, straw hats bobbing as the bamboo poles across their shoulders creaked under the weight of their baskets. Clothes were drenched with sweat, which seemed to attract the sticky black flies that swarmed after the column. Left unchecked, the flies would disappear into ears, nostrils and open mouths as people gasped in the thick air. He kept a constant eye on Mei who struggled on under the weight of her baskets, back stooped as she stumbled across the broken slate and dust. He knew not to offer assistance, as it would have been refused, if not by her then by the old man who kept a constant eye on her.

'This column's getting too spread out for my liking,' N'kawa said to Piper.

'It's as we figured,' Piper replied. 'Seen anyone following us yet?' he asked.

'Not yet. They'll be shadowing the Mounted Troopers up front,' N'kawa guessed.

The first day finally came to a welcome end at Macmillan's camp near a waterhole. Exhausted diggers and Chinese collapsed in the shade of the trees, while the horsemen hobbled their horses and walked sprightly about the camp. Macmillan announced that he would name this place King Jerry Waterhole, in honour of his black-tracker, Jerry. Nobody took much notice of the announcement, they were busy recovering and setting up campfires.

Piper found it difficult to contain himself further. He found it callous beyond belief that the leader of an expedition, through apparently hostile country, would allow his column to spread out and become exposed to any threat of hostility that may arise, whilst he was seated comfortably astride a horse and surrounded by armed Troopers.

'King Jerry, huh?' Piper said, so all could hear. 'Here we have a leader who has difficulty finding his own ass to wipe and already he's playing God with names. Reckon we should call this place Macmillan's Folly.'

Again nobody took any notice, except Macmillan, who cast an angry stare at Piper.

The next day started as the one before; humid and teaming with flies and mosquitoes. The terrain was tough, but they all knew that worse was to come. Everyone could see the mountain range ahead and knew that they would have to cross it. They trudged on until finally making camp at a large creek.

'Some of these diggers are close to collapse,' Piper said to N'kawa. 'They'll either have to lighten their loads or perish alone out here.'

'Chinese seem to be holding up Okay,' N'kawa said, surprise in his voice.

'We cross the range tomorrow. Those fools in the front of the column will spread us out over miles once they start the climb,' Piper said.

'If we are to meet the Merkins, this is where it will happen, in the hill country where they will be able to hide if fired upon,' N'kawa calculated.

'You're right again, my friend,' Piper added, as they marked out a campfire site before walking to the Chinese camp. 'Everyone holding up okay?' he asked in a loud voice.

A few exhausted men smiled weakly.

'Mei,' he continued, now much quieter as he knelt beside her. 'How are you?'

'Good, I suppose,' she replied, her exhaustion obvious. 'My feet hurt, though.'

She flinched as Piper lifted and turned her feet to inspect them. 'Oh, Lord,' he despaired, 'these blisters have burst; another day on the trail will cripple you, Mei. Old man!' he yelled over his shoulder, 'get some bandages and salve over here.'

The old man, although exhausted, still maintained his defiant independence on behalf of the group. 'No bandage. She be okay, walk tomorrow, okay.'

Striding to where the old man sat, Piper reached down and heaved him to his feet. Grabbing his long pigtail, Piper yanked his head backwards to allow the old man full view of the angry face that confronted him. 'Now you either get this into your thick old Chinese skull the easy way, or I'll belt it in,' Piper hissed. 'I'm more than tired of the shit you dish out to your people, day in, day out. Now you are going to bandage that girl's feet and you are going to watch as I carry her baskets on my horse tomorrow and until she feels fit enough to take them back. Is that understood?'

The old man rattled out a short sentence in Chinese.

'What'd he say?' Piper yelled to Mei.

'Something about your breeding, I think,' Mei answered as Piper dropped the old man.

'Okay,' Piper announced to the whole group now. 'Get a good nights sleep because we cross the hill country tomorrow. It'll be slow and possibly dangerous going. The lunatic running this fandango will clear out and leave us all behind, so we have to stick together and keep a sharp lookout.'

N'Kawa joined in. 'Don't keep walking with cut or blistered feet. Bandage all wounds first thing in the morning. Anyone unable to continue can ride with us.'

'We'll travel in pairs and keep close together as much

as the track will allow. N'kawa will ride the rear and I'll take point,' Piper continued. 'If we come under attack, and it's unlikely, do not bunch up too close, and seek cover wherever it's available. N'Kawa and I will deal with any attackers as fast as we can.'

Looking at the old man, N'kawa flashed his white teeth in a cheeky grin. 'Seems you been demoted, old man.'

As predicted, the early morning saw Macmillan and his riders head towards the high country, caring little about the protesting diggers who stumbled around calling for him to wait.

Moving through the cleared camp, Piper shook his head at the amount of gear discarded by the diggers in an attempt to lighten their load. Tents, tools, spare boots and even food had been strewn around the campsite. 'Damn fools,' he muttered to himself.

Following the trail of the lead group, they weaved their way upward over the rough terrain. Blood flowed freely from gashed knees and elbows as the Chinese tripped and fell under their loads. Piper led their horses and walked with the Chinese, the horses now laden with the baskets of those too exhausted to carry them. Diggers, too weak to keep up with the main group had taken their rest on the side of the trail before tagging onto the Chinese group. Nobody wanted to be left alone, no matter how difficult the struggle, they would have to go on, pushing themselves beyond the limits of human endurance.

Over the coastal range at last, the weary column entered the Normanby River Valley. N'kawa scanned the close escarpment and counted the Merkins lining its fringe. He made a mental note of around thirty or forty warriors, all carrying spears as they watched the column stumble down into the valley. Mei, her baskets aboard Piper's horse, limped beside Piper at the head of the group. She almost fell as Piper abruptly held out his arm and stopped his horse. Twenty five yards ahead stood half a dozen Merkins, naked and painted, spears in hand. The rest of the group bunched up as they halted. The Chinese, clearly terrified at the sight, chatted anxiously as they huddled even closer together.

'Damn,' N'kawa spat, knowing that it would be impossible to get them to spread out again. 'Back here,' N'kawa yelled to a couple of digger stragglers who immediately hurried to the rear of the group, snider rifles at the ready.

'Wait here,' N'kawa ordered, stripping off his shirt. 'If either of you fire a shot without my command I'll personally kill you … very slowly,' he promised as he trotted to where Piper and Mei stood.

As the semi-naked N'kawa arrived, Piper nervously slipped the leather thong away from the hammer of his holstered pistol. 'Time to meet these fellas N'kawa said coolly. 'Wait here, Piper. I'll go parley with the boss-man. For God's sake, don't shoot anyone, we can handle this.'

The Merkin group stared at the unusual sight before

151

them. The Chinese had by now all huddled together while the two diggers stood behind them, rifles ready, wide eyes fixed on the native road block. They were confused by the semi-naked black man with no hair that strode towards them. He carried no weapon save his belt knife.

As N'kawa approached, the leader spoke to his men, after which they all placed their long spears against the trees. He then yelled a message to N'kawa; a message in a language nobody understood. As he spoke he held his arm out and looked to the valley, then to the escarpment. Finally he gestured in a direction behind him, away from the trail blazed by Macmillan. All N'kawa could do was nod and present as friendly.

Eventually, the warriors picked up their spears and melted silently back into the scrub.

'What do you make of it, N'kawa?' Piper asked.

'Not sure, but I reckon they don't mind if we continue on straight ahead. I sure got the feeling that they didn't take too kindly to the track cut by Macmillan, just a hunch,' he said

'Okay, let's follow the track for today and talk to Macmillan tonight. Maybe we can get him to alter the course a little,' Piper offered.

'Not sure of the wisdom in that, but Okay, let's get moving,' N'kawa finally agreed.

The group was relieved that the Merkins had not lived up to the reputation as bloodthirsty killers who would spear intruders on sight. They were also surprised by their physique, tall and muscular, obviously healthy and agile as cats in their movements. Although this small group had met in friendship, as enemies, they would no doubt be formidable fighters.

Almost into the valley, Piper and N'kawa exchanged nervous glances as they heard the distant sound of gunfire. Perhaps a dozen rifle shots, all in quick succession, then silence. 'Pray that what you just heard was someone bagging wild geese for supper,' Piper said to N'kawa, who held a worried look and nodded.

Passing more discarded clothing and equipment on the trackside, Piper led the group to the Normanby River and Macmillan's camp. 'We'll be camping closer to the main group tonight,' Piper said as a matter of fact.

Macmillan shook his head as he loaded his pipe. 'I don't think so. The Chinks will camp downstream at least a hundred yards away,' he countered.

'Packs in a circle here, no more than four campfires,' yelled Piper to the Chinese, as if Macmillan's words had fallen on deaf ears.

'Perhaps you didn't hear me,' Macmillan interrupted.

'Oh, I heard you right enough,' Piper said, turning to face him. 'I heard you, but anyone who would lead an expedition and leave people strung out over miles of wild country doesn't deserve my ears and I sure as hell ain't going to follow any orders you might dream up. For the safety of this group, they are staying right where

153

J . R . G o r d o n

they are. If the diggers want to move, fine, plenty of country out there.'

'Inspector,' Macmillan yelled to Inspector Dyas. 'Over here if you would.'

'Inspector,' Piper yelled immediately. 'Consider your options, my friend. If you choose to enter this little parley, be prepared for a fight because that's what's about to take place here.'

Before Inspector Dyas could assess his predicament a group of Native Mounted Police cantered into camp. 'Blackfella gone back to hills,' one of them reported.

'Alright Corporal, keep alert tonight and have those bodies dragged to the river,' Dyas ordered.

'Bodies?' questioned Piper.

'That's correct,' Macmillan stated. 'Had to disperse a few blacks on arrival here.'

'Were you attacked?' Piper asked.

'Neither here nor there, they got too close and if we'd done nothing they'd have cut our throats in the night,' Macmillan said casually.

'You bloody fool,' Piper spat. 'We also had a meeting with the natives in the hills and parted company on a friendly note. Mind you, we gathered from their signs that they weren't too happy about the track you've chosen,' Piper said. 'It's my strong recommendation that you alter your course and head in a more westerly direction to avoid any further incidents.'

'Well now, General Campbell, you just go on back to your Chinese friends and leave the leadership issues with those who know something about leadership,' Macmillan said, with as much sarcasm as he could find.

It was Mei who took Pipers arm to prevent him moving towards the goading Macmillan. 'Come, Piper, it's better that we eat now and rest before tomorrow,' she said in a comforting voice.

'You're right, Mei. First I'll scout the river for a good place to cross,' he said as he walked towards the river.

The Normanby presented a few problems; it was deep in most parts and wide in others. As Piper continued down the sandy banks to mark a spot where everyone could wade across safely, he noticed the body of a native wedged between two fallen timbers. A closer inspection revealed several large holes in his back. Near a sand drift he spotted another, and yet another further on down in the trees that overhung the water. All bodies sported the ugly holes of the snider slug, a 410 grain projectile that ripped through flesh and bone like a warm knife through butter. The Native Mounted Police favoured this weapon because of the devastation it could wreak among those unfortunate enough to fall foul of the law. In this case, Piper thought, the only lawless activity that had taken place here was perpetrated by the police.

Returning to the camp, Piper yelled to Inspector Dyas. 'Just seen your handiwork down at the river. Your police must be damn good shots.'

'Well trained,' Dyas replied, not knowing how to take Piper's comments.

'Shoot, you must be so damn proud of them boys,

yes sir!' Piper continued. 'Sure takes some grit to gun down unarmed civilians.'

Not wishing to take the matter further, Dyas turned away and joined Macmillan and St George.

Returning to the Chinese group, Piper suggested that they take another route in the morning. They all disagreed strongly, and for good reason. Black Jerry was the only one who vaguely knew the way to the Palmer. There was still better than one hundred miles to travel, and there was obviously no way across the mountains and escarpments that lay to their left, even though the friendly Merkin had indicated that direction as the preferred one. 'We should try the direction suggested by the Merkin,' Piper insisted. 'They may even guide us across the escarpment, who knows.'

'I'd normally agree with you,' N'kawa said, 'but under the circumstances, I don't think that these Chinese would make it across, even if there was a track.'

Piper finally conceded. 'Okay, the terrain looks kinder for tomorrow's march. Seems to be much flatter across the river and easier under foot. We'll be able to keep with the lead group fairly easily, provided that lunatic up front doesn't proceed at a gallop.'

Mei's foot wounds were healing well beneath the bandages and salve. It was obvious that the Chinese were holding up well, as good, if not better, than some of the hardened diggers, who, although experienced in the Southern Goldfields and terrain, had never had to push themselves in such harsh country and weather conditions.

Most were down to the barest of essentials, some even lighter. Food sharing had become commonplace among the diggers while the Chinese had barely touched their rations, preferring to make use of the rations discarded along the way by the over burdened diggers.

As they settled in for the night, N'kawa confided to Piper that he held serious concerns about the weather. The sky had promised rain today and the humidity had risen sharply and uncomfortably during the early evening. 'If we get a cloud burst,' he said, 'this river and those beyond will be impassable. I've heard that once the wet sets in, the Northern wilderness is no place to be.'

'Wet shouldn't arrive before November sometime,' Piper said lazily.

'Piper, it is November!' N'kawa added.

'So it is. Ah well, we'll make the Palmer within a week or so if Macmillan doesn't get us all lost.'

'Or killed.'

'Or both. Lost, wet and dead,' Piper laughed. 'Hell, I could think of better places to die.'

Everyone spent a restless and uncomfortable night. The sickly sweet smell of sweat-soaked clothing filled their senses as they kept up their constant battle with mosquitoes and ants that stung the skin with every bite. Mounted Police patrolled the perimeter through-out the night while hobbled horses grazed on the grass close to the river bank. The eerie sound of a hoot owl echoed through the trees and across the water as the camp dozed fitfully.

CHAPTER ELEVEN

The next morning brought with it new concerns. A light rain shower crossed the camp and they could hear the distant rumble of thunder. Although it lasted only five minutes or so, it gave the diggers time to strip off and refresh their sweat sodden bodies in the cool shower. The Chinese looked on in disgust as the diggers pranced about naked, singing the crudest of sea shanties as they soaped up their crotches, deliberately facing the Chinese as they did.

Piper and N'kawa looked on, amused at their antics. Were it not for the Chinese women, they too would be enjoying a refreshing shower.

After testing the depth of the river again, the convoy crossed to the north bank. Some swam while others waded. The Chinese fashioned their poles into a raft and rafted their supplies across before wading after the diggers. Once safely across, Macmillan led off with the Mounted Police close behind. The going was much easier now due to the flatter land. Diggers kept close to the leading horsemen while the Chinese, Piper and N'kawa followed no more than one hundred yards astern.

Not half an hour out, they crossed a small creek and topped a low rise. Ahead of the leading horsemen stood a dozen Merkins, slightly off to their right. Knowing they had been spotted, the Merkins lay their spears down and stood watching the column, expecting it to pass them by. Macmillan called St George, Dyas and Connor to his position. 'It'll be the same group we chased off yesterday,' Macmillan said. 'Damned if I want these stragglers following us all the way to the Palmer. Let's show them we mean business.'

With that, the horsemen booted their horses to the gallop, Macmillan leading as they charged, screaming towards the dozen Merkins, revolvers firing, sending lead flying wildly into them. Terrified, the Merkins gathered up their spears and bolted for the trees. Those who escaped the flying lead disappeared into the trees, hotly pursued by the Native Mounted Police who ended their flight with the assistance of their snider rifles.

Macmillan and the other officials cantered back to the diggers, laughing as they rode. Some of the diggers cheered while others simply gathered up their packs and readied for the onward march. At the rear of the column,

Piper watched in total disbelief at the unprovoked cavalry-style charge and the slaughter of the friendly party. Furious, he cantered forward to the official group.

'You mad bastards. Don't be surprised if you haven't just started an all out war. Look to the escarpments; do you see the smoke signals?' he shouted angrily. 'They are signals calling every God-damn warrior in the region down on us, you mark my words. And another thing, the next murderous stunt you lunatics pull will see me and N'kawa riding in defense of the Merkins.

Macmillan looked to the escarpment and saw the smoke fires. 'Nothing more than campfires, Campbell. We're a hundred strong and they're now fully aware that we are not to be bothered; we've made sure of that right here. In any case, I would be very surprised if there were any more than fifty wild blacks left in this valley now.'

'Well, if you try real hard you might just be able to kill the whole damn lot of them off before we reach the Palmer,' Piper snapped back.

The column continued at a good pace. The digger's spirits were higher now that they were in touch with the leading horsemen. Piper and N'kawa rode in silence. They knew full well the consequences of slaughtering peaceful people … Australian Native or American Indian; the outcome would be the same.

They were the first to spot a large group of painted natives, high on the escarpment. N'kawa spoke first, 'One, possibly two hundred up there, all loaded down with spears. They're signalling others to our front and rear so God only knows their exact number.'

Two of the Native Mounted Police rode back to them, checking the column as they went. When they arrived, Piper seized the opportunity to speak with them away from their white masters. 'Tell me, lads, why did those Merkins lay their spears on the ground back there?'

'Sign of peace, Boss. Blackfella sometimes do that and chuck their spear when you go past. Some cheeky blackfella out here,' he grinned.

'Why do you reckon the blackfella on the hill wanted us to go another way?'

'Could be sacred ground here for them blackfella. Could be blackfella buried here or could be important corroboree ground; I don't know,' the black policeman answered with a shrug.

'You blackfellas like killing them wild blackfella?' Piper searched, tongue in cheek.

'Ah, you bet, Boss. Wild blackfella no good. They know soon as they see us good blackfella that we be killin' 'em pretty soon,' he answered with a hideous cackle.

Piper looked to the escarpment and pointed. 'Best you go get some other good blackfella and a passel of good whitefella because those bad blackfella up there don't look like they're on their way down to share your dinner with you.'

The two Native Mounted Policemen looked at the hills for a brief while, before galloping forward and talking to Inspector Dyas. Piper mustered the Chinese closer to the back of the diggers group and returned to the rear of the column with N'kawa.

'He sure has done it now. The fool probably thinks that these Merkins have no battle tactics. Thank God they don't have firearms or we'd be long dead and dried by now,' N'kawa said.

Piper nodded, a worried look came over his face. 'If they do attack, and I wouldn't blame them if they did, how are we going to protect the Chinese? They have no firearms and I'm picking that they will be the first targets because of it.'

'Even with firearms, judging by the numbers I've seen, the diggers are going to have to be damn good at reloading to hold them back. Guns ain't no good without ammunition, hey Piper?'

They watched as Macmillan rode towards them from the front, settling his horse to walk beside N'kawa.

'We'll be camping just up ahead for the night,' he advised. 'Seems we are being stalked by a large group of Merkins so we'd best take a few precautions. When we stop, the Chinese can help to cut saplings to build a barricade of sorts. Of course they can join us inside the perimeter for safety.'

'Well of course,' Piper replied. 'Couldn't leave the poor ol' Chinkies out in the cold, now could we?'

'No time to be squabbling among ourselves, Piper. We could come under a concerted attack at any time and I'd like to think that we can rely on you lads to help us through. I'm not asking much,' said a very worried Macmillan.

Yet again, Piper made clear his position on events. 'Seems you didn't give too much thought to dropping those few Merkins earlier today; and the ones yesterday. I don't think that they were asking for much either; simply to be left in peace. Be that as it may, I don't intend dying out here for you or anyone else. You've put us into this war and now we'll have to fight it. Be warned though, Macmillan, when next we ride into civilization, my story will be told.'

'Fair enough,' Macmillan replied before cantering back to the lead group.

'Hard to figure, hey Piper,' N'kawa said. 'I think that these crazies felt that they could go on slaughtering blacks every day along the track without fear of reprisal. I think they're about to learn just how wrong they were.'

The site chosen by Macmillan to camp and defend was a good one atop a slight knoll with a supply of old timber and sapling growth that could deflect spears. By late afternoon, the sapling barricades had been fashioned as a fort-wall to protect from attack, if it came. The horses were hobbled close to the camp and everyone was ordered to eat before sundown, after which time there would be no fires allowed.

The Campbell's figured that the attack would probably come from the treed area down by the creek. Once agreed, they positioned themselves and the Chinese facing the probable attack direction.

'Better to die facing an attack than take a spear in the back waiting for one,' Piper explained to the Chinese who sat around hanging off his every word. Even the old man nodded in agreement.

Piper had the Chinese sacks and baskets stacked high enough for cover and staked out canvass tent-walls to give them shelter in the night. Propping his saddle into the barricade he insisted that Mei try it for comfort.

'Well, that's just fine, isn't it? I thought that perhaps you liked me, now here you go putting a saddle on me!' she joked as the other Chinese laughed.

Piper knew that it would keep her safe from spears and if there was no attack, she would have a comfortable night. N'kawa arranged his saddle in similar fashion for one of the other ladies whom they believed to be the best Chinese cook in the land. 'You stay real safe, Ma'am. Shucks, anything happens to you and we all starve to death for sure,' N'kawa told all who listened.

As dusk approached, details were sent to replenish water stocks before all cooking was finished and fires doused. Mei cooked extra rice and some dried pork she had been saving. They ate some and stacked the remainder in bamboo steaming-packets, next to where they would sleep. She knew that neither Piper nor N'kawa would sleep much and figured that some food in the night would help them through.

Quiet fell over the camp, even before the last light had vanished.

'Towards the creek,' Dyas called, loud enough for everyone to hear. 'Merkins at the creek.'

Everyone strained to see what he'd seen. Shadowy figures moved silently through the trees, too far away to be considered good targets.

'At the ready lads; nobody fires until I give the command. Make every shot count and don't dilly-dally on reloading. When they come, they'll come in force,' Macmillan yelled.

'My hero,' Piper muttered to Mei who crouched, frightened, beside him. 'They won't attack just yet; we're far too prepared at the moment. They'll wait until we let our guard down if they come at all.'

A lone Merkin broke from the shadows of the tree line and walked into the open grassed area. Loading his eight-foot-long spear into his woomera he launched it with all his might. The heavy spear glided effortlessly through the air before arcing and burying itself deep into the soil about twenty yards from the barricade. Quickly he retreated back into the shadows and disappeared.

'God-damn!' Piper whistled. 'He threw that thing better than a hundred paces. I swear it's gone a foot into the ground.'

'Sure he ain't Karankawa,' N'kawa asked. 'Hell, we'd welcome him to the campfire any old night with a throwing arm like that.'

166

The diggers mumbled their concerns as they pushed closer to the packs at the barricade, rifles poking menacingly through the saplings, boxes of ammunition at the arm. Piper laid his repeating rifle in front of Mei and went through its action. She baulked at the touch of it but soon had it dry-firing with some confidence. Again, and again, they went through the loading procedure until Piper was confident that she would hold her own if sleep turned to battle. 'I'll be here beside you,' he comforted. 'If you have any problems I'll fix them. You mustn't fire until I say so, and remember the sequence we've just gone through. There will be a lot of noise, but put it out of your mind and concentrate on what you're doing. If we come under attack, under no circumstances are you to stand up.'

Although terrified, she felt comfort in Pipers strength and calm. It seemed that he was giving her a grocery order rather than lessons on how to kill people. Silently, she prayed that the attack wouldn't come as she settled back into the saddle to watch N'kawa open a bottle of dye and paint blue circles beneath each eye, followed by a broad band of red across his forehead and neck. Once painted, he carefully removed his long-bow and arrows from the Apache bow-boot and placed them near his saddle where the frightened Chinese cook huddled. Although the evening had become cooler, N'kawa removed his shirt and placed it over the cook. He stood there humming as he fingered the beads around his neck, his bare torso defying the evening air and biting insects.

'Why is he doing that?' Mei whispered to Piper.

'He's an Indian. He has just connected with his ghost warriors. He won't feel the cold or the mosquitoes tonight, and he probably won't sleep. His ancestral spirits will join him in the night and stay with him in battle, if there is to be one. Even the spirits of the Comanche and Kiowa he has killed will be with him, he has eaten their flesh and so they are part of him now.' Piper replied.

'He has given his saddle pistol to some of the Chinese. How can he defend himself with a bow and arrows?' Mei question, seriously concerned about N'kawa's safety.

Piper looked deep into her eyes. 'Mei, I'd rather have one N'kawa with a bow at my side than five diggers with rifles. He might run out of arrows, but they might also run out of ammunition, and that's when I want N'kawa at my side. If something happens and this becomes a hand to hand skirmish, I'll bet you my horse and saddle that N'kawa will be the last of the expedition standing.

As the minutes turned to restless hours, nothing interrupted the night song of the unseen creatures. Piper and N'kawa could read the signs. For as long as the crickets sang and the frogs croaked, there would be no attack. Any movement towards them would silence the night critters. Mei dozed uneasily against the padding of the saddle. Looking down at her, Piper reached slowly across and gently stroked her dishevelled hair. Her eyes opened momentarily, then closed again as she smiled and drifted into peaceful slumber. As he had done many times before,

168

but from a distance, Piper studied her beauty as she slept. He looked around the camp at the sleeping diggers, Mounted Police on patrol, and the restless Chinese. The old Chinese man was awake. He smiled his agreement as Piper continued to comfort Mei.

Piper was jolted awake by the early morning call of the birds. The camp dozed peacefully as he looked around. Mei's small hands were clasping his as she slept. N'kawa sat staring at the creek, the same position he was in when Piper saw him before dozing off himself. Once N'kawa saw that Piper was awake, he padded quietly to his position and urged him away from the sleeping Mei.

N'kawa spoke. 'Three maybe four hundred warriors, even more, will be up that hill soon, Piper. I scouted their camp last night. They're all carrying three or more of those long-range spears and a bunch of clubs and wooden swords. The spears seem to be tipped with some foul smelling concoction, so avoid getting nicked, they're probably poisoned. I gotta tell ya, brother, the situation looks grim.'

'Mmm,' Piper nodded. 'Guess we do the best we can, and N'kawa, if it goes bad for us, enter your spirit world as my brother, I'd like that.'

N'kawa flashed his broad smile. 'If I enter the spirit world it will be behind you. I'll pick you up on the way. You'd like my Karankawa family; they're looking over you at the moment, as they have done since we were new brothers roaming Argyll.'

Diggers started to stir, re-kindling campfires ready

for breakfast. As they went about their chores, N'kawa listened closely to the song birds in the trees lining the creeks. Mei brought hot tea for Piper, and N'kawa, as the other Chinese warmed the overnight rice packs.

'Macmillan,' N'kawa shouted out of the blue. 'Call your men to the barricades, we're about to come under siege.'

Even before the urgency of his call had registered, the morning air filled with the blood-curdling screams of hundreds of Merkins as they rose from the grass and charged the camp. Boiling cans spilled and food canisters fell to the ground as everyone scrambled to man their positions at the flimsy barricade. Piper knelt calmly beside a trembling Mei and loaded the first round into the rifle for her. 'Do as I taught you, Mei. Lie low and wait for the order to fire. You'll be fine … don't be scared,' he said as she positioned herself, rifle at the shoulder, staring across the sights at the wall of naked Merkins as they charged.

Macmillan, standing on high ground in the centre of the camp, watched and waited. 'Wait for it, wait for it gentlemen … FIRE!' he screamed as the Merkins closed to within thirty yards.

The first volley ripped through the Merkin's ranks. Skulls exploded and limbs were torn apart as the deadly slugs found their mark.

'To the back wall, Merkins to the back,' screamed Macmillan as another two hundred screaming Merkins joined the charge on another front. 'Select your targets

170

and fire at will,' Macmillan yelled as he dived for cover, narrowly avoiding a wave of spears that rained down on the centre of the camp. Diggers carefully selected their targets and sent lead to meet them. When one target fell, another appeared to launch yet another eight-foot spear, before he too was felled.

'Jesus' a digger yelled. 'More of the heathens from the right, someone give us a hand over here.' As another hundred Merkins charged the right wall.

Piper knelt beside Mei, revolver in each hand and waited for the charging warriors to get close enough for a comfortable kill-shot. Each shot found its mark as the dead and dying piled up in front of his position. He looked down as Mei rolled aside to reload her rifle, tears streaming down her face. Once loaded, she regained her position and took aim. Each squeeze of the trigger caused her slight frame to jerk violently from the recoil as the projectile journeyed forward and buried itself into the chest of a young Merkin. Deafened by Piper's gunfire above her head, she entered a world of total enclosure. The screams of the charging Merkins ceased to register as she methodically reloaded and fired into wave, after wave, as they charged.

N'kawa crouched near the Chinese cook, bow in hand, arrow nocked. A hardwood spear buried itself deep into his saddle and penetrated through to the Chinese cook's arm, causing her to yelp in pain. Almost casually, N'kawa stood, drew the bow and released the four foot arrow towards the spear thrower.

N'kawa stood motionless and watched as the arrow entered the Merkin's chest and exited his back.

Realising their dreadful losses, the Merkins withdrew towards the creek as bullets continued to rip through their ranks. Seizing the moment, St George and the Native Mounted Police hurriedly gathered their horses and chased the retreating group as they ran, unarmed towards the lagoon. Reining in their horses, St George's party looked at the forty or so Merkins who had waded, shoulder deep into the lagoon, and turned to face their pursuers. Raising his snider, St George took careful aim and fired. The brain of a young Merkin exited the back of his head as he fell backwards into the lagoon. 'Finish 'em off, lads,' he called to the police as he turned and galloped back towards the camp.

Gunfire from the lagoon echoed through the camp. Now and then a shot would ring out from the creek where diggers had followed a group of wounded Merkins. The smell of cordite, and death, hung in the air as the defenders nervously surveyed the damage. A spear sliced through the air and embedded itself in the thigh of a digger who fell to the ground, writhing in agony.

'The grass, they're still in the long grass,' Macmillan yelled as a dozen sniders emptied their loads into the grass to the right of the camp.

Piper had to pry the rifle away from the vice-like grip of Mei. As he did, she sat up and started shaking uncontrollably, tears streaming down her blackened face. 'It's okay, they've gone,' he comforted, embracing her shaking body in his arms and rocking her gently. 'They won't be back, you're safe now.'

N'kawa walked to the front of the barricade and out through the scores of dead and dying Merkins. Further down the slope he discovered a group of wounded warriors, huddled together and hidden in the long grass. He motioned for them to stay down and continued towards the creek. He hadn't taken a dozen paces when the roar of a snider rifle jolted him.

'Few live bastards here,' a digger yelled as he reloaded his rifle and placed it against the head of another wounded Merkin and squeezed the trigger.

N'kawa's hide-leather boot caught the digger square in the face as he reloaded for the third time. Before the dazed digger hit the ground, N'kawa was on top of him, knife in hand. In two lightening movements N'kawa had both of the digger's ears in his hand as he stood up casting an ear each to two young Merkins. 'You fought with honour. Take these to your lodge and remember what happened here,' he said.

'The black bastard took off my ears,' the digger screamed. 'Shoot the bastard, shoot him.'

A few diggers raised their rifles and lowered them again as they heard Piper's promise. 'I will surely kill any man who draws the hammer of a weapon against N'kawa. There's been enough blood shed here today, let it be.'

Looking around them, the diggers took in the

extraordinary sight of armed Chinese, rifles and revolvers aimed at those diggers who would consider shooting N'kawa.

'Enough, lads,' Macmillan calmed. 'There'll be no more killing here and well done lads. From this day on this place will be known as Battle Camp,' Macmillan bragged in a voice raised enough so everyone could hear. 'We've shown the hostile blacks that we are not to be taken lightly and any resistance will be met with force. You can all be proud of what you've done here today.'

Piper removed his comforting arms from Mei and walked to where Macmillan stood. He sneered, spat on the ground, then hammered his fist into the face of Macmillan who reeled backwards and sank to the ground as his knees buckled under the force of the blow.

'You would be reduced even further in my estimations if you stood up. 'Cos if you do, I'll put you back down again you son-of-a-bitch,' he growled. 'This is your doing, nobody else's, yours and yours alone. Luckily, you haven't lost any of your men, but there are a hundred or more dead Merkins out there that shouldn't be dead. Congratulations … you son-of-a-bitch!'

Piper turned away, knowing that a dozen revolvers and as many rifles were trained on his back. He didn't care, he'd done what had to be done. As he walked towards the Chinese group, Inspector Dyas defiantly stood in his way. He continued walking. When he could go no further he again launched a powerful blow that sent the Inspector crashing to the ground, blood spurting from both nostrils. 'Never stand in front of an angry Texan,' Piper snarled down at Dyas. 'End up getting' all sore and sorry for yourself you piece of raccoon-shit.'

Slowly the camp settled down. Rifles were lowered and diggers went about preparing to move out, all the while keeping a wary eye on Piper and N'kawa.

CHAPTER TWELVE

A n eerie silence fell over the camp as everyone nervously prepared themselves for the march ahead, all the while recounting the battle of that morning. The trigger happy digger, blood-soaked bandages covering his head where his ears were once attached, constantly levelled abuse and threats at N'kawa while another wounded digger bandaged his leg. Swarms of flies had already commenced feasting on the black corpses that littered the knoll, broken limbs askew, eyes glazed and mouths gaping in silent screams. A thousand spears or more stood embedded deep in the earth, testimony of the ferocity of the attack.

Macmillan's eyes, already swollen and red from Piper's battering, mounted and called the convoy into line.

'We'll leave here in a defensive column,' he ordered. 'If the Merkins attack again we'll be ready for them. Stay close … move out.'

The column moved off slowly into the dry, flat grassland. While the mid-morning sun shimmered on the ground ahead, they trudged onward, complaining at each gruelling step taken. March flies had joined the swarms of sticky, black flies and bit their way through any exposed skin causing an instant of pain and drawing a droplet of blood with each attack. Diggers cursed the weight of their packs and thoughtlessly discarded more and more of their treasured belongings with every hard earned yard they covered.

At noon, the convoy rested under whatever shade could be gained in the low-brush country. After a lengthy discussion with the other officials, Macmillan announced that progress was far too slow. At this defensive rate of travel their rations and water would run out within a few days and they would starve before reaching the Palmer. He announced that the official mounted group and police would move ahead at a quicker pace, blazing the trail as they went. The convoy could follow the trail and meet them at the next camp. A near riot followed. Diggers demanded that the mounted group remain with them, and rightfully so, they were fearful of another attack and knew that such an attack would best be fought as a consolidated group, not a fragmented convoy.

Gaining some control of the riotous diggers, Macmillan and the rest of the mounted contingent cantered off ahead as diggers continued to yell their discontent while struggling to follow.

N'kawa stood beside Piper and gazed upon the tired and clearly distraught Chinese. 'The last few creeks we've crossed have been dry. The further we go, the hotter it will get and I'd say that come nightfall, this convoy will be strung out over several miles,' he said to Piper.

'Damn you, N'kawa. I just wish you weren't so right all the time,' he replied.

'I disagreed with you yesterday about branching out, but now I'm not so sure. Maybe we should be looking to the hills; maybe taking the direction offered by the Merkins,' N'kawa said.

Piper, clearly surprised, looked at N'kawa seriously. 'I've seen the rough map that Macmillan is following. They have at least one hundred miles ahead of them to the north, then west around the conglomerate before wheeling south into the Palmer basin. That map didn't indicate a track over the mountains; in fact, I recall an inscription thereabouts stating 'impossible territory' with no water.'

'But if there is a way through, we'd save fifty or sixty miles,' N'kawa said. 'Believe me, as a kid being hunted by everyone else we came in contact with, we covered impossible terrain, mountain passes and deserts where no sane man had ever trod, and we always made it.'

'Did you have twenty Chinese tagging along?' Piper asked.

'No, but if we load our horses and alternate the load,

everyone gets a rest and we'll travel much quicker. I can scout ahead on foot and search for a track,' N'kawa planned. 'As long as we travel quietly and eat only dry rations, we may just avoid complications with the natives.'

'What do you believe they are doing right now … the natives, I mean?' Piper questioned.

'They'll be retrieving their dead and will go into a short period of mourning; that may last a week or two. Small groups will catch up to the convoy within a few days and attack them again, only this time it will be hit-and-run tactics … Comanche style.'

'So they won't be expecting us to break away and cut through the mountains?' Piper asked.

'My guess is as good as yours, but I don't think they would expect a small group to detach completely from the convoy, no. But I caution you, Piper, by heading into the mountains we are probably heading into their camps and that could be fatal,' replied N'kawa.

'I think that trying to follow Macmillan is just as flawed and every bit as dangerous. As I see it, we either turn back now or take our chances in the mountains. Following Macmillan simply isn't an option for me, I'm afraid,' Piper said resolutely.

The departure of the horsemen and scrambling diggers saw the Chinese gather their gear and fall into a single line, chattering loudly as they did. 'We go, we go,' yelled the old man, urgency in his voice.

'Hold on there,' Piper commanded. 'Ease your packs and listen up for a spell.'

After Piper explained the situation and offered the alternative, the Chinese went into their typical huddle and finally fell silent. Mei rose from the group and approached Piper. 'Not everyone agrees, but we will follow you and N'kawa through the mountains to try and find a shorter track to the Palmer. The old man thinks that we will die if we follow Macmillan. He also says we die if we follow you, but better to die with honourable people rather than die with silly people.'

Piper looked at her curiously. 'You mean the old man thinks that we are honourable?'

'Of course. But N'kawa is the most honourable,' she smiled.

Piper shook his head as he looked at the grinning N'kawa. 'Pleased nobody else heard that,' he said

As the Chinese gathered around, Piper and N'kawa went about arranging packs onto the horses and a rotation of free walkers without packs. Their idea was to share the load and keep everyone as fresh as possible as they would be travelling from sunup to sundown each day from here on in. It wouldn't be easy, but certainly easier than following Macmillan, who was by now several miles ahead.

Ready to move, Piper issued his final orders. 'We travel only as fast as the slowest walker. Report injuries as they happen and if need be we can have the injured ride for a spell. Nobody gets left behind. We move as quietly as possible to avoid being detected. Sound travels well out here so there will be no chatter, understood?'

The Chinese nodded and immediately set about chattering loudly. 'Hey, hey,' Piper calmed. 'I said no talking.'

With that, the small column turned to the mountainous west and silently marched on.

N'kawa scouted ahead on foot, moving quickly and quietly through the scrub as the terrain took on rises, gullies and waterless scars that would be raging torrents during the wet. Perspiration glistened on his bare back as the sun streamed cruelly down. He could read the lay of the land as good as any Australian Native. He picked his way through the ridges and gullies finding the best route before returning to the group to give directions. He was covering their distance a dozen times over as he scouted out, decided on the track, returned to the group and then scouted again, looking all the while for the tell-tale smoke signals indicating that the Merkins had discovered their movements.

By the end of the day they had coursed around the escarpment, crossed the parched gullies and entered a valley surrounded by red and yellow sandstone cliffs. N'kawa reported that there were caves ahead where they could shelter for the night before attempting a steep climb to the plateau in the morning. He was confident, that once they were on the plateau, the temperature would drop and travelling would be cooler, but no easier. Ahead lay steep climbs up slate rock that would be difficult to negotiate, especially for the horses, but if they kept going in the right direction, he was confident that a trail could be found.

Arriving at a large sandstone cave, they unloaded the horses and set the packs in a semi circle around its mouth. Inside they discovered that the walls were adorned with paintings that chronicled the life of a native group and its every day activities. Ashes from old fireplaces were scattered about and half completed spears and woomeras were stacked neatly against the rear wall of the cave.

'Got the feeling that we're intruding,' Piper said quietly.

'Those fires haven't been lit for a week or more. I'm picking that the inhabitants of this cave are lying down there on the plains with bullets in them,' N'kawa comforted as the wide eyed Chinese looked on and listened.

'As soon as it's dark we'll light a fire and get some food,' Piper said to the Chinese. 'The cave will hide the fire.'

The exhausted Chinese nodded their agreement and as darkness fell, a fire was lit and they soon had water boiling, rice cooking and weary travellers fed. Piper and N'kawa took up positions at the mouth of the cave overlooking the entry track. Their horses were hobbled outside but would not eat this night due to the total absence of grass in the slate rock country. Tomorrow, perhaps they would find more generous pickings along the way.

Everyone slept well after their exhausting day. Even N'kawa managed a good night's sleep. He was the first to rise next morning as a small lizard scurried across his leg. In the dim morning light he could see two figures sitting cross legged in front of him. He inhaled deeply, realizing that they meant no harm. If they had, he would not have woken. Standing, he stepped over the baskets and sat, cross legged, facing the two figures and waited for the sun to rise.

Piper was next to rise, followed by the old man who, upon seeing the two natives sitting at the caves entrance, woke the rest of the Chinese with his high pitched chattering.

N'kawa looked back and held up his hand to silence them. 'Quiet, keep quiet,' he ordered. 'That chatter can be heard for miles. These two mean us no harm.'

The two natives and N'kawa sat facing each other as if acting out some choreographed theatre movement. N'kawa could see that they were the two wounded youngsters he had saved from the now earless digger. The oldest, perhaps only eighteen, sported an ugly bullet crease across his forehead while the younger one, maybe fifteen, hung his right shoulder and cradled his arm, the upper muscle having been ripped open by a snider slug. His wound wept its sticky, fly attracting substance while the gnarled, raw flesh bulged hideously outward in ripe cauliflower fashion. The older of the two, showing no emotion, held out his hand and offered the two bloodied ears to N'kawa, who accepted the gift.

'Some jerked beef, water and iodine solution,' N'kawa called as he threw the ears over his shoulder to

Piper who caught them instinctively. 'And put those ears on the hot fire stones.'

The Chinese had now retreated to the rear of the cave in a confused and terrified state. How many more were out there, they wondered as they watched Piper take the jerked beef strips and small medicine bottle from his saddle pouch, calling for Mei to bring water.

Walking to the still smouldering fire, he placed the two ears on the hottest stone, causing them to crackle and contract into small, stinking bits of gristle. The Chinese gasped in horror as Piper took the ears from the fire and gave them to N'kawa.

N'kawa handed the pulled beef strips to the young natives and gestured for them to eat as he placed the first of the half-roasted ears into his mouth. Watching him closely, they both sat and held the jerky, not yet eating. Holding out the other ear to the oldest native and calling for his jerky back, N'kawa transacted a food swap that saw the native commence his ear breakfast while N'kawa swallowed and started on the jerky. They settled in for a silent breakfast of ears, jerky and water, all the while staring at each other.

'Everyone go about getting a good breakfast,' Piper commanded the Chinese. 'N'kawa will talk with these two for a while.'

'He doesn't understand their language,' Mei said in a shaky voice.

'Doesn't need to. I've seen Indians who don't understand each other's language talk for hours using signs.

N'kawa will talk to these people alright. Go on with your breakfast,' Piper said.

As they ate, N'kawa went about setting up a sign language the natives and he could relate, and respond to. Within minutes they were gesturing and scratching signs and pictures in the sand floor. It was clear that they understood each other perfectly. Deliberately knocking a recent graze on his hand open, N'kawa opened the iodine solution and applied it to the bloodied graze. He winced in pain as the iodine stung his raw flesh, and then smiled. The two young Merkins watched as N'kawa called Mei to them, instructed her to wet a cloth and nodded in acceptance on their behalf as she gently mopped their wounds. When the iodine was applied they sat motionless, although their eyes and expression declared the sting of the concoction. N'kawa nodded and smiled at them as Mei applied salve and bandages, smiling nervously as she did.

'Sit with us,' N'kawa said to Mei. 'C'mon over here, Piper. These young fellas have a story to tell.'

The Chinese group watched anxiously at the circle of people sitting at the entrance of the cave. Mouths full of jerky, the circle chewed and listened as N'kawa spoke. 'These two boys tell me that their people are in mourning. They also tell me that the white people who dig in the rivers will pay for their losses. They believe that I must be one of their spirits returning to guide the Chinese across the mountains to the place where people dig in the river.'

'Is there a way across the mountains?' Piper inter-jected.

'Yes, there is and they will guide us because we have helped them. Once we get there, they will leave and if we are seen crossing their land again we will be killed,' N'kawa answered.

'So much for the return trip,' Piper said.

'Hey, at least there's a way to get there.'

Once packed, the group left the cave and followed N'kawa further into the hills. Ahead of N'kawa walked the two native youngsters who seemed just as keen as N'kawa, Piper and the Chinese to keep their travel a secret. The small group pushed on silently, resting every couple of hours as they struggled up the steep ridges towards the top of the high mountain range. The natives often made a detour of the group to take in small rock pools of water that would have otherwise gone unde-tected. Mei constantly re-dressed their wounds, while Piper ensured that they ate as much as everyone else in the group. N'kawa kept close contact with them; they related well to him and quickly passed on native phrases in return for English ones.

After three days of torturous climbing and descend-ing the group faced their most arduous task yet. Ahead lay a steep climb across broken slate rock that slipped and cracked under weight. One step forward claimed half a step back as they slowly picked their way higher. The horses fared badly under their pack weight and often stumbled to their knees, almost losing their footing completely and taking the group with them back to the bottom of the horrendous slate staircase. Finally they reached the gaping corridor through the thirty foot rock formation perched atop the Range.

Exhausted, the group rested and took in their surrounds. 'Hate to get caught up here by a bunch of angry Merkins,' Piper gasped. 'This place is tailor made for an ambush. Nowhere to run and hide up here.'

'Think that's bad,' N'kawa said. 'Take a look out yonder at where we're going.'

Piper walked to N'kawa and looked west over the country they would now cover. 'Ah, shit. This could hurt,' he mumbled.

Ahead they could see the conglomerate plateaus and narrow ridges dissected by sheer rock faces that fell hundreds of feet into yawning chasms. If they could make it over that, they would enter the Palmer, somewhere down there in the distant, hazed blue landscape.

Resting as long as they dared, the group continued down the ridges. Although he never voiced his concerns, Piper held grave fears for the horses as they picked their way across an unstable surface. On many occasions, had they lost their footing they would have fallen to depths where recovery would have been impossible.

'Don't recall ever seeing country this bad,' Piper said as he wiped a river of sweat from his brow.

N'kawa slipped, regained his footing before answering. 'It's bad … very bad. Hell itself couldn't have dished up worse. Small wonder nobody has found a track over the mountains yet.'

Refusing to let fatigue claim him, Piper smiled, and then laughed. 'Hell, at least it ain't snowing!'

The old man suddenly erupted into high pitched, high volume chatter from the middle of the group.

'What'd he say?' Piper called to Mei.

'He's talking about your breeding again. I think we all agree with him now,' she answered sternly.

'C'mon, Mei. It's not too late to turn back, you know. Now we know the way, hell, we could be back in Cooks Town within a few days,' Piper joked.

Mei answered in Chinese.

'Best you leave it go for a while, Piper,' N'kawa offered intelligently, as they slid and stumbled down the ridge atop legs of rubber.

Finally, the two sprightly natives stopped at the end of a small ledge, still high in the mountains. Joining them, N'kawa looked down on the parched valleys below. Scantily clad trees only just hid the fire red ground that spread out before them and disappeared into the blue haze of the mountains. River courses were clearly identifiable and smoke drifted skyward from points further to the south west as he took in the vista. 'So, that's the other side,' he said, almost to himself.

'Ask the natives where the people dig in the rivers,' Piper said to N'kawa.

After a brief intercourse of sign language, N'kawa turned to Piper. 'We follow this filthy little pinch down and we should make contact with diggers at that first dry creek bed, according to our guides.'

'Okay, let's get moving,' Piper called back to the bedraggled group of Chinese.'

The two natives stood their ground as everyone passed them and slid down the steep incline. No matter how much N'kawa coaxed them, they would not go any further. Before turning, they waved to the group and then were gone, trotting barefoot over the roasting rocks.

After a gruelling descent, the group finally made the river bed they'd seen from the escarpment. The clear, inviting waterholes provided soothing relief to aching bodies. N'kawa scouted the opposite bank and found fresh boot prints and evidence of recent activity by diggers. Selecting a spot away from the river, hidden by the trees, they set camp for the night. Tomorrow they would continue downstream until they reached the diggings. In the meantime they would rest and reflect on their good fortune … to at least be alive, thanks to a couple of young natives who had repaid a debt.

CHAPTER **THIRTEEN**

I t had taken the group five torturous days to cross the rugged mountain range, hiding in caves and dry creek gullies by night and cautiously struggling throughout the burning hot days. The journey had taken its toll. They were weak and gaunt, and spoke little, using every opportunity to sit and rest their pain filled joints. At least now that they were over the mountains, they could handle whatever lay ahead. N'kawa estimated that they still had another two days march before reaching the diggings further downstream where he had seen smoke from the mountains. They took comfort from the digger's boot prints in the sand, and the scattered campfires. At least now they were not alone in the wilderness.

'I reckon that we're on the north fork of the Palmer,' Piper said to N'kawa.

'Still a day or two before we reach Palmerville,' N'kawa replied. 'Country is not so rough but a couple of the Chinese look completely done in. We can travel a little slower now and at least we'll have water.'

Mei walked towards the two, concern etched on her gaunt face. 'The old man and one of the women are very ill. They have a fever. Can we stay here another night so they can rest?' she asked.

'Best we don't,' Piper replied, noting her concern. 'They can ride up on the horses but we need to get as close to the diggers as possible today.'

Helping the two feeble Chinese aboard the horses they again got under way. The scattered trees gave little relief from the unrelenting sun as it continued its painfully slow journey across the sky. Slowly they picked their way along the river, often following tracks blazed by the diggers. By late afternoon, Piper called a halt at a small shaded area near water. Noticing a fresh gravestone beside the river, the Chinese insisted that they move on another two hundred yards before camping.

Piper looked around the second site and then back to the grave site. 'Has to be the third or fourth grave we've stumbled across this side of the mountains,' He said to N'kawa.

N'kawa nodded. 'There'll be more. This place gives new meaning to the word difficult,' he said.

'All for the chance of finding some yellow metal,' Piper said, shaking his head.

As night fell the old man grew weaker. Other Chinese nursed him and the sick woman throughout the night, but to no avail. By sunrise, the old man had gasped his last breath and the woman could not be moved. Sorrow and despair hung heavily over the camp as Mei lamented. 'To come all this way, endure all that he has, only to die here in a strange land. It doesn't seem fair.'

The group comforted each other as best they could while the ill woman lapsed into a coma. There was little they could do except sit by and watch as she finally breathed her death-rattle and drifted from this world into the next. Although there was some protest about leaving them there, Piper finally convinced them that the two should be buried on a small rise overlooking the river. The cause of their deaths was a mystery. Was it contagious? Was it some unknown plague that had also claimed those other unknown souls they had passed on the way, or was it just plain exhaustion?

The travel for that day had been halved by the time the two Chinese had been buried. After a brief but meaningful ceremony, the group was again under way and reached the river fork by nightfall. They were now on the Palmer River. Evidence of prospecting was everywhere but they had not yet encountered the first digger's camp. Throughout the day they had discovered campsites strewn with spent rifle cartridges where diggers had fought off intruders, whoever they may have been. 'I'll lead off tomorrow,' Piper told N'kawa. 'We'll reach their camps tomorrow and the last thing the diggers want to see is a black man riding in. I'm picking that they'd shoot first and ask questions later.'

He was right. The first group of diggers they encountered scurried for their rifles as the bedraggled group appeared through the scrub. At the head of the group, Piper waved and shouted his greetings. 'Don't panic, lads. No need for the rifles. Would someone be kind enough to point us to Palmerville?'

'Where in Gods name did you come from?' a scruffy Irishman asked, genuinely surprised at the sight he took in.

'Cooks Town. Through the mountains,' Piper replied.

The Irishman stared in disbelief. 'No track over the mountains. We've been up the left branch and there's no track. Even if there was, the Merkins would pin you to a tree. Thicker than flies on a dead horse up there, they are.'

'Well, that's true enough, but I'm here to tell you that there is a track through the mountains, although I'd caution anyone from taking it. Filthiest damn track on Gods earth,' Piper replied.

The group rested with the diggers who had stopped panning the river sand to hear their story. Although the Chinese were in poor shape, the diggers looked no better. Their rough and craggy features told a tale of hardship and desperation. Lack of good food and much toil under the burning sun had reduced their hardy frames to mere shadows of what they must have once been.

'Keep on the track down yonder and you'll get to Palmerville in an hour or so,' the Irish digger instructed. 'Oh, by the way, you couldn't be sparing some small piece of food for a hungry digger, could you?'

Piper thought for a moment before generously handing over some jerky, which the bony fingers snatched gleefully. 'Don't have a lot ourselves but it seems we have more than y'all,' Piper said as the rest of the diggers eyed off the bulging Chinese baskets strapped to the horses.

'People have been robbed along these trails for food,' another digger said with a deliberate threat in his voice.

'People also been shot robbing people,' Piper replied, matter of factly. 'Damn shame, ain't it?'

Leaving the diggers to continue their search for riches, the group travelled on until finally reaching Palmerville in the mid-afternoon. They had lost count of the days, but agreed that it had been ten, or eleven, since they departed Cooks Town.

There was no welcoming committee for them as they strode into the main camp of tents and shanties. The diggers were clearly not pleased to see the Chinese arrive and stared curiously at the tall Texan and his equally well presented black partner. Avoiding the constant requests for any spare food, they selected an area away from the main camp and went about unpacking and setting up their tents. They knew that staying too close to the diggers would cause problems. No digger wanted Chinese close by and would be quick to move them on, forcefully if need be.

Walking the dusty tracks between the shanties and tents, Piper and N'kawa soon learned that food was not only of poor quality but was in desperately short supply. Everything arriving from the Etheridge was snapped up immediately the wagons arrived. Prices were outrageously high and those who had won gold handed it over for their meagre rations. Those without the means to pay begged from other diggers.

Prospecting had denuded the river scape. Water that once teamed with a variety of fresh water fish now lay empty. Wallaby and kangaroo had long since been shot out for food. Diggers had reduced their food intake down to an evening meal of mite-ridden flour and sugar while they waited for the next wagons to arrive.

N'kawa looked to Piper as the sound of distant thunder rumbled across the land. 'If these people think that times are tough now, wait until the rains come. They'll be starved and locked in by floodwaters. No amount of gold in the world will help them,' he said.

'Seems it's not too far off, either,' Piper offered as he surveyed the heavy skies.

'The Chinese won't be talked into leaving now but at least they have food enough to see them through,' N'kawa said.

Piper looked concerned. 'I doubt that. Those baskets hold some food but not a lot, mainly equipment for them to build their shops and trade stores. If they stay, they too will starve.'

As they passed a rough shanty, a mildly well dressed creature held out a bottle. 'A wee dram for you gentlemen,' he sneered. 'Payment by gold or food, take your pick.'

Without answering or taking up the offer, Piper and N'kawa continued, shaking their heads as they went. 'Seen that gutrot before,' Piper said under his breath. 'One part liquor and two parts water; the rest kerosene.'

Back at the Chinese camp they watched as the Chinese hurried around selecting sites for tents and shanties. They had already scouted the area for timber good enough for support poles and were hastily setting up a makeshift kitchen, much to Piper and N'kawa's delight. When evening came, they would eat with the Chinese and discuss the future.

That evening, sprawled out among the squatting Chinese, they devoured a meal of fresh rice and jerky. Diggers could be seen watching as the smell of freshly cooked food wafted through their camp. One of the younger Chinese men had assumed control of the group in the absence of the old man who had perished. He held court and chatted seriously to the group as they ate. Piper and N'kawa watched on silently.

Finally, Mei, still grieving the old man's death, walked to Piper and sat at his side. 'The men are scared that diggers will rob them of their food and tools,' she said.

'Not as long as we're here,' Piper replied.

'We will start building our sheds tomorrow,' she continued. 'Once they are ready we will need to go back to Cooks Town for supplies to trade. The men are afraid to go back.'

Piper shifted uneasily. 'You don't have supplies enough to feed yourselves if you stay here through the wet season. You will either have to get supplies in, and quickly, or get the hell out of here and return in the dry.'

'We can't go now. They won't go. We need supplies,' she pleaded.

'We all need supplies, Mei. It's just that there aren't any to be had here. We have to go back and get them. You can understand that, can't you?' he said as sympathetically as he could.

She nodded. Her face reflected a mixture of fear, uncertainty and hopelessness as the harsh reality of their predicament filled her mind. 'Perhaps if we send some of the men to the Etheridge for supplies,' she offered

'Too far. Even further than Cooks Town and just as dangerous, apparently.'

'Now that we know how to get through the mountains, how long would it take to get to Cooks Town?' she persisted.

'Probably a week each way on horseback with pack horses, but I for one don't think kindly to making that journey again. The Merkins will be through their mourning now and will be out to take their revenge on anyone foolish enough to travel the Cooks Town track,' Piper warned.

'But you have guns,' she said.

Reaching for her hands, Piper looked deep into her eyes as he spoke. 'You Chinese are more stubborn than old mules. We will help you build your camp and get settled. Once that's done, we'll all head back to Cooks Town together over Macmillans track, if he ever gets here. Then, when the wet is over we can return.'

Mei did not have to consult the other Chinese for an answer. They had already decided that they were staying put, rain or no rain. Slowly she rose and freed her hands from Pipers. 'It will be a difficult time, but we will survive the wet here, you'll see.' She said before departing to help with unpacking.

Piper looked questioningly to N'kawa.

'Don't ask me,' N'kawa said. 'I don't have the answers.'

'Perhaps if we went back over the mountains and blazed a trail this time. At least it's dry country and supplies could start rolling from Cooks Town to feed the camp here through the wet,' Piper said.

N'kawa's expression was one of surprise and disbelief. 'I really don't believe I heard properly. You want to go back across that evil place after what it's just done to us? We damn near died up there!'

'Well, that's true, but if we can open up a shorter trail….'

'Hey,' N'kawa interrupted. 'Why not just come on out with it? What you really mean is that you feel the need to look after Mei. Ain't that the truth?'

'Hell, no!' Piper defended, feeling embarrassed. 'Didn't cross my mind once.'

N'kawa chuckled in response to Piper's embarrassment. 'Let's just get this place livable and then make a decision, huh?'

'Look after Mei,' Piper muttered to himself. 'What a God-damn stupid thing to say. Damn stupid.'

The next day saw the arrival of a dozen head of cattle and a wagon loaded with supplies from the Etheridge. There was cheering in the rough township as diggers left their panning and rushed the wagon, small leather pouches of gold dust waving in the air to prove their buying ability. Supplies were snapped up by the scrawny diggers as soon as they were unloaded. The teamster emptied the precious gold dust into his money sack as the outrageously priced sugar, coffee, tea, flour and liquor left the wagon. Holding up a hefty pouch of gold, a digger yelled his bid for one of the cattle. To everyone's surprise, the Chinese leader held up two pouches of gold and countered the diggers offer. Furious, the digger held up three, only to be countered by the Chinese leader's four.

At the end of the heated Dutch auction, the Chinese had parted with a dozen pouches of gold and won four of the cattle. The diggers jeered as the Chinese led the beasts away to their camp.

'Bastard Chinkies,' a digger spat as they passed. 'Eat 'em yourselves ya heathens, we'll not be buyin' from ya.'

'I'll be damned,' Piper said to N'kawa. 'No wonder those baskets were a little heavy. Wonder how much more they've got stashed in them?'

'Who cares,' N'kawa replied. 'At least now they have food enough to get them through the wet. They'll strip and smoke it if they're clever, that way it'll last.'

As a few Chinese passed them Piper yelled. 'Well, you folk won't go hungry now.'

'Not for Chinese, keep for selling. Get twice as much gold back when no cattle for sale,' one of them answered happily as he trotted along beside the cattle.

Piper and N'kawa were speechless.

CHAPTER FOURTEEN

The passing of each day saw more and more diggers struggle onto the Palmer after their arduous trek from the south. They told of attack after attack by Merkins and recounted how many had been lost during the trek. A call went up for an armed group to return southward a few miles and kill a group of Merkins that had camped there but it was soon forgotten as gold fever took over. The clouds were now becoming heavier each day with the promise of rain to come. Everyone knew that to stay on the Palmer too long would mean certain starvation if caught out by the wet season. They would have long days prospecting and wait until the very last minute to leave.

Piper and N'kawa's track through the mountains was

discussed with contempt among the diggers, who simply didn't believe them. Surely they had come from the south and became lost. That's how they ended up so far east of the Palmer. Crossing the mountains was an impossible task; crossing the mountains with a bunch of straggling Chinese without coming under attack by the Merkins was just too far fetched to make any sense at all. For that reason, the diggers kept a wary eye on the Texans.

Almost a week after their arrival, Macmillan, sitting high in the saddle and riding ahead of his Mounted Police, entered Palmerville presenting for all the world like a modern day Napoleon leading his troops. Spoiling the moment were the strung out diggers that followed, half starved and complaining bitterly. Riding near the river, then up the ridge towards the main township they passed Piper and N'kawa who were working on building a slab-hut. Macmillan stopped and stared, as if seeing a ghost. 'I didn't see you two pass our column,' he said as he looked to where the Chinese huts were well advanced. 'How long have you been here?'

Piper fought to contain his delight. 'Well now, you boys all went the wrong way. Seems like there was a command problem somewheres up front,' he chided. 'Hey, N'kawa. How long we been here? Five days or more I'd say.'

'All of that,' N'kawa confirmed with a grin.

'Best you go on up yonder and buy some of that sweet smelling food from the Chinese kitchen. It's the only fresh food shop in town and I'm here to tell y'all that the food is just dandy,' Piper said as the horsemen urged their horses forward to rid themselves of the taunting Texans.

The diggers straggled past silently in single file. One of them, looking quite hideous with no ears, looked to N'kawa and reaffirmed his intent. 'Your days are numbered, you black bastard,' he called. 'We'll not be forgetting what you done.'

N'kawa glanced lazily at the threatener, belched deeply and patted his stomach before continuing on with his work.

Later, the two routinely went to the Chinese camp kitchen for dinner. In exchange for protection and general assistance they were afforded each evening meal at no cost. Others, critically low on rations did not fare so well and parted with some of their hard won gold to secure a square meal from the Chinese.

Mei and the other Chinese women had planted an array of vegetable seeds that would soon be ready to swap for gold dust. A smoke-house had been built and one of the beasts slaughtered. Every part of the beast was put to use, not a scrap was wasted. Without panning an ounce, the Chinese had accumulated a substantial stockpile of the golden dust already.

Piper sat with Mei in the cooler evening air and gazed out over the campfires. The night sky flickered with distant lightening. 'This place has grown by around one hundred people since we arrived. Now, even the officials are here; how's it going to look in six months time?' he asked her, not really expecting an answer.

'The Cantonese will arrive in their thousands, maybe even before the wet arrives,' she said with confidence. 'We need to have our shops well established before they get here otherwise they will take over.'

'I've got no doubt that Cooks Town is already hosting a flotilla of ships full of supplies and diggers ready to make the trek inland. As soon as Macmillan gets back and tells them where the trail is, they'll be on their way,' Piper said, arching his back and rubbing his shoulder that ached from the days toil.

Mei noticed his discomfort. 'You have a sore back?' she asked in a concerned voice. 'Here, let me rub it … unbutton your shirt front.'

Surprised and delighted at the offer, Piper quickly unbuttoned his shirt and removed it. His eyes closed as Mei's smooth, soft hands firmly massaged his tight neck and shoulders. Moving to a more comfortable position, she squatted behind him and beckoned him to lean forward as she slowly glided her hands over his muscular back. 'Lay on your shirt, I can ease the tension in your lower back too,' she said quietly.

He lay there and felt the tension of the past few weeks flow from his body as her hands glided fluidly across his back. Moving from his side, Mei adjusted herself and straddled him as she massaged deep into his shoulder muscles. His mind tried desperately to control his heart as it raced wildly. The feel of her buttocks rolling slowly back and forth on his back as her hands glided its full length was taking him places he had only dreamed of.

How could anyone feel such bliss in such a God-forsaken place, he thought.

Raising himself up onto one elbow he turned quickly, taking Mei by surprise as he spun onto his back. She looked down at him, now straddling his lower stomach.

'Oh, front sore as well?' she questioned with a cheeky smile.

'Uhuh. Kinda stiff from digging post holes, I guess,' he lied unconvincingly as she started to massage his chest … more caressing than massaging.

He placed his hands on the outside of her thighs and gently stroked them as she continued caressing his broad chest. 'You must go back over the mountains,' she whispered.

His mind raced. Was this attention simply softening him to agree with her wishes to return and get supplies from Cooks Town? Would this goddess use such a weapon against him? Perhaps she thought of him merely as a tool to get what she wanted; something to be used and then discarded when the time was right. Disappointment entered his mind as she suddenly dismounted and slid to a position beside his head and began gently massaging his scalp. 'It's okay if you don't, but it would be wise. We will be in danger when food runs out, but if we leave, the Cantonese will take over from us and we will be left with nothing,' she said, almost in a whisper.

Piper, eyes closed, savoured the moment as her nails

combed his scalp slowly. 'If we did go back, me and N'kawa, who would look after you?'

'The government people are here now. They will stay here to protect us,' she answered. 'Are you worried about me?'

'Of course I'm worried about you. Guess I just wouldn't like anything to happen to you, that's all,' he replied.

'Then you will consider making the trip?' she persisted.

'I'll think about it.'

'Even if you don't go back …' she paused, leaned forward and kissed his forehead. 'I will still take care of your aches and pains.'

His eyes opened dreamily at the feel of her soft, full lips on his forehead. He reached up but she was already standing and smiling down at him. 'I must go back to my tent now. The others will wonder where I've got to,' she giggled, as she turned and swayed deliberately away, turning after a dozen paces to give Piper a small wave. His eyes followed her as she walked. Her hair now flowed freely down her back. When she'd first sat down, it was tied in a knot. He didn't recall undoing the knot.

Macmillan's voice moved him from heaven and closer back to hell. 'There you are, Campbell,' he said. 'Bit warm for you?'

Replacing his shirt, Piper stood and fronted Macmillan. 'What can I do for you?'

'How did you get here a full week before me? I know

that we took a few blind canyons and had sometimes had to cut back, but you couldn't possibly have made it here in the time you did without going across the Great Divide. Is that what happened?' he asked.

Piper felt malicious as he answered. 'Soon after you deserted us, not far from that slaughter camp, we got lost. Roamed the hills for days before finally stumbling into this hell hole. Don't know how we did it, but there you are.'

'Did you mark the track?' Macmillan asked anxiously.

'Hell no. We were too busy keepin' alive and fightin' off flies to worry about chippin' away at the trees,' he said. 'Besides, you done blazed a track yourself, didn't you?'

Macmillan could see he would get little sense out of Piper, who now clearly despised him. 'I'll find it, one day I'll find your track and when I do I'll be naming it Macmillan's Pass,' he said.

'Yep, reckon that'd be a good name for it. Just up the track from Macmillan's Slaughter Camp and Macmillan's Murdering Creek. Hell, y'all gonna be famous one day, Macmillan.'

'Remember one thing,' Macmillan cautioned. 'You assaulted an official on official business and that's punishable in this country.'

'Uhuh, I recall that each day when I'm taking a crap. I'm still wondering what gives me most relief … taking the crap, or belting your face. Both activities gave me so much pleasure it's a real hard one to pick.'

'You're an insolent man,' Macmillan growled as he walked stiffly off into the night.

'Well goodnight, y'all,' Piper yelled after him. 'Come on by any old time.'

Another small group of diggers arrived the following day bringing news that ships were headed for Cooks Town on the Endeavour. Paying no mind to the impending rain, even more diggers, possibly hundreds, would soon arrive from the Etheridge and Georgetown. As soon as they knew the track from Cooks Town they would be here in their thousands. Everyone listened with interest, and then went back to work getting as much gold as they could before they were overrun. The luckier diggers were now guarding more gold than they had ever imagined. The river, creeks and gullies were rich pickings with reports of new finds each day. Merkins kept them from venturing too far from the main camps and those who did, looking for the mother lode, never returned, their fate seemingly of little consequence.

On the eighteenth of November, during a short rain shower, Macmillan and his mounted guard left for Cooks Town. The track they had blazed would soon bring the wagons and supplies rolling in; there would be no way to stop them. Once there, they would be stranded as the rivers cut any chance of return, or more appropriately, their escape.

After a great deal of soul searching, Piper and N'kawa agreed to return across the mountains and mark the track. If nothing else it would provide an escape route for the diggers who would leave it to the last possible moment before leaving. If they took Macmillans track they could end up stranded between flooded rivers and perish. At least the track across the mountains gave a slim chance of survival. The only major crossing would be the Normanby.

They figured that they could make it back with their pack horses within six or seven days, load them with supplies and return before the wet set in.

Piper met Mei at the water point by the river to break the news. 'Now you had nothing to do with our decision, but we are going back over the hills to get supplies,' he told her.

She was clearly delighted. 'That's good, really good. Now we can have enough to get us through the wet,' she squealed excitedly

'Well hold on there, you're assuming that we will get through and make it back,' he said.

'Don't be silly. Of course you will make it. You always do,' she said confidently.

'Well, we're leaving in the morning before sunrise. Reckon you could rustle up some of that fine Chinese food for us to eat on the way?'

'Of course, I'll make it extra special for you,' she replied like an excited child.

She kept her promise. As they saddled their horses and prepared the pack horses for travel, Mei arrived with several packets of food. The rest of the township was still an hour from waking when Piper and N'kawa mounted. Looking down at Mei, Piper asked her if she could read. 'Of course I can read. Do you think I'm a fool?' she replied.

'No, of course not, just checking. Go to my camp, there's a letter there for you,' he said, turning his horse eastward and walking away from the camp, N'kawa following.

Rushing to Piper's tent she found a letter beneath one of his Peacemaker revolvers and a box of shells. She unfolded the rough bit of paper and read what he'd written.

Dearest Mei,

Keep this revolver handy to you at all times and don't be afraid to use it if you have to. You can stay in my camp if you wish. We should be back within the fortnight, all going well. As soon as we get the supplies we need we will return over the mountains.

I'm not much to write words but I need to say that I've become very fond of you. I know that the other Chinese don't much like the idea of me spending so much time with you but they will learn to live with that. I'd like to spend a lot more time with you when I return if that's alright with you. My intentions are very honourable and I won't do anything that you don't like the idea of. I'm a bit stuck for words now but I'll talk to you when I return. Please be careful and stay close to your people while I'm gone.

Affectionately yours,
Piper

She smiled to herself as she tucked the letter into her shirt pocket. Hiding the revolver and shells inside her shirt she walked away from his camp, her sight blurred by the welling up of tears. They had just departed and already she was feeling a little lonely.

Piper and N'kawa rode silently past the diggings and on to the Northern Branch of the Palmer. It wasn't until they reached the point where they had descended the mountain that they started to mark the trail. Climbing, as quietly and quickly as they could travel, they inched their way up the mountains, along the narrow pinches and ledges that overhung the yawning chasms, forever upwards to the craggy summit and pass through the rocks, all the while scanning the surrounds for Merkins who could unleash a deadly attack at any time.

They reached the summit exhausted, but pushed on. That was no place to linger. Descending the rocky hillside, they crept passed the caves where they had slept a couple of weeks previously, not wishing to disturb anyone who may be there.

Sleeping beside their unhobbled horses, they were ready to move at any time if attacked. Surprisingly they saw no Merkins and made the flat ground of the valley in good time. Passing the lagoon where Macmillan had slaughtered innocent Merkins and on to the Normanby they rode, as fast as their horses could comfortably go.

After four days of gruelling travel and a day out from Cooks Town, the horses started to show signs of exhaustion. Both riders battled to remain awake in the saddle as one pack horse dragged them to a halt. 'We'll have to camp here,' N'kawa said. 'The horses are done for and we're not far behind them.

Piper looked around nervously, but agreed. 'So damn close and yet so far away. We're sitting ducks out here if the Merkins show.'

'Okay, let's walk for a while and let the horses catch their breath,' N'kawa replied as the horses kicked and swished their tails at the biting flies.

They walked on until they could go no further. Man and beast had reached the point of utter exhaustion and rested beneath a shady rock overhang, where they stayed till morning.

When they awoke, Piper looked across at N'kawa who was sitting beside his horse. 'Got any spear holes in you?'

'Not that I can feel, but we do have company,' he replied, gesturing ahead to a thicket of brush where a handful of Merkins squatted, spears rising into the morning sky above them.

'Ah shit,' groaned Piper.

'The horses are rested and fresh. Let's just mount up and go about our business,' N'kawa suggested.

'Okay, but if they start launching those spears I'm going to shoot back. Damned if I'm coming this far to be speared without a scrap,' Piper warned.

'Agreed,' N'kawa said. 'As long as we don't start it. C'mon, let's move,' he said as they headed towards the group of Merkins.

The natives rose to their feet as they approached, but didn't lay their spears down. Piper unthonged his revolver and took a few deep breaths as N'kawa led on. As they drew level with them, N'kawa yelled a greeting in their language and waved. Confused, they looked at each other before one of them yelled something back. 'What'd he say?' Piper asked anxiously.

'How the hell would I know?' replied N'kawa. 'I only learned hello and goodbye from those young bucks on the way in.'

'Well for Christ's sake yell goodbye. Maybe they'll take the hint and bugger off.'

N'kawa again yelled in their language. Piper guessed that it was goodbye but changed his mind when one held his spear high into the air as if signalling. Instantly the grass erupted with screaming Merkins on their other side, not fifty yards from them. Spears filled the air as Piper and N'kawa let their pack horses loose, knowing that they would follow, and booted their mounts forward, splitting up as they went. Piper fired his revolver wildly into the air as he rode, choosing not to select targets. N'kawa deviated towards the group and galloped headlong into them, screaming his own war cry as he went, sending the surprised Merkins leaping for cover.

Avoiding the spears they galloped on and were soon out of range of the Merkins who stood, watching the riders escape. Reining their horses in they waited for the pack horses to catch up. N'kawa's pack horse had taken a spear in its rump and trotted around nervously, fear blazing from its eyes.

'Secure the horses,' N'kawa yelled as he slid his bow from its pouch, took two arrows and ran back towards the Merkins who stood their ground, wondering what this black man was up to.

'N'kawa!' screamed Piper. 'What the hell are you doing? Get your ass back here you idiot.'

N'kawa ran on, hurdling loose boulders as he did. When he was within spear range he stopped and faced the Merkins who were now yelling among themselves as they launched a few spears towards the easy target that was N'kawa. As the spears buried themselves into the ground behind him, all narrowly missing, N'kawa nocked his first arrow, drew back hard on the bow and sent the arrow screaming through the air at lightening speed. The closest Merkin stumbled backwards as the arrow impaled him. N'kawa screamed another war cry and bounced around in a small circle as the other Merkins watched. The second arrow took the leader of the Merkins square in the forehead, snapping his head backwards before he fell slowly to the ground. Again N'kawa howled his war cry and charged, as fast as he could run towards the remaining Merkins who fled into the trees.

Reaching the dead Merkin leader, N'kawa took his knife and removed his genitals. Holding them high in the air he yelped his war cry, knowing that the Merkins were watching from the cover of the grass and scrub. Blood surged from the body as N'kawa commenced butchering it. Cutting the inner groin and circling his blade deeply around the buttocks he removed a large portion of the thigh and buttock muscles and draped it across his shoulder before trotting back to Pipers position.

'What in the name of God was that?' Piper yelled angrily. 'You were damn near killed.'

N'kawa, blood soaked to the waist, placed his bow back into the saddle pouch and climbed up onto his horse after removing the hardwood spear from the pack horse's rump. Yelping the Indian war cry again he swung the loose slab of bloodied meat in circles above his head. Only moments before, that piece of meat provided the Merkin leader with transport, now it was a trophy and as far as the Merkins were concerned, food for this very unusual black rider who killed with a weapon they had never seen before.

They made the rest of the journey at a canter, slowing only when the wounded pack horse dragged them backwards. 'Any Comanche or Kiowa would think twice about attacking us after seeing what we do to them,' N'kawa explained. 'I'm hoping that these Merkins will hold a similar view.'

'Crazy Karankawa bastard,' Piper growled again. 'What the hell are you going to do with that lump of meat?'

'Hang onto it for a while. They'll be watching,' N'kawa replied as they crossed a small creek. Dismounting, N'kawa quickly washed the pack horse's wound before cleaning the slab of Merkin meat. Soaking wet, he rejoined Piper as they cantered into Cooks Town.

The Endeavour was a mass of ships masts and smoking steamer stacks. Tents were everywhere as a few hundred diggers went about unloading the ships. Cattle and horses milled in makeshift pens while bullocks and drays were lined up at the rivers edge awaiting their cargo.

'Unbelievable. This place is a small township,' Piper said as they rode past some diggers resting in the shade of a sail tent.

'Hey, did you just come from the Palmer?' an eager digger yelled as everyone turned to look at the unusual looking duo.

'What you got there, some roo meat? Another added, spotting the slab of fresh meat now resting across N'kawa's saddle.

'Can you show us the track?' yet another yelled.

Piper chose his words carefully. 'That's right; we've just come from the Palmer. It's absolutely pissing down there now and by weeks end it'll be flooded. Best you lads make yourselves comfortable here for a month or two before you head out. It's a three week slog through desperate country and only the hardiest will survive the trip.'

'Bullshit!' came a voice from the rear of the group. 'There's no rain out there, it's dry country. You just want to spook us away from your claim, don't ya?'

'Well, we ain't miners, we're farmers and don't give one squirt of a skunks ass about prospecting. Hey,

N'kawa, throw these boys a bit of that roo meat for their supper,' Piper replied.

N'kawa raised the slab of meat and threw it to a digger, who caught it and walked away smiling. 'Now ain't that what I said,' he called to the other diggers. 'Plenty of game to be had up these parts, we'll not go hungry in this country.'

Piper and N'kawa rode on to their makeshift camp. The cattle were still held in the yard and their wagon was where they'd left it. A man climbed out of the wagon as they approached. 'You'll be the Campbells?' he asked.

'That's right,' Piper replied. 'And who might you be?'

'Captain Saunders asked me to look after this place till you returned. Said you'd be along bye and bye.'

Both men smiled. 'We're mighty obliged. Once we clear these horses and clean up a little we'll buy you a bottle … and join you in it's drinking,' Piper said.

'Said you were fair men, yes sir, that's what he said,' the stranger chirped happily.

Cleaned up, the three of them headed towards one of the many makeshift bars that had commenced trading up from the waterfront. Passing a crowd of diggers, they watched as one plucked a piece of meat from the slab on the roasting steel. Avoiding burnt lips, he juggled the meat in his teeth before finally chewing it. 'Roo's up here a damn site sweeter than those on the Southern Fields,' he managed, through his steaming mouthful. 'Bloody tough lads, but sure is sweet.

Thanks boys,' he yelled to a smiling Piper and N'kawa as they strode past.

'What'd ya say that was?' their companion quizzed.

'Black roo. Only get them up this way. Damn hard to hunt 'em down but well worth the trouble, hey N'kawa?' Piper answered.

CHAPTER **FIFTEEN**

The ships came and went daily. Piper put to good use the bank bills he held by buying up more land along the river for cattle and horse yards. Cooks Town was taking on the look of a thriving town as ships offloaded lumber and iron for buildings, which were commenced as soon as the materials could be hauled to the site. Charlotte Street was a mile long and the traders snapped up plots where shops, hotels and whorehouses would soon stand.

Ladies of the night had already arrived and were plying their trade among the settlers as they waited anxiously for the first diggers to arrive from the Palmer.

The Campbells had secured enough provisions and draught horses to haul their wagon across Macmillans track to the Palmer. The whole town waited patiently for Macmillan's return. Those tired of waiting, set off in small groups and vanished into the wild scrub. A fresh Chinese contingent, one hundred strong, prepared for the march as Macmillan finally rode into town with his Native Mounted Police, weary diggers at their heels.

New chums, eager to gain information about the Palmer, swarmed the bedraggled lot and offered food and drink for information. A Palmer digger, holding up a sizable pouch heavy with gold, called to the crowd.

'This is only part of it, lads, there's tons more where this came from. Be warned, though, there's every danger known to man between here and the burning gullies of the Palmer. You'll need good supplies and a good rifle, lest the darkies drill you with holes and feast on your remains.'

The town buzzed with excitement as people gazed through the pouches of coarse gold, which was quickly traded for supplies, and in a few cases, passage aboard a departing ship. Some had made enough for the time being and would possibly return when life on this particular field became less arduous. Only the strong and the foolhardy prepared for the trip back to the Palmer. Diggers knew full well that this venture inland, and their stay on the Palmer field would be short lived due to the impending rains, but prospecting had always been a risky business and diggers were all about taking risks to win their fortune.

'I'm looking at a very confused man.' Piper said quietly to N'kawa as Macmillan walked towards them.

'So, I was right. You do know a way across the mountains,' he said.

'Well now that's not necessarily the truth,' Piper replied. 'You see, you government folk like a sleep every now and then but us Texans, well shucks, we can just ride all night long. Passed you during the night, not more than a day into your trip. Really ought to post more sentries around your camp, Macmillan.'

'If you know a track, as Government Surveyor in charge of opening this country up, I demand that you disclose it,' Macmillan commanded.

'Yes sir,' Piper replied as he stood more erect and gave a two finger salute. 'Y'all turn around, follow the track backwards and go on for a day or two. When you see the Merkin smoke in the mountains, head straight for it. When you get to their campfire, you ask pleasantly for directions … hell, that's all we done!'

'I'll find it, by God I'll find it, and when I do I'll have you two jailed for obstructing a Government Official … and for assault,' he threw in, as he marched away from them.

Piper raised his voice. 'Hey, N'kawa. Notice how big his ears are?'

Macmillan flicked a glance across his shoulder, his face now red with rage. 'And attempted slaughter of an Australian digger.'

The Campbells looked at each other, shrugged and continued their preparations.

The seemingly half witted caretaker who had minded

their supplies was only too willing to remain at the camp and repeat the duty while Piper and N'kawa returned to the Palmer. Piper had enlisted the assistance of a reinsman and several diggers to escort the heavily loaded wagon. It would be the first wagon across Macmillans track. There would be a lot of clearing to be done along the way. The helpers didn't mind; it meant they would not have to carry their own heavy packs on their back.

At first light, the convoy moved off. An official party with troopers and Native Mounted Police led the way followed by a hundred or more diggers and a similar number of Chinese who shuffled along in single file, well back from the main group. The leading official had been instructed by Macmillan to keep a close eye on the Campbells. A couple of troopers were to follow them if they broke from the convoy.

When Piper and N'kawa turned and headed back for Cooks Town at the beginning of the second day, the officials sat pondering their predicament. Deciding against sending two troopers back to Cooks Town with the Campbells, they regained momentum and pushed on.

Piper and N'kawa rested in the shade of a large tree on the outskirts of town, far enough away so as not to be discovered. 'This lot of Chinese are quite different to Mei's,' N'kawa said.

'Cantonese, I guess. They're miners, not like Mei's group who are from Hong Kong. From what she's said, there's certainly no love lost between the two,' Piper replied.

'Wonder how many more will come?'

'Who knows? Hundreds, maybe even thousands,' Piper guessed.

They waited until the next day before mounting up and moving back along the track towards the Palmer. This time they didn't have the pack horses to slow them down and could move at speed if necessary. They would not camp at the established campsites, knowing that the Merkins would be watching the convoy and known camp sites. Hopefully, the Merkin raiding parties would be too interested in the convoy to notice a couple of lone rider's branch left and head for the mountains.

Finding their marks, Piper and N'kawa soon picked up their track. Unknown to them, the Merkins had already launched their first attack on the trailing, and unarmed Chinese coolies, dragging several of them screaming into the scrub, as the remainder of the Chinese dropped their packs and fled to the safety of the diggers ahead of them. The captured Chinese were roughly spirited away towards the high country, hands bound with grass as they stumbled behind their captors, using their long Chinese pigtails as lead ropes.

Piper looked upwards at the steep rocky track before them. 'I'll say it again, the devil himself built this place,' he cursed as the horses stumbled and slipped, lathered in sweat and dust. After the first steep climb, came the next, only steeper and more dangerous as it coursed up to the summit between the rock walls.

They quickly took cover in a rocky outcrop when

they heard the sound of Merkin voices. The voices were close, too close they thought as they sheltered. Quietly they gave the horses water and had a drink themselves while they waited for the voices to pass. They didn't.

'I'll go across the ridge and see what I can,' N'kawa whispered.

'Hold on, I'll come with you. The horses will be okay here.'

'What if they're spooked? Reckon you can run all the way back to Cooks Town?' N'kawa asked.

Taking his rifle from the saddle boot, Piper dismissed N'kawa's comment and followed on quietly.

The smell of fires and cooking meat caught their nostrils before they saw the mouth of the cave below the ridge. Settling behind some rocks and scrubby trees, they peered into the cave. Neither man spoke as they took in the theatre below them. Four Chinese hung by their pigtails, arms bound behind them, their mouths gagged with knots of grass. Wide eyed, the Chinese watched as the Merkins carved a leg from one of the prisoners and threw it onto the hot rocks that overhung the fire. The pungent smell of the Cooley's gut roasting on the second fire filled the cave as the Merkins picked through it and feasted, swatting the brigade of flies as they did. In all, thirty yellow and white painted Merkins squatted around the feasting fires. As the roasted carcass of one Cooley was devoured, another had his skull smashed, gut removed and fed onto the fires.

'Jesus,' was all Piper could finally offer.

'Back away quietly and we'll leave this place,' N'kawa suggested.

'But those poor bastards are still alive down there, watching their friends being eaten,' Piper protested.

'We also, are alive,' N'kawa said. 'If we're discovered, we'll be next on the fires. Get the hell out of here … NOW!'

They crept silently back to where the horses stood and continued as cautiously as they could up the steep track, cursing each stone that broke loose and rattled its way back down the decline. Finally, gasping for air, they reached the gate through the stone cliffs. Normally they would have rested there, but under the circumstances, they pushed on across the pass, onto the narrow track and down the steep decline, travelling as far as they could until darkness hid their trail.

They rested on the warm earth and chewed through some dried rations, ready to move at a moments notice. 'Karankawa only ate their enemies for spiritual reasons,' Piper said, deliberately not questioning N'kawa.

'That's right. These natives are clearly eating humans for food. Didn't see too much spiritual activity back there,' he said gesturing back up the track.

'Adds a whole new problem to these parts,' Piper said.

'You have to understand, though,' N'kawa explained. 'The creeks don't have fish in them anymore and most of the game has been shot out. These natives have to eat something, so I guess that they figure eating the people who took their food away is a fair trade. Beats the hell out of starving.'

'Maybe they've always been cannibals. Maybe it just comes natural to them,' Piper said.

'Could be right,' N'kawa added. 'If that's the case, they've got easy pickings for a long time to come while the diggers enter their land. Once the Australians find out they're cannibals, they'll hunt them down and slaughter them to a man.'

They both knew that N'kawa was right in his prophecy. The time would soon arrive when expeditions would seek out the Merkin camps and slaughter them. They wouldn't stop until the whole of the vast Palmer Valley region and beyond was clear of the savages that stood between them and riches. As the two continued their nervous ride towards the Palmer they discussed the similarity of events that had taken place in Texas and what was now taking place in Queensland. The only major difference was the geography, most else remained the same.

Finally, they reached the North Palmer and made their way easily towards Palmerville. Diggers had moved further up the dry gullies and worked away at their dry-blowers while one stood guard with his rifle at the ready. It was clear that more had arrived overland from the Southern Fields. They had heard about the Campbells, one white and one black, and paid them little attention as they passed. They all knew of a track across the mountains but had yet to discover it. Nobody was brave enough to venture up there. On the few times they had, they'd come under attack and lost a few diggers, causing them to pull back to the safety of numbers on the diggings.

Piper couldn't control his excitement as they trotted their weary horses into Palmerville. The town had grown almost as dramatically as Cooks Town. Substantial buildings were now being completed, streets had been marked and trading posts dotted the landscape. The Chinese had wisely taken up even more ground and had the makings of a small Chinese settlement well under way. Gardens were growing and yards held good cattle. A Chinese kitchen stood near the end of the long street. It had already become a favourite eating place for diggers who had scratched enough gold from the sandy beds to pay for good, fresh food. 'They've done well,' Piper said like an excited kid to N'kawa as they neared their camp.

'Piper!' Mei yelled from a garden. 'Piper, you're back.'

The Chinese looked up at the two riders and Mei, running from the garden to greet them, throwing her arms around Piper's neck almost before he had dismounted. 'Hold on their, Mei,' Piper said as she hugged him.

'So good to see you back, and safe,' she continued happily, before running to N'kawa and hugging him also. Looking around behind them she asked anxiously, 'The pack horses with supplies. Where are the supplies?'

'They'll be along presently, Mei. Got a wagon load of stores for you on the way up Macmillans track. Should be here within the week I'd say. I'm pleased that you've marked out more land; there's another hundred Chinese on the way, Cantonese I think,' Piper said.

The other Chinese within earshot commenced their chatter when hearing the news. 'Canton Chinese no good,' one yelled. 'Cause plenty problem.'

'Ah well, they're on their way so you'd best get used to it,' Piper replied, as he unsaddled his horse and turned it into the corral.

'We had trouble here,' Mei said.

Piper turned and looked at her with concern.

'Trouble?'

'Yes. Cantonese from the South are on the fields and jumped someone's claim, so they say. The diggers think that we are also Cantonese and burnt one of our sheds. We would have been run off if it wasn't for an Irishman, Mulligan, who stopped them,' she explained.

Still concerned, Piper placed his hands on her shoulders and asked, 'Where can I find this man, Mulligan?'

'At the trading post or the hotel tent next to it I think. He's a good man,' she replied.

Striding up the hotel steps, Piper stood at the entrance and caught the eye of a group of men seated at a table drinking whiskey.

'Aha, the Texas cowboy, I presume,' Mulligan greeted, standing and walking to Piper.

Piper looked at the rugged explorer and immediately

believed all he had heard about this man who had discovered the river of gold.

'Sure is,' Piper replied with a smile, holding out his hand. 'Hear you broke up a little skirmish down at the Chinese camp the other day.'

'Mmm,' he replied nodding. 'Seems the diggers have difficulty telling the Cantonese from the Hong Kong breed. All damn Chinese as far as they're concerned. Lucky there wasn't too much damage done, although I hear that a few Chinks have been lynched downstream.'

'Well, just thought I'd let you know that I'm obliged to y'all for looking out for them,' Piper finished.

'Tell me, Texan, how'd you get over the mountains? Damned if I could find a way through. Did you mark the trail?' Mulligan asked.

Piper knew that they would find the trail sooner or later and he didn't mind passing information on to someone like Mulligan, knowing full well that some Government Official would eventually be praised for finding it. 'Uhuh, cuts around seventy, to eighty miles off Macmillans track as far as I can make out, but ah, shit, what a track it is. No water, and about as dangerous as sleeping with a rattler. I'll bet you that bottle of whiskey and another that the parched bones of humans and beasts will line the ravines up there before the next summer passes.'

'You'll have to give me some directions,' Mulligan said. 'These diggers will have to be moving away from here pretty soon, or be trapped by the floods. A shorter route across the mountains will save a few lives.'

'Depends which way you look at it,' Piper replied. 'Came across a Merkin feast up there on the way through and they sure as hell weren't eatin' hogs. But yes, I'll scratch out the trail for you.'

Piper turned to leave, but stopped as Mulligan spoke again, this time uneasily. 'By the way Tex, might be a good idea to move away from the Chinese camp. Folks just aren't keen on Chinese and I'm fearing that they could take unkindly to you if you seem to be in tight with them, if you know what I mean.'

'I hear ya,' Piper replied. 'But if it's all the same with y'all, me and N'kawa will remain with them. Perhaps you'll come on by this evening and share some of their cooking with us, best food in Queensland.'

'Okay, I'll respect your judgement, but don't say I didn't warn you. Maybe I will drop by tonight,' he said as Piper left.

Back at the camp, Piper hurried to his saddle bags and cleared them. Taking a small parcel and dusting off the flour and sugar, he walked to the garden where Mei was digging. As he approached, Mei looked up and beamed her smile. 'I kept your tent clean. You should sleep well tonight,' she said.

'Well thank you kindly, ma'am,' he said, holding out the parcel. 'There were ships all over the river at Cooks Town; ships from everywhere you could imagine, even families with children are landing. I thought I'd grab this little gift for you,' he said, feeling a little awkward.

'A present?' she asked, dropping her hoe and wiping her hands on her brown Coolies jacket.

'Well, it's nothing really, just that I thought, well … nah, it's nothing really,' he struggled as she eagerly opened the wrapping to reveal a hair brush, comb and small table mirror.

Delighted with the gift, Mei removed her hat, untied her hair and started brushing it, all the while looking into the small mirror. 'Thank you, Piper,' she said softly. 'It's lovely, I will treasure it.'

'Okay then. Well, we ought to be looking at a dinner plate soon, huh?' he said in a cocky tone.

'Of course, I'll call you in an hour or so,' she replied happily.

Mulligan and his men joined them for dinner at the Chinese kitchen, along with several of the diggers who needed a wholesome break from boiled flour and sugar. The general topic of discussion moved from the Palmer goldfields to the tales told by Piper and N'kawa. Their youth, growing up, battles with the Indians and then the Civil War. Their travels around the world aboard leaking ships drew laughter from the group as tale after tale was eagerly heard. As the evening wore on, the group thinned, until only Piper, Mei and a few other Chinese remained. Piper again tried to convince them to leave the Palmer and return to Cooks Town to set up shops there, but again, to no avail.

Within the fortnight their supplies arrived down Macmillans track. Yet again the travellers were astonished to find Piper and N'kawa there before them. They recounted the attacks along the way where two diggers had been speared to death. The group bringing their wagon and horses guessed that the Chinese had lost at least a dozen men. Those killed were simply left on the trackside, abandoned and unburied by their countrymen. They couldn't be absolutely sure, but thought that some Chinese had been bundled up and taken away by the Merkins. To be used as slaves, they suggested innocently.

Christmas on the Palmer was like any other day. Diggers feverishly hunted their wealth amid constant rain squalls. They all knew that they would soon be leaving. Mei's group had supplies enough to see them through; they need not rely on the gold that lay in the river, now rising slowly by the day. They would stay high and dry in Palmerville and could continue building through the wet, ready for the thousands who would arrive later.

Piper finally convinced the Chinese that at least some should return to Cooks Town. At last, he had finally made them see sense.

'We have agreed that Mei and two other Chinese will go back with you,' the leader explained. 'You are right; there will be money to be made in Cooks Town if we have butcher shop and trade store. We can make money here, and there,' he said to a relieved Piper.

As if to clinch the deal, Inspector Douglas rode into town the day after with his troopers to claim a track across the mountains. It provide the perfect escape route for diggers who could make the journey to Cooks Town in little more than a week with only the large Normanby to cross. No mention was made of the blazed trees he had encountered along the new track, which he described dramatically as the Douglas track through Hells Gate.

The rain continued to fall daily while Piper, N'kawa and the three Chinese prepared to leave for Cooks Town. They would take all four horses. One for packing and one each for Piper, N'kawa and Mei, who had become quite comfortable on horseback. The two Chinese men, both young and fit would carry only minimal back packs and would travel fast. Enough supplies could be had on their arrival to set up an enterprise, and if not, they could soon get them from Townsville.

In the early morning they set out through the valleys that were heavy with mist as the sun transformed the wet earth into a steam bath. On they went, sinking into the track where no stones lay, then slipping and skidding across the rocky slate when it was reached. They had chosen to move out alone. The diggers would wait another week. They had fared well travelling alone before and considered it the safest option.

Piper vowed that the next time they entered this valley it would be behind a herd of cattle and horses.

CHAPTER **SIXTEEN**

ain slowed their progress during the first two days and made for uncomfortable evenings, which saw them huddled beneath a canvas sheet, their body heat slowly drying their clothes to an uncomfortable state of dampness.

Struggling past the sheer cliff walls with valleys hidden by mist; the group finally crossed the last pinch and entered Hells Gate. Piper turned to show his relief to those walking close behind.

Without warning, boulders the size of large watermelons rained down from thirty feet above.

'Rockslide!' yelled Piper, realising the futility of the statement as soon as it left his lips.

A boulder struck Piper's horse on the rump, causing

it to rocket forward, pulling the wet reins out of his hands. N'kawa's horse struck Piper in the back, as it also broke free and galloped wildly forward, away from the falling rocks that thudded heavily onto the ground around them. Mei's horse, further to the rear, opted to spin around and head back down the pinch, losing its footing and tumbling over the edge of the cliff.

'Against the wall,' Piper screamed. 'C'mon, run through.'

Running forward, keeping as close as possible to the rock wall, they tried desperately to clear Hells Gate. The boulders stopped falling; now there were only large rocks descending on them. 'What the hell?' Piper yelled as a rock grazed his shoulder.

Then it started, the blood-curdling screech of the Merkin's war cry as dozens of them appeared from the pillars above Hells Gate, launching their deadly hard-wood spears towards the intruders who ran for the cover of the next row of boulders

The horses continued on ahead of them, slipping and rolling completely over, bouncing down the track that resembled a giant, wet staircase.

Spears bounced off rocks as Piper aimed his revolver carefully and fired until the chambers were empty. Only then did he realize that his revolver was the only weapon they had left, other than N'kawa's belt knife. He had strapped his other revolver to Mei's saddle and his rifle and saddle revolver had just bounced down the track ahead of them. As he fumbled to reload, another pack of screaming Merkins appeared and was upon them within seconds, their broad four-foot wooden swords hissing as they cut the air.

Almost reloaded, Piper felt the thud of a sword against his head, then another to his back, knocking him to the ground. Dazed, he tried to regain his feet and join N'kawa who was struggling under the weight of half a dozen Merkins wrestling him to the ground. Mei and the Chinese men had already been subdued, their hands and feet securely bound by vines.

'N'kawa!' Piper screamed, as another blow to the head made him fade into unconciousness.

Sharp rocks bit into Piper's chest as the Merkins dragged him, feet first, into the mouth of the cave. He could only vaguely make out the shapes behind him. He wondered if his friends were dead. The Merkins yelped their victory and prodded his back cruelly with their spears. He passed a row of slab fireplaces, still glistening with the grease and fat of recent meals, and was finally dumped at the foot of a large wooden pole, one of many inside the cave, connected by cross-bars and obviously there for one purpose only.

Pain wracked his body as they lashed his hands with vines and hoisted him high onto the cross-bar, hands above his head, feet securely hobbled. Above the din of the triumphant Merkins he heard Mei scream.

'Leave her alone, you bastards,' he yelled, before his mouth was gagged with knots of grass and vine. The only sounds now were those made by the Merkins and the crackle of the three fires which filled the cave with dense smoke.

Thirty or forty Merkins seemed to talk at once as they argued over which captive would be the first to face the rock ovens. Piper, and the now conscious N'kawa, hung from one cross-bar, while one of the Chinese males was hung with Mei from another. The other Chinaman, clearly dead, lay untrussed on the floor between them.

Unable to speak because of the gag, Piper grunted like an animal as he looked to N'kawa. He could see that N'kawa had taken a spear in the shoulder and stomach. Blood oozed from a vicious gash above his eyes, but at least he was alive. Mei was also conscious; her terrified eyes stared past soil smeared cheeks as she trembled uncontrollably. The Chinaman with Mei seemed only semi-conscious. Blood soaked from a wound beneath his tunic as he hung limply on the pole.

Smoke stung Piper's eyes as a Merkin with a hideous grin approached him holding N'kawa's knife. Piper knew that the knife was razor sharp as he closed his eyes, praying that the end would be quick. The grinning Merkin quickly sliced each trouser leg and the waistband of his trousers. Removing them, he threw them onto the fire. Other Merkins howled with laughter as all four of the live captives were stripped of clothing while the fires raged. Their boots and shirts had been removed outside and were now worn by a few of their captors,

Piper's struggle to free his hands brought a trickle of

blood down each arm. The vines held tight as he looked helplessly across at the naked form of Mei, who now seemed somewhat calmed, apparently resigned to her fate. Her pleading eyes locked into Piper's. If only they could speak, Piper would at least be able to tell her the words that he'd so far held back. Now the opportunity would be lost forever.

Piper blinked furiously and moved his head as best he could, trying to get Mei to close her eyes as the Merkins moved in on the dead Chinaman near the fires. Again and again Piper groaned like a trapped animal but Mei's eyes remained open, staring towards Piper across the earth floor as the Merkins butchered their kill.

Arms and legs were placed on different fires while bloodied hands searched through the gut to locate the kidney, a prize for the head Merkin.

Shovelling the intestines around the hot plate with their spears, they greedily sectioned off their portions as the putrid smoke filled the cave. Clearly the feast would only end with all captives being put to the fires. This many mouths needed more than one Chinaman to satisfy their hunger.

As limbs were turned in the coals, two well-built Merkins walked to the other Chinaman and cut him loose. Frozen by fear, legs unable to move, he slumped to the ground, urinating as he fell. Dragged to another of the fireplaces, he was dumped roughly beside it, before the blade of a wooden sword crushed the back of his skull. This fireplace was larger and was stoked even higher as the stunned Chinaman, still alive and semi-conscious lay beside it.

A scar faced Merkin, cackling like a hyena, trotted to Mei and stood in front of her, eating the remains of a scorched forearm as his ugly, bearded face peered into her eyes. Piper's blood boiled. The veins on his neck threatened to burst as he struggled to free his now bloodied hands, but still the vines held firm. He could do no more than watch as the heathen thrust his hand between her thighs, his grease covered fingers penetrating her violently. Mei stiffened at each violation but refused to close her eyes, preferring to stare defiantly at her tormentor, her defiance betrayed only by the tears that flowed freely down her cheeks.

In a final act of terrorism, the Merkin thrust the half eaten forearm of Mei's Chinese companion between her legs with such force that it lifted her off the ground. Laughing wildly, the scar faced brute ran to Piper, pulled the grass plug from his mouth and jammed the same forearm into his mouth; the jagged ends of the bone ripping his inner cheek and making him gag.

'You mongrel son-of-a-bitch. Free me and face me now, you bastard,' he spluttered through the blood.

The semi-conscious Chinaman on the floor groaned, and then screamed as he was hoisted to the sitting position onto the roaring fire. Flames scorched his body as he desperately scrambled to escape. The spears of half a dozen hungry Merkin held him down until the screams subsided.

Tears of rage and helplessness now flowed from Piper's eyes as he looked at Mei, slumped on her vine shackles. 'You bastards, you bastards,' he yelled, over and over as N'kawa suddenly slumped to the floor, his hands free. A few, enjoying their feast, looked at him as he lay motionless on the floor, then went back to eating and rolling the charred remains of the Chinaman around the large fireplace.

The creature that had violated Mei trotted back to her, a spear in each hand. Untying her ankles, he roughly pushed her legs apart. The semi-conscious Mei murmured and then screamed in pain as the Merkin pegged her left foot to the dirt floor with a spear. Now weak with pain, she tried to kick him with her free foot, which was grabbed and also secured to the ground by the other spear. Losing consciousness was a blessing for her as the Merkin went about violating her further.

Like a trapped panther, N'kawa, who had been slowly freeing himself, launched across the cave, knocking the rapist hard against the wall. In an instant, he freed Mei's feet from the spears that fastened them to the ground. Before the scar faced tormentor could regain his composure, N'kawa was on top of him, spear in his hand. The sound of crunching gristle was followed by a loud pop as the spear forced its way through his mouth and exited the back of his skull. Turning, N'kawa screamed his Karankawa battle-cry and launched the other spear into the now approaching Merkins, impaling one on its journey.

Crouching low, he ran towards them as they scrambled for their spears and wooden swords, half eaten limbs discarded to the dusty floor.

The first Merkin hit by N'kawa's rampaging bulk was the butcher with N'kawa's knife. N'kawa quickly relieved him of the knife and slit his throat, almost in one movement, before pouncing on another, opening his stomach with a wide sweep of the blade, spewing the contents across the cave floor.

'Over here, N'kawa,' Piper screamed. 'Cut me loose so I can help.'

N'kawa knew that soon the spears would come, and he would be dead. He had little time to cut Piper free; he would fight on and get as many as he could before joining his Karankawa family. Attacking again, he sliced only air in a broad arc as the spears held him away from his quarry. If he lost his footing, they would spear him where he lay. He chose not to die lying down and allowed the spears to run him backwards until he could go no further.

His back against the wall, he grabbed a spear and deflected it, all the while trying to attack the aggressors. Another spear pressed hard against his throat. The Merkin at the other end looked into his eyes, and then pushed forward with his weight. Blood sprayed everywhere as the spear cut through the front of N'kawa's neck and exited the back. Grimacing in pain, he struggled to keep his footing as Piper screamed in anger. Another Merkin took N'kawa's knife and reached forward, grabbing his genitals.

The sound of the pistol erupting in the confines of the cave momentarily deafened all those inside. The painted butchers, ready to finish off their captives, turned to see a dozen of their own kind, unpainted and led by a bearded white man standing at the mouth of the cave. The butcher facing N'kawa coughed blood and slid slowly to his knees, collapsing on the floor with a bullet in his back as the unpainted Merkins rushed into the cave. One of the aggressors rose to his feet, raised a spear and was instantly shot by the bearded intruder who barked his orders in their language to his followers. Moving swiftly to Piper, he cut his bonds and steadied him as he struggled to stand.

'Can you walk?' he asked.

'I can walk,' Piper replied as he staggered to Mei, who had been cut down and was being revived by her saviours. Seeing that they were comforting her, he staggered to N'kawa who sat against the wall, blood flowing freely from his neck and torso. 'N'kawa. Oh my God, N'kawa,' he cried. 'C'mon brother, we're going home,' he said as he tried to lift him.

'My boys will take care of him,' the bearded stranger barked. 'No time to mourn happenings here, we've got to get away as soon as we can,' he added, as his black followers lifted N'kawa, stemming the flow of blood from his wounds with chewed grass and mud.

Still dazed and confused, Piper turned to the man. 'Thank God you turned up. Who the hell are you?'

'Palmerston … Christie Palmerston, at your service, sir.'

'Christoforo? The same Christoforo we met in Brisbane? The singer?' Piper asked.

'Not the time for singing, but yes, the same person indeed. Now let's get the hell away from here.'

Outside the cave, Palmerston's Black soldiers quickly fashioned two stretchers and within minutes were trotting down the Devils Staircase with the unconscious N'kawa and Mei aboard, naked, but for the flies that swarmed their wounds. Piper recovered his buckskin boots from a dead Merkin and hurried along behind them, as naked as his wounded friends. 'How'd you find us?' Piper called to Palmerston, the only one on horseback.

'You've got friends you don't know about,' he replied, pointing to the two Merkins carrying N'kawa. 'Apparently you saved these boys a few weeks back. Well, lucky for you they are friends of mine; they led me to you.'

Moving about in the wild Cape York country at night would be an impossibility for anyone but Palmerston and his Merkins. Slowly but surely they picked their way through the hills and valleys before eventually arriving at a point on the Normanby unknown to any other European. Although the river was by now in light flood, it was relatively easy to cross at this point with the stretchers hoisted high.

During their dash for Cooks Town, Palmerston's Merkins cared for Mei and N'kawa. Piper was always at their side, but sat back while the Merkins administered their traditional medicines.

Within five miles of Cooks Town, Palmerston called a halt. As morning approached, Piper checked on N'kawa. He was in desperate shape. His wounds had not become infected, thanks to Palmerston's Merkins, but the severity of the wounds would have seen a lesser man dead. Mei had regained enough strength to walk slowly and sat beside N'kawa, mopping his battered brow with Palmerston's kerchief.

The only person not naked was Palmerston. Clothing didn't seem an important issue at the moment for Piper and Mei, as they sat among the naked Merkins trying desperately to keep their friend alive.

Regaining consciousness momentarily, N'kawa engaged in a brief discussion with Piper that the others did not hear, even Mei had allowed exhaustion to reclaim her and had slumped against a nearby tree. Afterwards, Piper spoke with Palmerston who quietly issued orders to his Merkins and within the hour there was enough white, yellow and red ochre to mix coloured pastes.

As the Merkins and Christie watched, Piper painted a white circle beneath each of N'kawa's eyes. A red band was painted across his forehead and neck, covering the grotesque wounds. The final painting was a large strip of yellow across each breast and down to his feet. Piper then sat back and chanted a Karankawa chant he'd learned as a child from N'kawa. As the chant continued,

Mei woke and moved to sit beside Piper who was holding N'kawa's hand.

Stirring, N'kawa asked to be raised to the sitting position. Once there, he fixed a blank stare towards the east. 'The Karankawa are calling me,' he said, words struggling to escape his mouth. 'I will enter their world ahead of you my brother. I will tell them of your bravery and love for me. You will be accepted into our spirit lodge when the time is right. We will be waiting,' he said as he commenced a weak spirit chant.

The Merkins moved away, uneasy at watching this man die. Piper gently moved Mei's hand from N'kawa's and placed his arm around her, drawing her naked body to his as they listened to N'kawa's voice fade and finally fall quiet. They wept as they embraced, grief pouring from their hearts.

The sound of a horse clearing its nostrils jolted them back to the moment. 'Oh Lord,' Piper exclaimed through his tears. 'It's N'kawa's horse.'

'I'll bring it in,' Christie said as he walked towards the horse, took the loose reins and led it back to them.

Rustling through the saddle pack they took N'kawa's poncho and draped it over Mei to cover her nudity. The groundsheet provided a wrap for Piper as they helped the Merkins fashion an Indian pack-draw behind the horse to take N'kawa to Cooks Town.

Industry took their minds away from their grief and they were soon on their way, Mei in the saddle, N'kawa's body roped onto the Indian pack-draw and Piper astride

Christie's mount as he walked beside them steadying Mei's leg to keep her in the saddle.

Palmerston's Merkins melted into the trees as they came in sight of the township. 'Come on,' Christie said to Piper, 'an old friend of mine is in town. She'll take care of Mei while we get settled.'

'I've got a camp to the north,' Piper explained. 'Maybe we could just go straight there.'

'The lady needs the comfort of another lady at the moment, my friend. Best we do it my way for this day at least.'

Piper looked across at Mei who managed a weak smile and nodded. 'Okay,' Piper said quickly. 'We'll do it your way for the day.'

Riding up the track behind the buildings that faced Charlotte Street, Piper heard the murmurs of the towns-folk. The Chinese girl, barely covered by a poncho, rode astride a horse pulling a frame with a painted black man. Now walking beside them, a half naked white man, bruised from head to toe and chatting with the man everyone in the North knew well … Christie Palmerston.

'A doctor to Kitty's place,' Christie yelled to a group of mumbling onlookers.

Before they had dismounted, the rear door of the building opened to reveal an amply bosomed lady, finely dressed with jewellery to match.

'Christie. What on earth are you doing back here?' she asked. 'And what in God's name have you brought with you?'

'Hello again, Kitty. My friends here stumbled into a Merkin kitchen in the hills. Seems they done his woman some sort of mischief. Perhaps you would be kind enough to tend to her needs,' he said in an aristocratic tongue befitting a Count.

'Well certainly. Bring the girl inside,' Kitty replied. 'Don't want that dead Merkin left here, though.'

'We'll take care of him, and oh, he's an American, not a Merkin,' Christie corrected.

'He's black, painted and dead. Best he moves on sooner than later,' she said. 'And Christie, since when did you go out saving Chinese people?'

'Just tend to her, Kitty. I'll be back soon.'

On the way to Piper's camp, Piper asked Christie what Kitty had meant when she said what she did about Chinese people. 'You'll here it sooner or later. Word's out that I don't like Chinese … and I don't. Problem is that I've been accused of doing things that I haven't done, mainly by the Chinese,' Christie said.

'Things?' Piper enquired.

'Well, all sorts, really. Supposed to have led the Merkins against them. That way, according to my accusers, the Merkins get a feast while I get their gold, that sort of scuttlebutt.'

'Is that what you do?' Piper again asked.

'Cast your mind back a few days, my Texan friend. Did I get any gold? Did my Merkin friends, and your friends I might add, did they feast on your Chinese friends? I don't believe so,' Christie answered, shaking his head.

'Well, whatever. All I know is that I owe you a debt I can never repay. If there's ever anything I can do to repay you, just ask, y'hear?'

Christie patted Piper's back as they walked. 'Forget it; you'd do the same for me.' He comforted. 'Best I help you prepare your friend here for the hereafter. I'll call tomorrow and get some clothes up to you.'

Once Christie had gone, Piper enlisted the help of the camp caretaker to get N'kawa inside the canvass and log hut. The caretaker, although thought of as a half-witted man, knew what Piper was going through and left him alone with N'kawa. No sooner had he gone, Piper broke down and wept uncontrollably as he held the cold hand of N'kawa. His grief continued to spill out until the tears simply dried up and he drifted off to sleep, crouched beside his Karankawa brother.

Sleep gave him little comfort as he dreamt of Argyll – sparks flew from the flint-rock as his horse sped into the clearing where Comanche warriors surrounded the Karankawa family; a lone youth, his black naked body glistening with sweat as he faced the superior Comanche without fear, knowing that death would soon be with him; Piper's killing of the Comanche, his first kill, and the years that followed, as he and N'kawa grew up together as black and white brothers.

He slept, unable to control the dreams that walked him, step by step through his youth at Argyll, of his life with N'kawa, his brother's Hamish and Rob, and his mother. As if in slow motion, he watched again as the canon grapeshot sent his beloved father to another world.

Sitting bolt upright, in a lather of sweat ended the tragic mosaic of pictures that rolled through his mind. Lighting a candle he saw that someone had placed a neatly folded set of clothes just inside his door. Putting them on, he checked N'kawa, peaceful in death, before walking through the drizzling rain to where Mei had been left. He figured it must be around four or five in the morning. The town was asleep as he trod up the creaking steps towards the door. He stopped, turned and walked back down before stopping again, turning and returning to the door. About to knock, the door opened slightly to reveal the muzzle of a pistol.

'Shit,' he cursed almost falling backwards down the stairs.

'Piper,' Christie whispered from behind the door as he eased the hammer of the pistol. 'Damn near got yourself killed twice in the same week. Come on in, but keep quiet, your girlfriend is down the hallway, one door from the end.'

'Thanks,' Piper managed. 'Sorry to wake you up, really, I'm sorry. Couldn't sleep.'

'Forget it. The doctor has seen your friend and given her medication. Probably won't be able to wake her. Those bloody Merkins gave her a good seeing to,' Christie said, genuinely concerned.

Piper looked at him. 'Can you wait while I go in? I mean, if she's okay I'll stay, or leave, I don't know, but can you wait?'

Christie slowly opened the door and waited as Piper crossed to the bed where Mei lay sleeping. His ruptured mouth hurt as he leaned down and kissed her on the forehead. Gently, he took her soft hand and stroked it, fighting back the tears as he gazed at her.

Her face was bruised and there was swelling on her cheek, but her natural beauty could not be hidden. Holding her warm hand to his rough, unshaven face he gently kissed it.

A comforting hand rested on his shoulder. Turning, he gazed into the sympathetically smiling face of Kitty. In his eyes she could see the loss, the hurt and the anger that he was feeling at this moment. She bent and kissed him. 'There, all the demons have been kissed away. Stay here with her, she needs you. She'll be okay, few minor injuries that you can help her heal in time, but right now, she really needs you.'

'I don't know how to thank you,' Piper stammered to Kitty and Christie, who had now joined them.

'Tell you what. After you get cleaned up, use my bathroom, you can be the first one she will see when she awakens, but only if you get your American arse down there and clean it up!' Kitty joked in a whisper. 'My man here will show you around, won't you Christie?'

Nodding with a smile, Christie guided Piper to the bathroom and then left to hunt down someone who could cook; but first he would make sure that Kitty got herself safely back to bed.

CHAPTER **SEVENTEEN**

Mei awoke to the sound of distant thunder as the township came to life under heavy rain clouds. There was nothing Piper could do for her other than to maintain his bedside vigil, but there were other things to be taken care of. Leaving Mei in the comfort and care of Kitty, he headed back to his camp. Townspeople stared as the battered Piper strode purposefully along the muddy street, his solemn face not caring to acknowledge them.

News of the incident had already spread throughout the shanties and camps along the river. Palmerston had held court during the night and painted the grimmest of pictures of the rescue from the Devils Kitchen below Hells Gate. 'Skinned alive and roasted,' he told the spellbound listeners.

'Do we go up there in force and shoot the heathens out?' a voice called, receiving immediate support from the others.

'It's the Chinese they're after,' Palmerston replied. 'Let them take their revenge. My best advice is for everyone to keep well clear of the Chinkies and travel the hills in groups of no less than a dozen.'

The group nodded their acceptance of Palmerston's advice.

Arriving at his camp, Piper was greeted by the caretaker. The greeting was by way of silent gesture as he slowly entered and crossed to N'kawa's body. Piper sat beside the body of his lifelong companion and as if not knowing what to do next he quietly reflected on their life together. The hours rolled by unnoticed before the silence was finally broken.

'Piper,' the caretaker called quietly from the door. 'Some of the townsfolk are here to help with the burial. The grave has already been dug up on Cemetery Hill.'

N'kawa's body was quickly loaded into a rough wooden coffin, carried outside and placed atop a trolley. A dozen or so of the townsfolk, diggers, sailors and merchants followed the trolley up the hill to the cemetery, already the resting place for two dozen or more souls that had made it no further than Cooks Town on their way to riches. A preacher sang N'kawa's praises as he bid him goodbye and confirmed his entry into the almighty kingdom above.

Piper helped the diggers cover the coffin and worked with them to place the final site markings. Christie Palmerston offered his assistance. 'I know of a good Italian stonemason in Victoria,' he said to Piper. 'I'll have a headstone shipped up. What should the epitaph be?'

Piper thought for a while before replying. 'Diego N'kawa Campbell. Texas Ranger, last of the Karankawa,' he replied. 'Don't worry about dates, as far as he was concerned he died a long time ago along with his people. He just hung around a while longer to make sure that I was okay.'

As they walked back to Kitty's place, Palmerston nodded, pretending to understand.

Piper winced as he eased himself into a chair beside the sleeping Mei. The sound of hammers belting nail heads rang through the town as carpenters worked frantically. The town was a hive of noisy activity, in contrast to the silence of the cemetery Piper had just left. Gently brushing Mei's forehead, Piper whispered his hopelessness. 'What now, my beautiful Mei? What now? You're all I have left. Is the Campbell dynasty to end here in this wilderness? Maybe we could rebuild it … you and me, this could still become the Argyll of the South. We can start right away, soon as you are up and about.'

A doctor quietly entered the room. 'Mr Piper?'

'Campbell, Piper Campbell,' Piper corrected.

'Good Scottish name. I'm Doctor Stewart, not of the

Clan, but a Scott just the same,' he said in a typically dry medical voice. 'This young lady has a long way to repair. Her feet will be alright in time, as will the internal problems but I hold concerns for her mind.'

'Her mind?' Piper quizzed.

'She displayed certain signs of instability before I drugged her. The absence of any fever indicated to me that her experiences up there in the hills may well have affected her somewhat. We'll all have to wait and see,' he said in a resigned tone.

'Are you saying she's mad?' asked Piper.

'No, no. Mad is not a description I use. A traumatic experience can sometimes alter the thinking and behaviour of people, strong and weak alike. She may wake in a fine frame of mind, but I caution you, be attentive to the possibilities during her convalescence and let me know about any extraordinary behaviour she may develop.'

'I saw soldiers go mad during the war in Georgia. They were totally mad, running around deliriously until they were shackled,' Piper said.

Doctor Stewart glanced at Piper across his spectacles as he dressed Mei's foot wounds. 'Not likely to happen here Laddie. And you … do you feel any psychological effects from the incident?

'Few bumps and bruises, but they'll mend, I'll be fine,' Piper replied.

'You know, it's not only the fairer sex that suffer hysteria after being dealt with in such savage fashion. I've seen the symptoms present in the minds of even the hardiest. Unfortunately, such manifestations, if left untreated, can lead to long term disorders. Be mindful of that Laddie,' Doctor Stewart cautioned.

'Of course.' Was all Piper could manage.

'You can be off now while I see to the young lady's other disturbances,' Doctor Stewart ordered.

Piper quickly left the room and went to the kitchen where half a dozen ladies sat around talking with Kitty and Palmerston.

'Ah, *buon giorno*,' Palmerston greeted, causing the ladies to turn and watch Piper enter.

Under different circumstances, Piper would have greeted them with a smile; instead, his still swollen mouth managed only a grimace as his tired, blood-shot eyes watched Palmerston stand. 'Come on, Piper. Come with me, you can help fetch a few items from a ship.'

Piper nodded. 'Be pleased to help.'

'Well then, we're off,' Palmerston announced to the room full of ladies.

Outside, Piper looked up at the shingle that had just been erected above the door. PALMER KATES, the bold, gold lettering yelled. 'Who is she?' Piper asked.

'Who? Palmer Kate? That's Kitty. Thought that PALMER KATE had a certain ring to it, don't you think?' Palmerston laughed

'She's a lady of the night?' Piper asked.

'Best in Australia, and the most enterprising,' Palmerston replied.

'So I'd be correct in saying that Mei is recovering in a whorehouse?' Piper enquired.

'You'd be very correct. It was either the clean sheets of a whorehouse; round the clock care by Kitty and her girls and good food, or sharing that squatter's shanty with you. I know which one I'd prefer.' Palmerston replied.

Piper nodded his agreement as they walked on towards the wharf.

After discovering that the goods had not arrived, Palmerston and Piper strolled through the town, talking to the diggers, merchants and others that made up the cosmopolitan outpost.

Throughout the day, weary diggers arrived from the Palmer as others set out to replace them. Pouches of gold were swapped for food, booze and supplies. With the tangible essentials taken care of, the diggers headed for the hotels and Palmer Kates to offload even more of their hard won gold, and plenty of it.

It was well into the evening before Mei opened her eyes and gazed around the room. Piper smiled down at her, relieved to at last see her awake. 'Welcome back, stranger,' he smiled.

'Where am I?' she asked weakly.

'At a friend of Palmerston's,' he answered. 'It's okay, you're with friends here. How do you feel?'

'I'm fine. How's N'kawa?' she asked.

Piper paused before answering. 'N'kawa's dead, remember? We buried him at a proper service this morning.'

Mei's eyes widened as she clutched the sheets tightly. Piper knew that she was now starting to recall the terrible events of the past few days. He took one of her hands and stroked her forearm as her eyes closed, causing a tear to roll down across her cheek. 'It's okay, now. You're safe,' he said calmly.

Her eyes remained tightly closed as she breathed heavily, almost sobbing. Kitty entered the room ahead of Palmerston who carried a bedroll. 'Stay here with her tonight,' Kitty ordered. 'Doctor Stewart will be along presently. She still needs rest and you can't take her back to your camp just yet.'

After thanking the two, Piper set up his bedding so that he could hold Mei's hand. Doctor Stewart administered his potion which made Mei slip back into a deep, fearless sleep. Ignoring the sounds of passion that invaded the rooms as diggers parted with their hard won gold, Piper settled into another fitful nights sleep. He was a light sleeper and each new customer at Palmer Kates momentarily woke him. Drunken street brawls erupted each half hour as diggers discovered their gold stocks empty, spirited away by the card sharks, bootleggers, pickpockets and pimps. This was a place where the undertaker was fast becoming the most sought after tradesman in town as bodies, covered in mud and blood, discarded in the lonely ditches greeted each sunrise.

Piper maintained his bedside vigil as the days slipped by. When not by her side, his time was spent securing timber and iron for his house. A bank-agency had opened and was doing a brisk trade. Piper now had direct access to his considerable wealth rather than relying on bank promissory notes. That wealth had allowed for certain influence which he used without apology in establishing prime real estate and employees who were paid above the going rates of pay without question. Although Piper had suffered the most horrific personal setbacks imaginable, he never lost his wit, sense of humour or his ability to get along with almost anyone.

Mei grew stronger each day and was finally ready to leave the care of Doctor Stewart and Kitty. With the aid of Piper, she limped slowly to his camp where she was taken completely by surprise. The shanty hut had been converted into a timber home, quite fashionable under the circumstances. Although far from complete, it was substantial enough for comfortable habitation. Carpenters continued at their brisk pace as Piper led Mei up the steps and onto the partly finished verandah.

He smiled as he led her through the door. 'It's not much yet but it'll take shape soon enough,' he said with some excitement.

'I'm sure it will be lovely when it's completed,' Mei replied as she walked through the timber shavings.

'Over here. Have a look at your room,' he urged.

She saw that it was the only room that was completely finished. A fine bed with a colourful spread dominated the room. There was even a glass window, neatly draped with curtains, a wardrobe, table and chamber necessities. Opening the wardrobe, Piper stood back to get her response. 'A fine wardrobe for a fine lady,' he said, displaying a wardrobe full of dresses, shawls, shoes and other odds and ends. 'And you thought I'd been standing idle.'

'They're lovely. It's all lovely. Is this my room?' she queried, but yet to smile.

'Of course. Your room, your house … our house. I'll sleep in the other room while the house is being finished. I figured you'd be more comfortable with that, for the time being leastways,' he replied, tongue in cheek.

'That will be fine,' was all Mei added as she rustled through the wardrobe and checked the bed.

She had yet to recover fully from her ordeal; however Piper felt a little deflated at her lack of outward appreciation. Her eyes that once flickered like black diamonds were now dull as soot. Her smile that once lit up a room had deserted her and the spring in her step was replaced by a painful shuffle.

'I'll get some water for the bedside table,' Piper said. 'Some food, you'll need some food. I'll go to the Chinese camp and get fruit.'

'Fruit would be nice,' she said as she lowered herself onto the generously sized bed.

Obtaining a good supply of fruit and vegetables, Piper walked briskly back to the house. Both Kitty and Doctor Stewart had told him that good care and time was all Mei needed to return to her former self. His plan to seek her hand in marriage was shelved for the moment. He would wait until she was well enough and the house finished. The thought of their union put a spring in his step as he skipped up the steps. The Campbell line would continue from this place, he thought, as soon as the time was right.

'Piper,' she called from her bed as he sliced the last piece of fruit into a bowl.

'Just about there,' he said, walking to her room with the fruit.

'Oh, it's good to smell fresh fruit again,' she said sitting up.

'All you can eat. If you want more, just holler,' he said cheerfully.

'Piper, I'll be up and about within a day or so. How many Chinese are here?' she asked, surprising Piper.

'Ah, could be no more than a thousand or so. Why do you ask?'

'Just curious,' she answered. 'Are you returning to Palmerville?'

'Not until the wet has ended. I think we should make good use of our time here in the meantime. I've ordered more horses and cattle from Townsville, but that's not what you need to be talking about until you've rested,' he replied, confused by her line of questioning.

'I won't be going back to Palmerville,' she said resolutely.

'Of course not, and I wouldn't expect you to,' Piper replied quickly.

'We can stay here in Cooks Town,' she decided.

Not willing to discuss the 'we' and it's possible

meaning at this time, Piper smiled and urged her to eat the fruit. 'Plenty of time to map out the future when you're up and about,' he said, wondering if he was repeating himself.

'Sleep will be easier here,' she said finishing her fruit and rolling herself comfortably under the bed covers.

'Sure it will. If you need anything I'll be right out there,' he said pointing to nowhere in particular. 'You get some rest, y'hear?'

Mei's recovery took Piper by surprise. In no time she was up and about although she never left the house, preferring to tidy up after the carpenters and add feminine touches to each room as it took shape. At night she slept alone while Piper occupied the other large bedroom across the hallway. During the days while Piper was busy negotiating deal after deal with bankers, government officials and traders she often sat on the verandah chair gazing out towards the Chinese camp. Wearing the clothes Piper had given her, from a distance she could pass as a European woman. It still bothered Piper that she had yet to smile or display any affection towards him, unlike the Mei of Palmerville.

Returning early one afternoon Piper declared that they would be guests of an old friend, the skipper of a large clipper that had just moored at the wharf. 'It'll do you good to get back out and away from the house,' Piper said.

'Perhaps you can go there on your own,' she suggested.

'Nonsense, you'll enjoy yourself and I can show you around a real ship. Besides, I'd like to show you off now that you are well again. Let's dress up a little, huh?' he said.

'I really don't feel like it but if it means so much to you, yes, I'll come,' she said without enthusiasm.

Piper dressed in his finest clothes. Parading in the main lounge before a tall mirror, he looked more the English gentleman than a Texas redneck in his knee-high leather boots, moleskin trousers, red shirt and jacket and his finest white hat. As an afterthought, to complete the charade, he took the steel pommelled riding crop from a hallway vase and tapped it against his leg. 'This'll do just fine,' he said quietly to himself as Mei entered the room.

'Ah, you look stunning,' he said, turning to face her.

'I feel like one of Kitty's ladies. Can I get some Chinese finery soon,' she asked.

'Sure can, just as soon as I can arrange it,' he answered.

'No need, I'll arrange it tomorrow with the Chinese merchants,' she responded looking at herself in the mirror. 'I look cheap.'

Reassuring her that she looked terrific they walked through the town and down to the Calcutta, a fine three-master that dwarfed the other ships at anchor. They were met at the rail by the master who had crewed with Piper and N'kawa only a short while before, or so it seemed.

The evening went well. Old times were visited, and revisited by the two as Mei sat by and listened, not once registering a smile as the two men often roared with laughter. Not willing to set about the second bottle of rum, Piper excused himself and guided Mei back to Charlotte Street for the shuffle home, past the hotels, whorehouses and card saloons. 'N'kawa would have enjoyed seeing that old dog finally at the helm of his own ship,' Piper said as they walked.

Passing one of the darker bars at the end of the street, a Chinese merchant called to Mei, causing the two to stop. Mei engaged in a lengthy discussion in Chinese as Piper stood by listening, not understanding a word. The merchant eventually nodded his goodbye and departed towards the now flourishing Chinatown.

'What was that all about?' Piper asked.

'Oh nothing. He's from Hong Kong and knows my family. He was curious as to why I was living with you,' she answered.

'What did you tell him?' Piper added curiously.

'I told him that it was my house and that you were living with me as a paying boarder.'

'Uhuh. How'd he take that?' Piper continued.

'He called me a whore and offered me a job in his whorehouse. Of course I refused the offer and told him that I owned the land he was squatting on, and that I would see that his lease payments would be increased from tomorrow,' she said.

'You what?' was all Piper could think of.

'We do own that land, don't we?' she asked.

'Well yes, I do … I mean yes, we do but we can't just increase the lease. There are two dozen shops down there, not to mention the scores of shanties.'

'Then we will raise the lease on all of them. They are wealthy Hong Kong merchants and will pay, or they can move further up the river to live with the Merkins,' she said coldly.

'Perhaps we can talk about it tomorrow,' Piper said as they entered the house.

'We've just talked about it now. There'll be other things to talk about tomorrow,' she said as she walked to her room. 'Don't worry, I'll go and tell them tomorrow if it embarrasses you.'

'Well no, it doesn't embarrass me. I just think that it's unfair to ask for more money from poor people when I have quite enough as it is,' he said, his voice still well tempered.

Mei turned her expressionless face to Piper. 'You have money. You have influence and of course you now have an almost hero status. You are the famous Texas Ranger who rides with Christie Palmerston and rescues Chinese whores from the ovens of the Merkins. You are the famous Piper Campbell who can command respect from all of the bankers in Queensland,' she said, her words cutting through Piper's very being and taking him completely by surprise.

'Mei…' he started, but was cut short.

'Let me finish. I'm Australian-born and educated,

and I will not stand by and let Chinese migrants accuse me of whoredom. I will establish myself here as someone the Chinese will respect and I'll start by raising their lease payments, if that's alright with you!' she finished and walked to her room.

'Shit!' Piper muttered, unable to locate a correct emotion for the occasion.

True to her word, Mei spent the next day extorting raised lease contracts from the Chinese. She promised the wealthy merchants that if the poorer Chinese suffered she would make sure that the merchants were removed from the land. Merchant after merchant screamed their disapproval while Mei dictated the terms of their lease. As some consolation, she promised that work would start immediately on a grand hotel that could be built and staffed by the Chinese. She would also meet the cost of building a laundry and bake house.

In the late afternoon, Piper returned home to find Mei dressed in a fine silk Chinese gown. Her lithe body moved graciously beneath the smooth silk as she welcomed him to the dinner table. For the first time since they'd returned from the Palmer she looked radiant. Colour had returned to her cheeks and her hair shone brightly in the lamp light. Sparkling eyes and a radiant smile were all that was needed to complete the picture of old.

'That's a fine dress, Mei,' he ventured.

'A whore could not afford a dress like this,' she said.

'Mei, you ain't no whore. Get that notion out of your head straight away,' Piper said, feigning anger.

'In the eyes of some, I am,' she replied.

'To hell with them,' he yelled. 'Alright then, if you need to change your status, marry me! You can't be called a whore if you're married.'

Mei spooned another mouthful of food. 'I've promised a new building or two in the Chinese leases,' she said, completely evading Piper's proposal. 'I'd also like us to buy the big hotel across from Kitty's place as soon as we can.'

Piper stopped chewing food and shook his head slowly. 'Mei, I'm a cattle man. I came here to start the new Argyll, and I'll do it. What the hell do I, we, know about running hotels? And while I'm on the 'we' subject, unless 'we' decide to make the 'we' a commitment, 'we' are going to have to ease off on spending 'my' money,' he said, inadvertently raising his voice.

'We will get married only when we have enough assets in place to sustain the marriage,' she replied calmly. 'Go ahead and start your Argyll, but let me deal with the business of securing some honour for us, me in particular.

He was not accustomed to such a calculated viewpoint from Mei and struggled for a reply, knowing that any reply would probably erupt into a full scale argument. Choosing to remain silent he gracefully cleared the table and adjourned outside with his pipe.

The lamp in Mei's room was dimmed and she went

to bed. Piper walked inside and extinguished the large room lamp then crossed the floor to Mei's bedroom. Perhaps it was courage he lacked in the matter of courtship, he thought.

Persuading himself that he was correct in his assumption, he entered the room, crossed to Mei and kissed her forehead. 'Goodnight,' he said softly.

'Goodnight,' she said, looking up at him and then rolling onto her side, pulling the covers around her neck.

'What would you do if I suddenly jumped into bed with you?' he joked.

'I would leave and go to your bed,' she answered firmly.

'Just kidding around,' he said, as he left her on her own.

Again he found himself wondering what on earth had gone wrong. Was this the mind-switch that Doctor Stewart had cautioned him about? Perhaps she would respond differently if he acquiesced and openly supported her entry into the hotel business, a business about which he knew nothing.

What he did know, was that losing her would devastate him. For the first time he confessed his love for her, if only silently to himself. If the events of this evening were any indication, he had best hold off announcing his feelings until he could be sure of at least a little reciprocation.

Confused, Piper retired. He made a mental note to

call on Christie Palmerston and Kitty in the morning. They did not seem to have the difficulties he had. They were kind, understanding people to whom he owed a great debt. They would help him and Mei through this turbulent time, of that he was certain.

CHAPTER **EIGHTEEN**

octor Stewart answered the door to greet Piper. 'Up bright and early,' he said.

'Thought I'd call by and ask your opinion,' Piper replied.

'Mei?'

'Uhuh. You said to keep an eye on her. Well, seems she's had a complete character change. Rarely wants to talk, and is as cold as ice towards everyone,' Piper said.

'Under the circumstances, quite understandable. My advice hasn't changed. Keep an eye on her and expect a little irrational behaviour until she completely repairs. Trauma sometimes plays tricks on the mind,' he said.

'So how long before she returns to her normal self?' Piper asked.

Doctor Stewart sharpened a pencil as he considered his answer. 'Who knows? Changes of the mind, as an outcome of trauma, can be permanent, but I'm confident that Mei will get over it.'

Piper was relieved that he had discussed the problem with someone, even though the answers were any thing but conclusive. He would do his best to accommodate Mei's moods, and for the meantime at least, would go along with her overly ambitious plans. He could always sell the hotel and other buildings at some later date.

Kitty met him at the door of Palmer Kates and invited him in for morning tea. As she poured the tea, Palmerston looked at the unusually quiet Piper. 'Look to have the weight of the world on your shoulders,' he said.

'It's Mei. Just can't figure her out these days,' he replied. 'Damned if I know what's in her mind. She's acting weird as all hell.

'Well, she's been through a bit, you know,' Kitty said, joining in the conversation.

'I know that, but she's taken on a completely new character. She's got me buying up buildings all over town, even down in the Chinese camp. Hell, I've even bought the hotel across from here; God only knows who's going to run it,' Piper said. 'She even thinks that she's a Chinese whore!'

'Certainly got yourself some problems,' Palmerston said over his tea cup.

'I told her that she was just being spooked by shadows,

but she won't have any part of that. As far as she's concerned, she's living with me, outside wedlock and that makes her a whore. Even offered to marry her, which is what I've always wanted to do, but she seems not to agree. Doc Stewart thinks that she'll get back to an even keel in time, but hell, I'm not so sure,' Piper said.

'So what are you going to do?' asked a concerned Kitty.

'As the Doc suggests. Just have to sit it out and go along with whatever she decides. Not much choice, really,' Piper answered.

Feigning a couldn't-care-less attitude, Kitty raised the subject of the hotel. 'Has she told you what style of hotel she wants? Liquor, accommodation, whores … what?'

'Your guess is as good as mine. Accommodation and liquor hopefully. I'm here to raise cattle, not whores, besides, you have that line covered pretty well,' he answered.

'Oh well, let's see what she comes up with,' Kitty said as she cleared the cups and saucers from the table.

'None of my business, Piper, but if Mei opens a whorehouse and hotel right across the street for Chinese customers all hell will break loose, with you in the thick of it,' Palmerston said. 'See what you can do about changing her mind.'

Piper stood to leave. 'I will, but I will also support what she does, you know that. Hell, I don't know where all of this is going and I wish I had no part in it, but I have. What would you do, Christie?'

J . R . G o r d o n

'What I always do, disappear into the hills for a few months. Things seem to have a way of sorting themselves out,' he replied with a grin.

'Maybe that's what I'll do, just as soon as this damn rain eases up,' Piper said as he walked out into the muddy street and headed home.

More confused than ever, Piper removed his boots and walked inside. Mei was busy in her bedroom. 'You there, Mei,' he shouted.

'In here,' she replied from the bedroom.

It wasn't until he entered the bedroom that he realised there was another woman with Mei. He looked at her, a Chinese girl from the Hong Kong section, watching as she loaded the last of Mei's clothes into a sack.

'You're giving your clothes away, Mei?' he asked.

'No, I'm moving to the Chinese Camp,' she replied without looking at him.

'What?'

'I said I'm moving to the Chinese Camp … today, now,' she confirmed.

'But why? This is where you live; this is your house here. What about all your plans?' he asked, voicing his despair.

'I can run our business affairs from the Chinese Camp just as easily as I can from here, in fact, better. At least if I live down there I won't be known as Campbell's whore,' she said.

'Ah, not that whore thing again,' Piper said, becoming angry. 'I've already told you how we can fix that. For

276

Gods sake, Mei, even your friend here can see that we are not living as husband and wife. Tell her to go back to the Chinese Camp and spread the word.'

Mei did not answer. Still limping slightly she bundled a sack onto her shoulder and walked from the house with the other girl at her heels.

'C'mon, Mei,' Piper pleaded. 'You're proving nothing by doing this, nothing at all. Mei, turn around!'

Frustrated and angry, Piper paced around inside the house like a caged animal. Slipping back into his boots he walked quickly to the cemetery. Perhaps N'kawa would have the answers.

Arriving at N'kawa's grave he was surprised to see a fresh bunch of wild flowers, neatly placed near the stark wooden cross. It puzzled him. Had someone mistakenly placed the flowers on the wrong grave? The small footprints around the grave could only fit a woman, but which woman? Mei, he concluded. She must have been there earlier in the day and if she had, he was pleased. He aborted his intention to ask N'kawa for guidance when the undertaker appeared with another coffin.

That evening, after a great deal of soul searching, he seemed resigned to the fact that he had little to occupy himself with in his empty house and decided to call on Palmerston at Palmer Kates.

As the ladies traded their favours for gold under the watchful eye of Kitty, Piper and Palmerston set about the agreeable task of becoming slightly more than merry with the assistance of some fine whiskey from Kitty's private collection. Stopping just short of solving every problem known to man, they both staggered to empty rooms and passed out.

On returning to his house the next morning with a splitting headache, he saw Mei and several Chinese approaching. 'Good morning Piper,' Mei greeted.

'Yes, good morning, Mei. Off to do some shopping?' he asked.

'We're taking over the hotel today. These people will be helping with the redecorating and there's supposed to be a ship from Hong Kong today or tomorrow. Why not come down and visit tonight?' she replied.

'Maybe I will,' he said. At least she was doing something and keeping her mind active. Doctor Stewart had told him that industry would push the trauma from her mind and so should be encouraged. 'Perhaps I'll come down for tea,' he added as Mei continued on.

Piper had almost forgotten the flowers on N'kawa's grave. 'Oh, Mei,' he yelled. 'Thanks for the flowers on N'kawa's grave. That was nice.'

Mei half turned and waved to him before hurrying on her way with her Chinese entourage. Piper watched them walking for a while before diverting his course and heading for the Chinese Camp. After locating the Hong Kong merchant's headquarters, he entered through the haze of joss-stick smoke to where four of the influential merchants sat talking.

'Came to talk to you about Mei,' he said as he pulled up a chair and made himself welcome.

'Not nice lady. All rent go up, must pay for everything now,' the older Chinese statesman complained.

'Well, I understand that you will be getting some new buildings and there will be employment in the hotel, shops and laundry now,' Piper defended.

'No want employment, want to own shop but cannot do on her land. She take best house and treat Cantonese like slave, no good for Chinese camp,' the old statesman continued.

'Well, you can always talk her into coming back up the hill and sharing my house with me,' Piper said.

'Haa, where you put all Chinese prostitute at your house? Mei buy all best prostitute for her. When diggers start coming again we get no money for prostitute any more, no good.'

Piper held his emotions and facial expressions in check. 'How many prostitutes does Mei have now?' he asked.

'Too many for one hotel,' the Chinaman replied. 'She also say she get more for Palmer gold field. Very dangerous. You must tell her, very dangerous.'

'Okay, I'll tell her,' Piper said, standing. 'The rains will be easing soon and the track will be open to the Palmer. You might tell your Chinese people not to leave for the Palmer until after the first wagons leave. Meanwhile I'll have a word with Mei.'

That night, Piper learned that Mei had indeed enlisted the services of a stable of Chinese whores to work from the hotel. Treated as a novelty, they traded throughout the night at prices above Palmer Kate's establishment. Cheap booze, gold and sexual favours were being traded at an alarmingly high rate when Piper entered the hotel. The décor was a mixture of fine European and Oriental. Piper embarrassed himself by inwardly admitting that the Chinese whores seemed better value for money than the older, more experienced ladies across the road at Palmer Kates.

Walking to the bar, he ordered a scotch from a grinning Chinaman. Turning to take in the surrounds, he noticed Mei for the first time as she greeted a couple of sailors and ushered them to a semi-private booth by the street window. She smiled her beautiful smile as she chatted and ordered them a drink. At last, Piper sighed, at last she had learned to smile again.

As she approached the bar, Mei looked at Piper and smiled again. 'Hello, Piper. Good to see you here. What do you think?'

'If this is what it takes to see you smile again, yes, I like … I really like,' he replied.

'So, do you want a girl?' she asked.

Piper's amusement at the question soon faded to dismay as he realised she wasn't joking. 'Tell me you don't mean that,' he said

'What are you talking about? Why did you come here if you don't need a girl?' she asked.

'Mei, I do need a girl. For Christ's sake, I need you, when are you going to see that?' he half shouted. 'Next you'll be telling me that you work here as well!'

'No, I'm too busy, but because you own the hotel,

perhaps you can drink free. You'll still have to pay for the girls though,' she said as if Piper's concerns had fallen on deaf ears.

Piper burst into sarcastic laughter. 'I don't believe this. Is that what it's all about? Money? Well alright then, I've got a thousand pounds here that says you will come to my house tonight when you've finished playing the madam here. If all I have to do is pay you, then that's what I'll do.'

He was outraged, confused and feeling downright ornery as he stomped out of the hotel, almost knocking Palmerston to the ground. 'Whoa, steady on old man,' Palmerston yelled.

'Don't tell me you're going in there to get some Chinese ass as well,' Piper yelled back.

'Not in there, out there,' he replied, pointing towards the track away from town. My boys have just told me that a bunch of Chinese are trapped on the high ground between the two flood channels out at the Normanby. Figured I might take a ride out there tomorrow and take a look-see. Want to tag along?'

'Damn right I do. I've about had this place up to my ears. When are you leaving?'

A grin came over Palmerston's face. 'Be ready at daybreak, rain or shine. See you then,' he said.

Piper took one more look through the window of the hotel. Mei laughed as she flirted with the sailors and escorted them to the hallway for some important introductions. He was disgusted. She could do as she pleased, he thought, he would have no part of this any-more.

Whiskey had just induced sleep when Piper was awakened by someone knocking at the door. Good God, he thought, Mei had taken up his offer. Fumbling for his trousers he hurried to the door and opened it to find a beautiful young Chinese girl standing there. 'Miss Mei say to come and sleep here tonight,' she chirped happily. 'She too busy.'

Piper groaned as he leaned against the door jamb. 'Oh no. Go back and tell Miss Mei that I'm sleeping with my horse tonight. Tell her it worked out cheaper,' he mumbled. 'Oh, and you can tell her the horse still has a reasonable opinion of me.'

A puzzled look came over the girl's face as she struggled to make sense of Piper's message. 'You like horse better than young girl? Ai, you no good man,' she said as Piper bid her goodnight and closed the door.

Early morning saw Piper and Palmerston on the track to the Palmer. Although the track was boggy in places they made good ground and the weather stayed calm. 'Rains will be gone altogether soon,' Palmerston said. 'That'll see a mass exodus to the Palmer. Will you be going back?'

'I need to set up better holding yards for the stock near Palmerville, and then I'll be looking to some of the fertile land close by to start a larger herd. Unless I'm a poor judge there'll be better than ten thousand on the Palmer before the next wet sets in,' Piper replied.

'Could be right,' Palmerston nodded as he pointed to a small thicket of trees where half a dozen Merkins stood. 'My boys, they'll lead us to the stranded Chinkies.'

'How come you have your own army of Merkins?' Piper asked.

'Don't ask,' Palmerston replied as they walked their horses behind the spear-carrying natives.

Arriving at the swollen river they looked across at a handful of emaciated Chinese squatting on a mound. 'I'll be damned,' Piper mouthed. 'Those poor devils are on their last legs for sure. Damn near skeletons.'

'They have been there for nearly a month now. My boys have watched them eating grass and bark off the trees like animals,' Palmerston said.

Seeing the two horsemen, the Chinese stood groggily to their feet and waved their arms about, pointing to their mouths. Although half dead from starvation, they held up their heavy bags of gold, offering them as payment for their rescue.

'Whew,' Palmerston whistled. 'That's one hell of a lot of gold dust they're waving around there. Best we get to saving these creatures and take some as payment. Piper, we'll need more rope, can you go back for another couple of rolls while I wait here?'

The thought of returning to Cooks Town alone didn't impress Piper all that much and it showed on his face.

'Don't worry, you'll be safe. The Merkins know that you're with me and will do you no harm,' Palmerston guaranteed as Piper remounted and departed at a slow canter.

After collecting the ropes and selecting a fresh mount, Piper headed back to the river. Almost there he met Palmerston returning to Cooks Town. 'What happened?' a confused Piper asked.

'Couldn't wait any longer. Those poor devils couldn't go another day so we tried to make do with the rope we had. Current was just too strong and swept them away. Damn near lost two of my best men trying to save them,' Palmerston said.

Piper found the story quite incredible but stopped short of suggesting that his friend was lying. 'Where are your boys now?' Piper asked.

'They got across alright, always do. They'll head back into the hills.'

'And the gold?'

'Ah, leave it there. Someone will have a rich find when the flood waters recede. Plenty more out there in the rivers,' Palmerston answered as if the small fortune of gold was neither here nor there. 'Besides, recovery would be just too damned dangerous.'

Arriving back at Cooks Town, Palmerston rode towards Kitty's and invited Piper to join him for a shot of Rye.

'Be right with you,' Piper said, 'soon as I've fed the horses.'

'Right then, see you in the private bar,' Palmerston called back over his shoulder.

Palmerston's story played heavily on Piper's mind. Almost to the horse yards, he turned and looked back to Palmer Kates. Palmerston had just climbed from his horse and was now carrying two very heavy saddle bags up the rear steps to a smiling Kitty.

He was disappointed. All his life he had been an open book, a say-it-as-it-is type of person. He had never found the need for deceit or lies, it just wasn't him and he didn't much like it in other people.

Why had such traits suddenly surfaced in those he held in such high regard, he wondered. People often said that gold fever changed men's lives, they'd even said that the wet season of the Northern Territories turned perfectly sane men into absolute lunatics … the silly season, they had called it. He held the belief that Mei at least had a reason for the dramatic change in her character, but Palmerston, why was he changing? Why?

CHAPTER **NINETEEN**

he dry season was fast approaching the now heavily populated Cooks Town. Chinese outnumbered all other races as ship after ship arrived from China. Chinese slaves, owned by wealthy merchants lined the banks of the Endeavour River waiting for the inland rivers to ebb enough for them to make the journey inland. Poor sanitation saw the outbreak of dysentery, while bouts of fever claimed all but the strongest. So appalling were the conditions that the Chinese soon had their own cemetery, as did some of the other Europeans who found themselves as susceptible as the Chinese to disease and fever.

Due to the swollen rivers, gold from the Palmer had long since dried up. Hotels and trade stores relied on cash from the new arrivals, which saw the price of food, stores and whores plummet. As they usually did during hard times, the Chinese fared best. They controlled the laundries, fresh food and breweries. For every pound earned by the Chinese, Mei took a percentage. Tensions grew between Palmer Kate and Mei, as Mei offered free liquor to anyone who took a whore for an hour. Although the presence of Police and a Magistrate managed to keep the two camps at arms length, tensions had become palpable with daily threats being levelled between establishments.

Piper saw Mei occasionally, but he kept his visits to her hotel to a minimum. It had become clear to him that his feelings for Mei were nothing more than wasted emotions. She had become wealthy in her own right and seemed to crave nothing more than that. Her reclusive nature was put down to the underlying current of hostility between the Chinese and Europeans. She, not the wealthy merchants, was regarded by the Europeans as the controller of Chinatown. It seemed that nothing happened in Cooks Town unless it had Mei's blessing, such was the power that accompanied wealth.

Deciding to travel south to enlist the help of good cattlemen, Piper booked his passage aboard a steamer to Maryborough. On the eve of his departure he called at Mei's hotel to find her in the back office talking with the wealthy Chinese merchants.

'A word with you, Mei,' Piper asked poking his head through the door.

She fired a string of directives at the merchants in Chinese, who all rose and left.

'Not the happiest looking bunch I've seen today,' Piper said.

She remained seated behind her desk. 'They'll never be happy as long as I have some control over their affairs. One tried to assassinate me the other night,' she said calmly. 'If it weren't for my loyal friends they would have succeeded.'

'Don't you think it's time for you to say that you've made enough money and call it quits?' Piper asked.

'Perhaps,' she replied. 'Maybe in a year or two I will step aside and let someone else take over. I know that you don't understand, but without me, the merchants would see half of the Chinese here starve or worked to death. Take my girls, for example. They are all healthy, well fed and happy and so are their families. I pay them more in a week than the merchants would pay them in a month.'

'But are you happy?' he asked. 'Has all of this power and wealth made you happy?'

'Of course I'm happy. You said that you had something to talk about.'

He had become used to her evasiveness. 'I'm going south for a few weeks before the track opens up again. I though that you might like to come along.'

'No, I'll be fine here. Too much to do,' she replied.

He felt that just this once he needed a reply that sounded something like more than a business response, but it wasn't forthcoming. He hadn't planned this discussion but decided to speak his mind. 'When I get back I'll be selling this hotel and handing the leases for Chinatown to the merchants.'

Mei erupted angrily. 'You can't do that,' she screamed.

'Well, yes I can. I paid for it all, I can sell it,' he said.

'You paid for something that was nothing. I've built it up, I've made it all work and now you say that you will take it away. You can't do that. It's mine,' she yelled.

'The profits and anything else you've put in are yours, but the land and buildings are mine, and I'll be selling them,' he said finally.

'I'll buy it all from you. Tell me your price,' she said coolly.

'Sorry, I already have a buyer in mind. I will not sell to you.'

She glared across the table at him. 'You would rather see me destroyed than help me, wouldn't you? Because that's what you'll do, destroy me.'

He wasn't enjoying the argument one bit. The last thing he wanted to do would be to hurt her. He found himself questioning the statements he had just made. Maybe she was right, maybe all she wanted to do was make herself independently secure, and then return to him. Was all this confusion his doing?

'Go south,' she said, now calmer. 'Do what you have to do to set up your Australian Argyll. One day you might reflect on the last few months and accept that what I've done was right.'

'One last time, Mei, come with me,' he pleaded.

'I've got work to do,' she answered, dismissing him as she went back to pencilling figures in her ledger.

He departed the office feeling defeated. The same heavy feeling weighed him down as he boarded the steamer bound for Maryborough. The voyage gave him plenty of time to reflect on the past and ponder the future. Was it all worth it? Why not just pack up and head back to Texas and do what his migrant father had done; marry a wholesome girl from a good Richmond family and set up a small ranch carrying breeding stock. The more he thought about it the better the proposition looked, but he knew that he couldn't do it. This is where he had settled and this is where he would stay. If only N'kawa were still here. If only Mei hadn't changed.

He had left instructions with packers and willing diggers to move his wagons and supplies to Palmerville as soon as the track opened, so didn't worry much that his return to Cooks Town was delayed by two weeks. He had secured good cattlemen and extra horses. Planning was also put in place to drive a small herd overland to the Etheridge and on to the Palmer. All he had to do now was seek out good land to establish his ranch.

It was with mixed emotions that he arrived back at Cooks Town. Ships of every description cluttered the harbour, more than half of them flying the yellow quarantine pennant from their aft mast. 'Half of China must be here,' one of his new cattlemen announced as he gazed in awe across the Port.

Once ashore, Piper could see that the first wagons and pedestrians had already left for the Palmer. Within the week there would be diggers pouring into town from the Palmer, bags loaded with gold after working the gullies during the wet. They would be hungry, but rich.

Walking up Charlotte Street he stopped outside Mei's hotel … his hotel, and thought about entering, then decided against it and walked through the doors of Palmer Kates.

'The traveller returns,' yelled Kitty.

'Can't keep a good man away for too long, Kitty,' he replied ordering a shot glass of her best. 'So what's been happening?'

'As you can see, just about everyone has gone to the Palmer. Gives us a bit of a break before they start rolling back in,' she said rubbing her hands together.

'Uhuh, and I bet y'all can't wait for that day,' he said laughing. 'What's been happening across the road?'

Kitty frowned. 'Don't really know. Haven't seen Mei around for a week or so, nobody has. Some say she booked passage for Hong Kong, others say Victoria. Don't rightly know. Can't say I was sad to hear it though, things were coming to a head.'

Piper threw his whiskey back and re ordered. 'Christie still in town?' he asked.

'No. He left for the Palmer not long after you went south. Don't expect to see him for a few months now.'

Throwing back the second whiskey Piper excused himself. 'Like to stay and chat, Kitty, but I'd really like to find out what's happened to Mei,' he said.

'Still in love with her, aren't you?' she said.

'No point in lying to a savvy girl like you, Kitty. Yep, silly as it sounds, reckon I am.'

She smiled. 'Then go look for her. If you can't find her … come back and we'll have another drink, on the house,' she said.

Crossing the street he entered the bar and walked towards Mei's office. A finely dressed Chinese merchant called to him. 'You look for Mei? Mei no here. Ah Chee now own hotel. You want girl?' he asked.

Taken aback, Piper looked at the man and then around at the patrons who were all Chinese. 'Ah Chee? Where can I find Ah Chee?' he asked politely.

'Red house in Chinatown. Everybody know Ah Chee. Take over from Mei Ling Siu.'

'And Mei? Where's Mei?'

'Ask Ah Chee, he maybe know,' the Chinaman replied.

Arriving at the red house in Chinatown, Piper asked for Ah Chee. Once inside, a relatively young, neatly dressed Chinese man bid him welcome and ushered him inside to a grand table and chairs. 'I'm Ah Chee,' he said as he directed Piper to be seated in a plush chair. 'What can I do for you?'

'I understand that you now own the hotel that Mei managed,' Piper said. 'Actually, the hotel belonged to me.'

'Ah, there must be a mistake. I bought the hotel from the person with the deeds. The transaction was witnessed and stamped by the Magistrate. Included in the sale was the laundry, baker's shop and a parcel of land here along the river,' he continued.

Piper had difficulty believing what was being said and would certainly be checking with the Lands Office to verify the claim. 'Let's assume that a transaction of some sort has taken place, for the time being at least. Tell me, do you know where the person is that sold you the businesses and land?'

'Ahhh, sorry, cannot help you there. She left soon after being paid. I hear that she may have gone to Brisbane,' he said.

'Out of curiosity, where exactly are you from?' Piper asked.

'Hong Kong, of course,' he replied.

'Of course,' Piper said standing and excusing himself. 'I'll be in touch.'

Entering his house, he half expected Mei to greet him. It was wishful thinking; the house was empty as a tomb and just as lonely. 'Where the hell is she, N'kawa?' he said out loud as he looked at N'kawa's bow-pouch leaning against the wall. He looked again at the pouch. Something was wrong; something was missing. Then it struck him, the neck beads that he had taken from N'kawa's body before burying him were gone. He fingered the identical necklace around his neck and checked again. He had hung N'kawa's across the end of his bow and now they were gone. In a state of near panic he rustled through the odds-and-ends around the floor, but the beads were not there.

He felt irrational doing it, but off he trotted to the police station and reported that he had been robbed. He also filed a report that Mei was missing. Not letting the matter rest there he called at the Magistrates Office to make him aware of his loss. I'll get the whole damn town looking for the necklace and Mei if I have to, he thought as he rushed from shop to shop, hotel to hotel until he could tell no more.

Returning to Chinatown, he called on some familiar faces and asked them if they knew anything or had heard anything. All shook their heads and walked from him as if he were a man possessed, a madman, perhaps.

It seemed that a wall of silence had been put in place and nobody was brave enough to break it. What was confirmed was that she had indeed sold the properties in her capacity as joint tenant and signatory to the estate. Piper knew that some clever skulduggery had taken place but was not prepared to pursue it now, and maybe never.

On a daily basis he did what he could to find Mei, but to no avail. There were no more fresh flowers on N'kawa's grave. The headstone ordered by Palmerston arrived and was laid in place with some ceremony. Piper remained in Cooks Town, or Cooktown, as it had become known, while his hired hands set up the grazing land around town and kept the beef supplies flowing as well as they could to the thousands that were now roaming the Palmer in search of gold. The sale of his holdings by Mei, he put down to experience. He decided not to dispute it. He was not bitter, she had done what she had to do before she lost it; if anything, he blamed himself.

His life became busier than he had planned. Spending time in his office in Cooktown seemed to dominate his life as he supervised Shipping orders, supply wagons and land purchases. As the gold fields grew, so did the need for supplies. The tracks to and from the Palmer remained lethal to those travelling in small numbers. Merkins attacked and killed when, and wherever they could. Diggers would joke as they sprinkled salt and pepper on the complaining Chinese as they left Cooktown. 'Hey, Merkins. Here comes another feast for ye,' they shouted, knowing full well that the natives had made their liking for Chinese flesh well known.

The wet season of '75 was drawing near. Piper discussed freight with the master of a ship bound for Brisbane that evening. About to leave, he stopped and looked at the Chinese woman gathering her belongings on the wharf. 'Cookie,' he said. 'Is that you, Cookie?' The name that he and N'kawa had given the Chinese cook that had travelled with them to Palmerville over the mountains.

She looked up briefly before scurrying behind some wagons. A coincidence, he decided and continued to finalise his directions to the skipper. Still curious, he walked to the area behind the wagons to speak with the woman who now sat with her baggage, head covered by a broad coolies hat.

'Pardon me, but I thought you were someone else,' Piper said as he again peered down at the woman trying to hide her face. He bent, and slowly raised the brim of the hat so he could see her face.

It was her; it was Cookie. 'I'll be damned. How have you been, Cookie?' he asked happily. 'Never thought I'd see you again.'

'Good,' the frightened woman replied.

'Something wrong, Cookie? You scared of someone?' he asked as he looked quickly around.

'No, not scared,' she replied still cowering beneath her hat.

'Then come on, stand up and give me a big hug … c'mon,' he said loudly as he tried to coax her to her feet.

Reluctantly she stood and accepted the hug. As she pulled away, Piper again noticed her strained look. 'Now c'mon, Cookie, tell me what's wrong,' he demanded.

'No can tell. Must go on ship now,' she wailed as she picked up her bag and trotted to the ship.

Piper waved to the skipper and beckoned him over. 'When do you sail?' he asked.

'On the tide, 'bout an hour I'd say,' he answered.

'Can the trip be delayed?'

'Not for long, maybe an hour at the most. Why do you ask?'

'I'll be back,' Piper said hastily. 'Do not set sail

without me, I'll be back,' he yelled as he ran towards Charlotte Street.

His mind was still racing as he neared his house. Cookie was one of Mei's family. Why was she sailing south and why was she upset? Why couldn't she say anything? Something was wrong. Maybe she knew something about Mei's disappearance, and if it meant a trip to Brisbane to find the answers, then so be it. Cooktown could wait, he thought as he made it back to the ship with his bags just in time.

'Damn near missed us Piper,' the skipper shouted as Piper leapt aboard as the last line was cast off, freeing the ship as she slid away from the wharf.

'Don't mind being deck cargo, skipper,' Piper yelled back. 'Where can I stow the bag?'

'Take the Mates rack, damn fool jumped ship and ran off to the Palmer. We'll be punching into it a bit on the way so I'm picking there won't be too much room on deck,' the skipper shouted. 'Old salt like you won't mind a few bumps in the night.'

As soon as he was settled, Piper hunted down Cookie and sat with her. She was not in the mood for conversation, but he persisted and finally had her relaxed and chatting about Palmerville. Mei's group had done well there, thanks to the help from Piper and N'kawa. Everyone on the goldfields had heard about their fateful trip through Hells Gate and there was great mourning over N'kawa's death. She sobbed when talking about Mei.

'Do you know where Mei is now?' Piper asked her gently.

'No. Cannot say,' was the only answer he could get from her.

'But you do know, don't you?' he insisted.

'Cannot say, please, cannot say.'

At least she was alive and hadn't vanished into thin air, Cookie's evasive answers proved that. She knew where she was, he was sure, and he would either get it out of her during this voyage or follow her, even if the next boat she boarded was to Hong Kong.

He felt excitement at the thought of meeting Mei again. After all she had done; her deliberate shunning of him, going against him and the final act of deceit meant nothing. After all that, he would like nothing more than to hold the Mei he used to know and take her with him to wherever she wanted to go. Damn fool, he thought. She's a God-damn thief! Was he trying to find her simply to conclude that chapter in his life? Would he really take her back and risk the same again?

He didn't have the answers, that's why he was aboard the ship sailing south to Brisbane. If she was there, and he found her, only then would his inner-self reveal itself and provide the answers. All he could do now was stand at the bow and enjoy the salt air as it coursed through his hair, the way it had during his travels that had brought him to Australia.

During the trip he spent many hours with Cookie but decided not to raise the issue of Mei too much for fear of distressing her again. She was relaxed and seemed quite excited as the ship tied up at Brisbane.

'Do you have somewhere to stay tonight?' Piper asked.

'Hong Kong friends meet me. Plenty of places to stay then,' she smiled and thanked him for asking.

'Right then, Cookie. Good to see you again and we'll probably meet again up on the Palmer,' he said as he hugged her and watched her walk quickly towards town.

He followed, not letting her get too far ahead, all the time remaining out of her sight. Crossing the parkland she hurried on through the streets, past the hotel where Piper and N'kawa had stayed, over the hill and down through the shops, finally stopping and resting under a cluster of palms. As she wiped her brow a well dressed young Chinaman approached and spoke to her. Piper was too far away to hear the conversation but could see that the young man was nervous, all the while looking around, but for what?

A carriage drew up beside them and within a moment they were being drawn back towards town, past Piper and on towards the upper river suburb, a very fashionable part of town it seemed. Piper could do little else but run after them and hope that the destination was not too distant.

Within ten minutes the carriage had entered the driveway of a grand house facing the river. Piper collapsed into the shrubs of a neighbouring house. His shirt dripped sweat under his jacket while his feet throbbed in his boots. He couldn't remember the last time he had run for ten minutes without anyone chasing him. Gasping for breath, he looked up at an old face peering out from a pure white handlebar moustache.

'I say, careful on the shrubbery old chap,' the face said.

'Sorry. Just thought I'd rest here a while,' Piper answered.

'Damn queer place to rest, don't you think? American, aren't you?'

'Yes, American,' Piper said still wiping his sweating brow.

'Not having a turn are you, by any chance?' The craggy face asked.

'No, I'm okay. Who lives in the large white house up there?' he asked, pointing to where the carriage had disappeared.

'Damn celestials. Moved in, oh, maybe a year ago now, maybe less. Could be a hundred of the swine in there, who would know? Breed like bloody rats you know. Could even be an opium den,' he concluded with raised eyebrows.

'Can you describe the people who live there?' Piper asked stupidly.

'Oh too right. Smallish, pale skin, slanted eyes and black hair. Used to be a Chief Constable in the old country, you know. I take notice of these things,' he said. 'Methinks she's into subversiveness or contraband.

Always a footman or two about and gardeners make good wages each day there.'

'You said she. Is there a he living there as well?' Piper quizzed.

'Let me see. No, I don't believe there is. Always just the she celestial and maids; mainly other celestials. Are you onto something, old chap?'

'Could be,' Piper said, feeling much better after his rest. 'I believe that she's the sole heiress to the Throne of Siam. She doesn't know it, but she's the richest and most powerful woman in the world at the moment,' he said playfully.

'The devil you say! Good lord,' he whispered, eyes wide as he turned quickly and trotted off towards his house. 'Audrey! Audrey dear, I've something to tell you.'

Piper chuckled to himself as he plucked twigs from his jacket and walked towards the house where the so-called celestials lived.

He was met at the door by the carriage driver. 'Good day, sir. Can I be of assistance?'

'And a good day to you sir. Just called to see the lady of the house, Mei Ling Siu,' he replied.

'You must be mistaken, sir. There is no one here by that name.'

'Oh? Surely this is the right address. Perhaps you could enlighten me. Who is the lady of the house?' he asked.

Piper could only just hear the voices inside. The

greeting was tearful but happy. Cookie wailed in gratuitous tones while a softer voice calmed her. His ears strained to recognize the voice but it was too soft.

'Sir, if you don't know the lady's name you'd best be on your way,' the carriage driver said firmly.

Piper hadn't come this far, with this much hope, to be fobbed off by some richly dressed carriage attendant. 'Tell you what,' he said to the carriage driver. 'You get your pompous little ass in there and tell the lady of the house that Piper Campbell is waiting outside or I'll shove your scrawny little head up that horse's ass and go on in unannounced.'

To Piper's amazement, the pompous little ass whistled a shrill whistle before bolting towards the side of the house. In an instant, two burley Chinese guards seemed to materialise from nowhere, closely followed by another, polished heads glistening in the sun as they surrounded Piper, their intentions clear.

'Whoa, hold on a minute …' was all he could say before the fists and boots thudded into him. He swung wildly but was no match for these very fast, very effective and very fit exponents of Asian styled fighting as they landed blow after blow. Struggling to maintain his feet, Piper reached for a garden spade. He never got to use it on his attackers as they set about him in earnest, beating and kicking him into unconsciousness.

CHAPTER TWENTY

Piper's recollection of being dragged across the track and thrown unceremoniously down the river embankment was vague. He lay there as his mind slowly cleared, bringing with it the registration of pain. The thugs had done a good job. His torso, legs and neck felt as if they had been kicked by a dozen wild horses, but outwardly, there were no signs of damage.

Climbing the steep bank, he gazed across at the house from where he had just been evicted. Two of the thugs stood guard by the entrance gate and watched as he slowly regained his footing and dusted his jacket. Discretion being the better part of valour, he turned and walked gingerly back to secure lodgings in a waterfront hotel for a week.

The following day he called on the bank manager to determine ownership of the house. 'Looking to buy up some quality houses,' he told him. 'In particular, that white mansion down yonder near the river.'

'I know the one you mean. That one and many more like it around there are owned by a Hong Kong businessman – Ah Chee I believe his name is,' the manager replied. 'Would you like me to make some enquiries, Mr. Campbell?'

'No, it's okay. I'll locate him and discuss any potential purchase. Do you know where he is at the moment?' Piper asked.

The bank manager smiled and shook his head. 'You won't believe this, but he left for Cooktown only a week or so ago, two weeks at the outside. You probably passed him in the harbour up there,' he said.

'Be damned,' Piper said, acting surprised. 'Guess it'll have to wait until he returns.'

Satisfied that he had confirmed ownership of the house where Cookie had gone, he set about the task of wondering why. Was Mei there as well? Of that he was sure. Why would Cookie be so evasive, why the secrecy? Indeed, why the security and what part had Ah Chee played in Mei's disappearance?

Nothing seemed to make any sense. More than anyone, he understood that Mei had suffered tremendously. He could accept that her behaviour and coolness toward him, or any male for that matter, was justified. He could almost understand her reclusiveness leading up to her unexplained departure from Cooktown, but as much as he tried, he could not figure out her continued desire to remain reclusive. Perhaps she belonged to Ah Chee as a traded chattel; perhaps she had been threatened by Ah Chee and needed to leave quickly or suffer his wrath. But how could that be? She was now living in one of the Ah Chee mansions. Perhaps, he finally concluded, just perhaps she left Cooktown to rid herself of him and his grandiose ideas, half-hearted advances and dreams.

It took three days and all the influence he could muster to convince the Magistrate to issue the Constables with a warrant to search the Ah Chee mansion for contraband from China and Hong Kong. Although the Constables protested his presence as they entered the property, Piper insisted that he remain at the mansion while they searched it, after all, he had knowledge of the goods and may be able to identify them.

Almost to the door, two burly Chinese appeared from the side of the house and hurried to block their path. 'Step aside, sir,' one of the Constables ordered as he displayed the search warrant, continued on and knocked on the door, leaving Piper to again confront the thugs that had so professionally set about him earlier in the week.

Cookie answered the door and was told their intent. Brushing past the protesting Cookie, the Constables entered, again ordering Piper to remain

outside. Cookie glared at Piper before slamming the
door and rushing past the Constables to the master
bedroom.

'Oi, what's in there then?' one asked as he followed
her into the large bedroom.

Piper waited a few minutes before stepping forward
and opening the door. The two Chinese thugs started
their protest but were silenced by the sight of a handgun
protruding from his belt.

Closing the door behind him he walked quickly
across to the formal lounge where one of the constables knelt, rummaging through a glory box. He glanced
around quickly before moving to the dining room and
then on to the kitchen. Passing the sewing room his
eyes flicked back for a second look at the odds and ends
around the dresser.

'At last,' he whispered as he crossed to the dresser
and picked up N'kawa's necklace. 'She's here,' he said
quietly, then turned back into the hallway.

His mind raced. Obviously she had taken the necklace before leaving Cooktown, thinking it was his. So,
there was still some feeling there for him, he thought
as he entered the grand lounge and turned to where he
could hear voices. Following the voices, he entered the
master bedroom to find the constable replacing his hel-
met and bidding the lady good day.

Piper's heart pounded as he looked past the Constable at Mei, reclined on the bed with cushions supporting
her, a small bundle of wraps in her arms.

'Off we go, sir,' the Constable ordered. 'Thought I told you to stay outside.'

'Mei,' Piper called. 'Tell him I know you, please!' he pleaded.

Her look was a combination of fear and embarrassment. She gazed at him for what seemed an eternity before speaking quietly. 'It's alright, Constable. Mr. Campbell can stay and visit for the time being. Thank you for your understanding,' she said.

After withstanding a less than generous utterance from the Constable as he passed close to him, Piper walked awkwardly to the bedside. It eventually registered that the wrap Mei held was a sleeping child, not more than a day or two old. He looked at Mei and the child in disbelief. 'It's a baby,' he managed, slowly lowering himself onto the bedside chair as Cookie gently took the baby and spirited it out of the room.

'Yes Piper, a baby,' she confirmed.

'Yours?'

Of course he's mine,' she answered, now smiling.

'But how? When? Who …?' he asked, totally confused.

Mei looked at him, noticing that he held N'kawa's beads in his hands. 'I thought that you would have known,' she said.

Immediately his mind flashed back to the cave near Hells Gate where Mei stood spread eagled, feet cruelly fixed to the ground by spears as the black heathen violated her. 'Oh God,' he said, cupping his face in his hands. 'God, I'm so sorry, Mei. Really, it was thought-less of me to ask.'

She held out her hands and gently took his. 'Piper, can you now understand why I couldn't get close to you? Can you understand now that I had to do everything in my power to secure a financial future for myself and this child, knowing that it would be black? Think about it, a Chinese woman with a black child and no husband. There was no future unless I could make it happen, and I did,' she said.

'But this could have been avoided. If you had mar-ried me when we were in Cooktown, at least you would have been secure,' he said.

'A Chinese woman, black baby and a white, well-to-do husband! Admit it; you would have been the laughing stock of the North. I had to be cruel to be kind, I had to leave there.'

'But nobody even knew that you were with child in Cooktown. I certainly didn't,' he said.

She laughed again. 'It's amazing what those flowing Chinese robes can hide. I really did like the clothes you bought for me but knew that I couldn't wear them with-out showing my pregnancy,' she said.

'What about Ah Chee? How did he and Cookie get involved?' he asked.

'Ah Chee is related to me. He was moving to Cook-town anyway and summoned Cookie to take care of me during the birth. He knew of the pregnancy long ago; Cookie told him.' She explained.

'Hate to say this, but your relative has seriously undermined your prospects of living comfortably. He owns all of the land and businesses in the Chinese sector that I … we used to own in Cooktown,' he corrected.

'Oh Piper,' she replied. 'You really don't know Chinese, do you? Ah Chee does own the land and the businesses, yes, but I now own this house and a healthy annual income from his entire stable of businesses, not just here but in Hong Kong as well. My child and I will be well taken care of, even if it is a black child.'

He sat there, nodding as she spoke. He had given her little credit for her business skills and ability to cut a deal to her advantage. He was slowly starting to understand the last few confused months, however, there was still one matter to clear up, her feelings for him.

'Mei?' he said, wrestling for the right words and hoping that the time was right. 'You and me, how do you see you and me now that everything is out in the open?'

She slid from the bed and stood before him, her hands again clasping his. 'You're a good man with a very good future in the North. Your Argyll will one day be famous and you will be very proud of it. How can that happen if you have a Chinese wife with a black bastard holding your coat tails? You must be realistic and remove me from your dream.'

'You said yourself that nobody other than Ah Chee and your family, Cookie included, knew of your pregnancy. Is that what you said?' he asked.

'That's right,' she answered, a little puzzled.

'Then that's it, by God that's it!'

'What? What are you talking about?'

'The child, the black bastard child, we'll tell everyone that you adopted it. Someone found it out there in the bush, dead parents, that kind of thing and you, being the benevolent lady of substance that you are, adopted it. That would work,' he said as he jumped to his feet excitedly.

She smiled up at him and took a deep breath. 'You are a stubborn, impossible man,' she said.

'So it's a deal?' he asked.

Please, let me think about it. There is so much to consider and you haven't yet seen the little black bastard child,' she joked.

'Well c'mon then, what are we waiting for?' he said as she led him to the dressing room where Cookie was rocking the baby.

Looking down at the bundle, he felt himself momentarily lost for words. 'Now there'll be no more calling the little chap a black bastard, y'hear? Shouldn't his hair be curly?'

'He's obviously taken on my hair,' Mei explained. 'How does your scenario account for the slightly slanted eyes?' she asked.

'Mmmm. Reckon you got a point there,' he said as he scratched his head.

'There is an orphanage of sorts in Victoria that often has half breeds dumped at their doorstep. Perhaps I could visit Victoria?' she offered cleverly.

'Then you did. Nobody knows you're here, hell, I

didn't. You just arrived back here with a baby from the poor-house in Victoria. Ah, mother you were right, there is a God,' he laughed as he looked skyward.

'I will still need time to think this through. A story like that could look a little silly if I were to tell it breast feeding the baby.'

Piper, unable to hide his joy, took her in his arms and kissed her. 'I've waited for what seems a lifetime just to see you smile like that again, Mei. Whatever is in the past can remain there; we'll completely erase it and start fresh, right now.'

'Have you no manners? In front of Cookie and the baby!' she joked.

'A name, we'll need a name,' he said.

'What would you have him called?' she asked cautiously.

He stood for a moment rubbing his chin, all the while looking at the baby sleeping comfortably in Cookie's arms. 'Is his family name to be Campbell?' he finally asked.

'Well, for the time, let's assume that it could be,' she teased.

'Would you prefer the name to be Chinese?' he asked.

'No, I would prefer not, I'm Australian, remember? Perhaps …' she paused, and then continued in a more serious voice. 'Perhaps he could be called Diego, Ah Chee, N'kawa Campbell. If it weren't for N'kawa, there would be no child.'

'That would honour Diego and me,' he replied, pausing a while in thought before continuing. 'Diego, how did you know N'kawa's name was once Diego?' he quizzed.

'He told me. So it's settled then, Diego, Ah Chee, N'kawa Campbell,' she said.

'Sure is. Oh, this necklace you souvenired from my house, it wasn't mine, it belonged to N'kawa,' he said, holding it up before her. 'Reckon he'd have no problem with young Diego inheriting it now.'

Mei did not comment as she took the necklace and handed it to Cookie.

Breaking the silence, Piper rubbed his hands as he again looked at the sleeping Diego. 'This calls for some celebration; I'll go fetch some fine champagne for us.'

'Hold on, I haven't made my mind up yet. You go on back to town and do your celebrating. If you are doing nothing on Sunday, perhaps you could call for dinner around noon. Cookie can make those dishes you always talked about.'

'Be delighted, Ma'am,' he said as he walked to the door, not bothering to hide his boyish exuberance as he skipped high and clicked his heels.

Outside the mansion, two Chinese thugs watched him as he removed the pistol from his belt, cocked it and aimed at the first one's head, sending them both diving for cover behind the shrubbery. 'Damn good thing the baby's asleep,' he grinned as he eased the hammer and placed the pistol back into his belt.

Ignoring the bruises he still carried, he strolled up the street whistling Dixie. The old ex-Chief Constable appeared over his gate. 'Did you get to the bottom of it, old chap?' he called in a dramatic tone.

'Sure did, old timer. Reckon there'll be a marrying in the town soon, yes sir, reckon that'll be the case,' as he reached across to shake the old man's hand.

'Gad!' he said, jerking his shoulders upright and fixing his eyes as wide as they could go. 'You'll be the King of Siam, lad, royalty no less,' he said before turning and trotting towards the house. 'Audrey, guess what old dear?'

CHAPTER TWENTY ONE

A contented Piper surveyed the remains of the Chinese banquet that lay on the table between him and Mei. Cookie had treated them to a royal feast, and now busied herself with baby Diego in the sitting room.

'If that's what life is all about, let's hope we live it for a long while yet,' Piper said, as he placed a crumpled napkin beside his empty bowl.

'Pleased you enjoyed it,' Mei said with a smile.

'You know, I've been doing some serious thinking lately,' he said.

'Oh. About what?'

He stood and motioned for her to follow him to the small occasional table by the open bay window. 'Had news from Richmond a few days back, seems that Ma's family is doing very well with cropping. Apparently Cousin Benjamin has entered politics and all but one of the family mansions have been restored to their original grandeur. From all accounts they seem to be doing very nicely.'

Mei looked into Piper's distant eyes. 'Do you miss Texas?' she asked.

'Reckon I do. Even thought about returning after N'kawa's death and, well, when I had given up all hope of your companionship,' he replied. 'What I'm trying to say is that there seemed little to keep me here, but now, well, you're back and I'm kinda thinking that the future looks a hell of a lot more agreeable because of it.'

'The future? Tell me what the future will be?' Mei asked.

'Well, the way I see it, Argyll homestead will be finished in Cooktown, we'll get married and move back there to raise young Diego. That about sums it up,' he said as a matter of fact.

Mei raised her eyebrows and smiled at his simplicity. 'What an uncomplicated scenario. You are assuming that I agree with your plans.'

'Well, you do, don't you?' he asked.

'All boys need a father and all women probably should have a husband, especially if they have a child. Yes, Piper, we will be married but not for another six months. You go on back to Cooktown and tend to Argyll. I will return with Diego when he is strong enough to travel.'

Piper's face lit up. He stood and raised Mei from her chair. 'Mei, you've just said something I've been waiting to hear for a long time. I'll arrange a wedding and grand reception for next weekend,' he said before kissing her lips gently.

'No, I don't want a big wedding. Under the circumstances, can't we just have a small ceremony here, just us, with Cookie as witness? If you want, we can be married before you leave for Cooktown,' she agreed.

'Well, I did kinda want to show you off, but if that's the way you want it, so be it,' Piper replied.

She now returned his kiss. 'Mr. Campbell, you'd better be off now, you have plenty of arranging to take care of and I have a hungry baby to feed,' she said.

Delighted, Piper took his leave and hurried back to town to arrange the ceremony. The preacher would attend the gardens of the mansion to perform the ceremony. It would be nothing grand and without a reception; that could take place at some later date at Argyll. They would live as husband and wife for less than a week before his return to Cooktown, but Piper felt now that his life had new meaning.

As planned, the wedding ceremony was brief but meaningful. Mei promised him that there would be a reception in Cooktown, but for now, the fact that they were married would do. The evening meal was taken late on the porch after Diego had been fed and whisked away by the fussing Cookie. The bottle of French champagne they had shared now stood empty. Anxiety

J . R . Gordon

mixed with excitement as the newly weds slid beneath
the expensive satin sheets. Talking gave way to intimate
murmurs as the two explored each other's bodies. The
hours passed delightfully. Childbirth had been such a
recent event that complete consummation of the marriage was deliberately avoided, although all other sexual
gratification was attempted.

'You have something on your mind?' Mei whispered.

'I'm not sure. I can't figure out what's wrong. I can't
seem to, well, you know, get prepared enough,' he stammered nervously.

'Is it because of what happened to me in the cave? Is
that weighing on your mind?'

'No, not at all, I wasn't thinking about that at all,'
he replied. 'Hell, I've been waiting for this night for a
long time, and now it's here, I can't seem to rise to the
occasion.'

'We cannot have sex yet anyway,' she consoled.

'Yeah, I know, but I don't seem to be able to get ready
for anything else either,' he replied sheepishly.

Doing her best to comfort and console his poorly
timed sexual failure, Mei stroked his hair gently and
suggested that he was just too excited at the moment.
'We have a lifetime to do that, go to sleep and we'll start
tomorrow where tonight ends.'

Mei's morning caresses and gentle kisses ended Piper's sleep. The feel and smell of her body filled his senses
as she slid on top of him; her long hair tickled his chest

as she rolled her hips gently back and forth, straddling him expecting her actions to arouse him. Again they realised that even if they had wanted to, sex was certainly not an option.

'It's my fault, isn't it?' Mei said quietly.

'No, really, it's not your fault. I just don't know what's going on,' a frustrated Piper replied.

Mei slowly climbed from the bed, providing him with a view of her exposed breasts, lithe body and perfectly rounded buttocks as she walked to the dressing room.

'I'd better check on Diego,' she called over her shoulder.

'Yeah,' Piper replied as he looked down at his peacefully dozing manhood that should have been dozing for other reasons. 'Guess I'll go and get things moving in town.'

Within the week, Piper was aboard a steamer headed for Cooktown. Mei bid him farewell from the mansion rather than the wharf. It was a worried Piper that stood at the bow on his own. He was finally married to the Chinese beauty he adored; he had experienced her kisses, caresses and fondling in their most intimate moments and yet he had been unable to consummate the marriage. Had the events in the Merkin's cave set up some psychological barrier that prevented him from being aroused? Unable to answer his own questions he concluded to call on Doctor Stewart upon his arrival at Cooktown.

As the steamer tied up at the wharf, Piper looked with disbelief at the hundreds of shanties, tents and houses that now filled the Port and beyond. The smell of overflowing ablution-pits mixed potently with the humid air as people busied themselves making ready for the next trip to the Palmer. After unloading supplies and checking the progress of Argyll homestead, Piper called at the cemetery to visit N'kawa's headstone. Well satisfied, he made his way back to town and Palmer Kates Saloon. Almost there, Ah Chee called to him from the Chinese hotel.

Crossing the street he entered the hotel and sat with the smiling Ah Chee.

'Welcome back, good to see you here again,' Ah Chee greeted.

'Place has kinda grown since I left,' Piper replied.

'Ah, plenty Chinese here now, maybe five thousand or more, and same at the Palmer,' Ah Chee said.

'Damn, that's a lot of Chinese. How many diggers?' Piper asked.

'Perhaps the same as Chinese, but I know that another five thousand Chinese are due here any day,' he replied. 'How was your trip to Brisbane?'

Piper poured another scotch before replying. 'Nice house you have on the river down there. Met a few of your lads when I visited,' Piper said.

Ah Chee looked a little surprised. 'House not mine,' he added quickly.

'Nope, belongs to me now, just like this hotel was once mine and now belongs to you,' Piper said.

Ah Chee's frown identified his confusion. 'House in Brisbane belong to Chinese trader, not you,' he said blunt.

Piper poured yet another drink and ordered a meal as Ah Chee sat waiting for his explanation. 'You see, Ah Chee, I married that Chinese trader, member of your family, I believe. Hell, we're now family.'

'Ah so! You find Mei and marry her,' Ah Chee chuckled. 'You get bargain; beautiful woman from wealthy Hong Kong family, servant and child as well.'

'You know about the child?' Piper asked, not letting on that he already knew the answer.

'Of course, Ah Chee know most things. You very understanding man to marry Mei.'

Over dinner the two discussed the wedding and pending reception at Cooktown. Ah Chee agreed that the story of child adoption was sound and should be held secret.

'Perhaps we can even do some business together,' Ah Chee told Piper. 'Christie Palmerston is robbing our Chinese convoys and stealing gold. He uses his blacks to attack us, when we run he takes the gold, then his blacks take Chinese to the caves and eat them. Not good. You can help,' he said, pulling a folded sheet from his vest pocket and spreading it out on the table. 'This is wanted poster for Christie Palmerston, written in Chinese. Magistrate has put reward out for his capture.'

Piper was taken by surprise. 'Be damned, the stories were true, huh? So, what makes you think I can help, and besides, you already know that he is a friend of mine.'

'You can go with the next Chinese convoy and protect them from Palmerston,' replied the excited Ah Chee. 'You kill Palmerston you get paid his weight in gold.'

'Mighty generous offer, but I've got work to do here,' he said. 'Mind you, I will need to get across to the Palmer soon so maybe I can ride with your convoy if that makes y'all happy.'

'I will see that you are paid,' Ah Chee said, clearly happy with the idea of securing Piper's services.

Leaving the Chinese Hotel, Piper strode into Palmer Kates and joined a group of sailors and diggers. Not a lot had changed. Buxom wenches flitted from group to group securing the best offer before leading someone out the back door, while diggers scraped through their near empty gold pouches for enough to secure a bottle.

'Piper!' Kitty called across the room. 'Welcome back you handsome devil!'

'Damned if it ain't my favourite lady,' he replied as she settled onto his lap and threw her arms around his neck.

'Too noisy in here, Piper; come on back to my parlour where we can have some fine wine and catch up on things,' she said.

'Don't need to call twice,' he replied as he followed her into the plush parlour, complete with oversized four poster bed.

As they settled into the couch, Kitty offered a toast

to the person responsible for the gold band on his finger. Piper displayed it proudly as he told her of the recent wedding to Mei in Brisbane. Kitty was impressed when she learned that they had adopted a black breed from an orphanage, but slightly confused as to why they didn't just get down to business and grow their own family. Piper quizzed her about Palmerston and his activities, particularly the killing of Chinese and gold stealing. Kitty simply shrugged it off but confirmed that the Magistrate had ordered his detention in order to clear the matter up.

'So nobody knows where Palmerston is?' he asked.

'Well he's out there somewhere but I haven't seen him for a few weeks now. His dislike for Chinese is well known but I doubt that he's leading attacks on them,' she said casually as she emptied her champagne glass.

They sat together drinking and talking for hours. Amid fits of laughter she recounted some of the happenings while he was away. The drunken shoot-outs in the street, naked men wrestling each other in the mud for a particular whore's favours and the scuttling of ships to prevent them from getting their cargo to their destination first.

Piper surprised himself when he touched on his embarrassing problem. 'Can I trust you, Kitty?' he asked.

'Why sure you can. Two people I can trust up here, you and Christie Palmerston,' she replied. 'Why, what's on your mind, sweetie?'

'Seems I have a little problem with, well, with getting ready,' he said uncomfortably.

'For what? Getting ready for what?'

'Ready for women, you know, getting ready,' he said gesturing casually towards his crutch.

Kitty couldn't help bursting into laughter. 'Ah shit, I'm sorry, Piper didn't mean to laugh but you'd be the last person I would have thought to have that kind of problem. Look at you! Any woman would fight over you, you handsome thing.'

'Well yeah, I've seen men fight over a good handgun but at least the damn thing worked,' he joked, feeling more comfortable now. 'Here I am a married man and I can't even satisfy my woman's needs.'

Kitty took his empty glass, turned the lamp off and joined Piper at his end of the couch. 'Consider this remedial activity,' she said, unbuttoning her blouse and freeing her ample breasts. 'Not that I don't believe your story mind you, but if you think you have a problem, then I'd best do all I can to assist. Isn't that what friends are for?'

The steamy session reached marathon proportions as the two moved from the couch to the floor, the bed, the table and any other vacant space that might trigger some scrotal activity in Piper. Finally, lathered in sweat and after exhausting all of her talents as a madam, Kitty lit the lamp and poured another drink.

'Sorry, Kitty,' he said meekly.

'No, don't be sorry. Sure seems that you have a

problem but that isn't the end of the world, you know. There are other ways to satisfy a good woman and that's what you'll have to do if you want Mei to stick around,' she said, gulping her drink down and turning out the lamp again.

Piper wasn't sure that he agreed with her resolve, and didn't much care for near suffocation as Kitty's broad hips ground his head deep into the couch, followed by an assisted inner exploration that left him feeling like a doctor making a late call. After what seemed an eternity they collapsed on the bed and slept.

First light saw Piper walking towards Argyll homestead. The musky aroma of Kitty's more private regions wafted over him as he relieved himself against a hitching pole, secretly checking for possible skin damage he thought may be present after the hours of vigorous manipulation that had, much to Kitty's disappointment, returned little in the way of results. At least she had enjoyed herself, he thought.

As he walked he found himself comparing Mei with Kitty. Mei, with her sweet smelling beauty, softness and understanding and Kitty with her no-holds-barred bedroom acrobatics, self gratification and sexual appetite. Early risers would have wondered at the sight of the dishevelled Piper walking home at daybreak, laughing to himself as he went.

CHAPTER TWENTY TWO

I t had been a long time since Piper last sat in a saddle, and even longer since he'd carried the arsenal of a Texas Ranger. Left and right cross-draw belt pistols, one secured in the saddle pouch, and a repeating rifle in the boot, had him reminiscing the old days.

The Merkins were still a force to be reckoned with when travelling over their country, especially through the hills. Although their numbers were dwindling, their resolve and courage was not. They were shot on sight. Small expeditions actively hunted them down like animals, running them to ground and slaughtering them. It seemed not to matter if the quarry was male, female or child; if it was a wild black then it was shot. On rare occasions a black child would be spared and taken to the camps where they were placed in religious care to be raised as Christians.

The convoy Piper joined was fully three hundred strong, of which only fifty or more were diggers, the rest being Chinese. Just past the Normanby, Chinese and pedestrian diggers branched left and headed for the Hells Gate pass while the wagons continued on to traverse the longer Conglomerate Range track. Although it would take longer, Piper decided to go with the wagons this time. He felt a certain uneasiness about returning to the Hells Gate track and the caves where he had nearly died, but knew that he would need to face his fears sooner or later.

The wagon track was now a well worn road. Each day they passed the grave stones that littered the trail, most of them simply marked with initials scratched lightly on their surface. Broken wagons and equipment of every description littered the brush, while waterholes were polluted from the oils given off from the lard based soap carelessly left by passing diggers. Fish that once swarmed the waterways were now gone; birds were rarely seen and kangaroos were indeed a rare sight. Yet amid the environmental disaster, the Merkins had managed to hold their ground and survive, albeit in rapidly diminishing numbers.

The trip was uneventful although Piper had often seen the smoke signals in the hills. The Palmer was a sorry sight. The landscape had been altered so much by digging, clearing and building that it was totally unrecognizable. Small settlements had sprung up and considerable houses and other buildings were now well established. Chinese outnumbered other diggers five to one, which was causing more than a little concern. Claim jumping was rife and hangings had become a mundane affair in the now heavily populated river basin that only a year or so before was a wilderness populated only by aborigines and animals.

Piper was welcomed into the Chinese settlement at Palmerville where Mei's group had settled. They were keen to hear news of Mei and Cookie and set up a banquet to celebrate his marriage to Mei.

'You now part of Chinese community,' the head Chinaman announced as the celebration moved into the night.

After checking his holdings, Piper called on the Gold Commissioner who confirmed that Palmerston was on the wanted list and any information as to his whereabouts would be greatly received. Not wishing to remain on the Palmer any longer than necessary, Piper arranged to escort a group of thirty Chinese across the Hells Gate pass. Relaxing at a shanty hotel, Piper noticed Sub-Inspector Dyas staring at him over a shot glass.

'Why not join me,' Piper called, holding up a half full bottle of whiskey.

Dyas slowly walked to where Piper sat and eased onto the wooden chair. 'Haven't seen you here for a while,' he said suspiciously.

'Been a bit busy with one thing and another. You still out there killing natives with Macmillan?' Piper asked sarcastically.

'When it's required. These days we seem to be more tied up with Chinese fighting Chinese and diggers lynching claim jumpers,' he replied.

Piper filled his glass. 'I hear that an old friend of mine, Christie Palmerston is on the wanted list,' he said.

'Wouldn't have taken him for a friend of yours. Seems he takes great delight in killing Chinese, you live with them, don't you?' Dyas replied with equal sarcasm.

'Not sure what proof you have, but I'll be sure to pass on your regards when I see him day after tomorrow,' Piper said.

'You'll be seeing him?' Dyas quizzed. 'And where might that be?'

Piper gave Dyas a questioning look. 'You don't know? Well I'll be damned, thought everyone out here knew his cave up there near Hells Gate.'

'There are a hundred caves up there, which one is Palmerston holed up in?' Dyas asked, not expecting an answer.

'Hard to explain. It's just up the top, down the other side a piece, and off to the left, that sort of area,' Piper replied.

'And you say that you're going up there day after tomorrow?' Dyas tried to confirm.

'Sure enough, I'll pass on your kindest regards,' Piper

said. 'Well, gotta be movin' on, time's a gettin' away again.'

Piper returned to the Chinese camp and discussed the next small convoy back to Cooktown. Because of recent attacks, they were reluctant to send the gold back, which meant that stocks had increased to a dangerous level. Of the last four shipments, only one had got through to Cooktown, the other three were apparently safely secured in Palmerston's cache.

Piper finally convinced the Chinese that twenty men could carry the gold if he supplied four rifles and rode with them. While they knew of his friendship with Palmerston, they trusted him, especially now that he was one of their kind by marriage and Palmerston would not attack his friend … surely.

Leaving the camp behind, the Chinese group and Piper were aware that Sub-Inspector Dyas was following. Piper knew that Dyas would continue on his trail in the hope that he would at some stage break away from the Chinese to meet with Palmerston. The arrangement suited Piper fine. If the Chinese were attacked, Dyas would be within a few minutes to their flank and would join the fight.

As the group neared Hells Gate, Piper looked over the cliff where Mei's horse had fallen. It came as no surprise to see the bones of several other horses littered the floor of the gaping chasm. He felt nervous as they entered between the rocky towers and passed through the gate, all the while expecting the boulders to start raining down from above as they had done the last time he had passed. His nervousness continued as they started the descent down the Devils Staircase, nearing the cave where his life had almost ended in a fire pit.

Without knowing why, he called a halt and ordered the Chinese to fall into a defensive circle. Choosing to ignore their complaints he dismounted and stumbled down the track to the cave. It was as he remembered it. The large fire pits and rock slabs that lay thick with layers of roasted human fat. He shook off a cold shiver as he entered the cave, his eyes slowly adjusting to the dim light inside. A noise towards the right had Piper on his knees; a cocked pistol in each hand as he strained to make out the figures crouched against the wall.

'Stand up and come forward or you'll surely die,' he commanded in a cool voice.

The chatter of a female Native and children filled the cave as an old woman and two children stood and walked towards him.

They chatted as they approached, holding out a woven bag. He could not understand them but eased the hammers on his pistols and replaced them in their holsters.

'What? You want me to take the bags?' he asked.

The old woman again chattered in her nasal tongue and reached the bag forward, motioning for him to accept it.

Reaching forward he took the bag and opened it.

Inside was a scalp of hair and small packages of offal wrapped in leaves.

'Good God almighty,' he whispered. 'You poor devils have resorted to eating offal to stay alive. Come on, come with me,' he motioned as he handed back the bag and led them out of the cave and up to the nervous Chinese who immediately voiced their disapproval.

As the Chinese watched, Piper dug food from his saddle sack and handed it to the pathetic, naked creatures that grabbed it and immediately started eating. Leaving as much as he dared spare, Piper waved to them and followed the Chinese group as they trotted hurriedly down the steep incline, pleased to be away from the evil place.

Piper had forgotten about Dyas and his Native Mounted Police until the sound of distant gunfire echoed through the hills behind him. 'You bastards, you uncaring bastards,' he said under his breath, knowing full well that his act of kindness had just been nullified.

Leaving the main trail, Piper led the Chinese to the Normanby crossing used by him after being rescued by Palmerston. Set for the night, he could almost feel the presence of N'kawa. The campfire was doused before darkness to avoid detection. Alone with his thoughts, Piper lay there, eyes wide open as the memories flooded back.

'Not many people camp here.'

The voice caused Piper to jerk upright as he grabbed his pistols. 'Who the hell's there?' he yelled.

'We camped here a while back, remember?' came the now recognizable voice of Palmerston.

'Damn you, Christie, you scared the life out of me. Where the hell are you man?' Piper said angrily.

'Here, old boy,' he replied as he walked to where Piper crouched and sat down. 'Got some wild berries here. Want some?'

'What the hell are you doin' scarin' the shit out of me?' Piper asked again in a more temperate tone. 'Hell, I could have shot you.'

Palmerston suppressed a laugh. 'You … shot me? We've followed you from the Gate, my friend. At any time I could have shot you and your Chinkies before you could have raised a hand to defend yourselves.'

'So why didn't you?' Piper asked. 'Word is that you rob Chinese on their way back from the fields. Care to tell me about that?'

'Sure. From time to time I've enriched my life by ridding it of a few Chinese. And yes, I've relieved them of their gold on such occasions. Now if that makes me a bad man, then I guess I'm bad; but no worse than the law official that earlier today blew holes in an old lady and her grandchildren as they sat eating a gift from a kindly passer by.'

Piper was lost for words momentarily. 'Well, sure, but you ain't got the right to go about shootin' Chinese and stealin' their gold now, have you?'

'Ah Piper my old friend. The name Carandini means little to you, I know, but to me it means a lot. You see my father, Count Carandini, the Marquis Di Carandini Di Sarzano to be precise, entered this country full of hope. He could bring little with him due to his exile from Italy by the Austrians, but quickly collected enough to take care of his family well. His mistake was making a deal with the Chinese in Melbourne who fleeced our family of everything we owned. We had to take a travelling musical show on the road to make ends meet because of it. Can you imagine such an important Italian family being forced to play tunes on the roadside for their supper?'

'I'm sorry to hear that, Christie,' was all Piper could find.

'And so you see, my friend, my hatred for the Chinese is well founded. Your lady friend, as beautiful as she is, is of the same Chinese group that caused my family's downfall but did I kill her? No. In fact I saved her life, and yours, as I recall.'

'And for that I'll remain forever in your debt,' Piper said. 'Is there to be a vendetta against Mei?'

'Absolutely not. I can see that you are smitten by her and will respect that. In fact, after a good breakfast in the morning you can be on your way with your Chinkie friends, safe as a church,' Palmerston replied.

'Oh, incidentally, Mei is now my wife and we have adopted a black bastard. And that breakfast in the morning, just make sure that it ain't one of my Chinese carriers.'

Piper awoke to the terrified screams of Chinese as

they huddled together in the camp, rifles at the ready. Palmerston sat beside him and shook his head. 'Tell them to relax, my boys won't harm them,' he said.

The camp was completely surrounded by natives, perhaps forty or more, all carrying a few long spears each.

'Nice surprise,' Piper said to Palmerston.

'Come on, breakfast,' Palmerston shouted as he walked to the natives and took a dead Goanna to the dull fire coals. 'Get these fires going and we'll all eat before the day starts.'

The Chinese remained in a huddle defending their gold while Piper and Palmerston feasted on the lizard. Natives busied themselves with another lizard as Piper and Palmerston sat to drink their coffee.

'Let me put this to you, Piper. Your Chinkie friends walk away from here on the proviso that ten percent of what they're carrying is given to you,' Palmerston said.

'What! I don't want their gold,' Piper objected.

'No, but Kitty might. You see, you get it and hand it on to Kitty and tell her it's a gift from me.'

'Bullshit,' Piper said.

'Well they may, but that's not the issue here. You see, it will take all my influence to allow the Chinese to leave here. My boys are starving, as are their families; they need to eat and at the moment they are looking at a week's supply of fresh food. Agree to the small payment and I'll convince them that you should all see tomorrow.

'You really are some son-of-a-bitch Palmerston. Alright, I'll talk to them and then we'll leave.'

'Hope so,' Palmerston replied.

After a heated debate the Chinese agreed to the proposal. Piper turned to Palmerston and nodded. 'It's a deal then. Ten percent of their gold goes to Kitty when we arrive at Cooktown.'

'Fine,' Palmerston smiled. 'Always a pleasure doing business with a gentleman.'

'My horse,' Piper said looking around the trees. 'Where's my horse?'

'Oh, well now that's the other part of the deal that I had no say in,' Palmerston answered. 'The natives have taken your horse for food … I told you, they're starving.'

'Damn you Palmerston,' Piper yelled as he drew both revolvers and levelled them at his chest. 'That ten percent just got reduced to five and if you disagree, then you never leave this place; I'll take my chances with the spears. Horse thievin' is a hangin' offence where I come from.'

Serious concern crossed Palmerston's face. He knew that Piper meant what he said and he was in no position to bargain with two pistols pointed at him. He smiled and motioned for his men to lower their spears. 'You drive a hard bargain, my friend but I accept. Only now, I'll take the five percent here; saves you having to call on Kitty.'

Working as fast as they could, the Chinese measured out five percent of their gold and handed it to Piper. 'There you go,' Piper said as he handed the leather bag to Palmerston.

'A small price to pay and I look forward to sharing a bottle of something smooth with you in a short while,' Palmerston said.

'Well I gotta tell you, I'm pissed off now and I reckon I'll be just as pissed off when next we meet. Let's hope it's a Sunday … Killin' don't come easy on the Sabbath.'

'Then I'll call some Sunday,' Palmerston joked.

'Be a pleasure; be sure that you stay on 'till Monday when you call,' Piper said as he joined the Chinese group and headed for Cooktown. 'Reckon killin' that son of a bitch would give me an erection,' Piper mumbled.

'What you say?' the Chinese leader asked nervously.

'Nothin', keep moving.'

It was late in the evening before Piper and the Chinese entered Cooktown. The Chinese trotted away to see Ah Chee while Piper went straight to the Chinese bath house for a hot bath followed by food at the Chinese Hotel. Mid way through his meal, Ah Chee approached and sat with him.

'Chinese carriers tell me of your losses. I'm very sorry but pleased you saved Chinese and their gold from Palmerston. I think you will kill him soon.'

'Maybe you're right,' Piper said as he wiped his mouth.

'For your troubles, all food and drink here free from now on. Cannot offer Chinese girl because you are married to Chinese but can offer free Chinese massage and opium.'

Piper stood to leave. 'Thanks, Ah Chee but the food

and drink will do for the time being. Oh, perhaps a little something for deep sleep, I hear that you have such powders.'

Ah Chee smiled. 'Of course, I will have a girl give you some on your way out.'

Leaving the hotel he paused for a while as he looked at Palmer Kates. What the hell, he thought, why not, as he walked across and entered

'Kitty, you exotic wench,' he shouted as he entered.

Looking up from a conversation with the banker she smiled back. 'Can we never get rid of you,' she yelled jokingly.

'Not without a good gun. Grab a couple of good bottles and show me the way to your parlour; got something to share with you,' he said.

She was obviously excited as she took his hand and walked quickly to the parlour. 'Drinks are already there,' she said.

Once seated on the couch, Piper accepted the glass and snuffed out the candle, leaving only the dim lamp alight. 'Got some news for you. Spoke to Christie just this morning and he's due here tomorrow. He's got a little present for y'all.'

'Oh you sweet thing,' she said as she wrapped her arms around his neck and kissed him. 'And how are you?'

'Ah, fine, just fine. Be better after an hour or two with you though.'

A cheeky grin covered her face as she stood before

him, let loose her breasts and dropped her skirt. 'Oh, you mean this?'

'Well I sure didn't come here to get my damn boots repaired,' he laughed as he reached for her.

Kitty descended upon him in a flurry of gyrating hips, buttocks and huge breasts; kissing, sucking and groping like a woman possessed. Again he found him self gasping for air between her thrusting thighs and then grimacing as she went like a rat at a mooring line on his flaccid manhood, all the while trying to avoid the unpleasantness of having his nostrils jammed into the less than perfumed undercarriage of a woman that had been strutting the floor for ten hours in a humid climate.

'Whoa there,' he finally called. 'Time for another drink.'

As the panting Kitty rolled aside he got to his feet and poured them a drink. Ah Chee's powder dissolved quickly in hers before she gulped it down and dragged him back onto the bed. 'Jesus, Piper, you don't need an erection. Hell, I didn't think that orgasms like this were possible,' she said excitedly as she commenced another onslaught.

Piper was fast developing an immense dislike for the sight of female genitalia rushing at him from all directions closer than eye focus. As his thoughts moved to wishing that her toileting could be more precise, she slowly collapsed on top of him.

'You okay, Kitty?' he asked.

'Mmmm, I'm fine,' she managed. 'Must be all pleasured out.'

As gently as he could he put more distance between his nose and her rear end and rolled her over onto her back. He was sure that there had been loss of skin around his non performing member, but ignored it for the time being as he sat up and looked at the smiling Kitty, now well asleep.

Turning the lamp completely out, he took a seat in the far corner of the parlour and massaged himself for comfort, wondering if his hunch was right. It didn't take long to find out. The door creaked as it opened. A silent figure crossed the room and bent to kiss Kitty, dropping the leather sack as he did. In the dim light, Piper watched as the figure undressed and climbed onto the bed. Kitty rolled over and murmured as the softly spoken figure mounted her. Piper continued to watch on as the shadow moved rhythmically above her for a few minutes.

It was either the sound of the pistol being cocked or the simultaneous feel of its cold steel being forced between the buttock cheeks that caused the shadow to cease its movement. There was silence. After what seemed like an age, Piper spoke in his lowest voice. 'You deprived me of a ride into town, now I'm depriving you of a ride in town. You also took five percent of my friend's gold, they didn't like that and nor did I. Way I see it, Christie, I take the gold back right now or you've just bought yourself another asshole. What's it to be?'

Palmerston started to roll over but was stopped by the feel of the colt being forced almost inside his anus. 'Ahhh, for Christ's sake, be careful,' he complained.

'Just checking the target, my friend. What's it to be? The gold or a second one of them there vents?'

'Come on, Piper. Shit, you've taken this too seriously. Come on let me up and we'll talk about it.'

Piper maintained the pressure. 'Do we have a deal?'

'Yes, for Christ's sake, yes, we have a deal, now let me up!'

Piper removed the barrel from Palmerston's sweating crevice and took a pace backwards before swinging the colt barrel hard down upon his head, knocking him off the bed. To allow the swarthy Italian up would certainly have been a mistake. Piper knew that he would be like a caged lion set loose if he did. He wouldn't kill Palmerston, that was never his intent, instead he would teach him a lesson he wouldn't soon forget.

Lifting the unconscious and naked Palmerston across his shoulders he struggled the two hundred yards to the mangroves where a ships tender lay tied to the bank. After bundling Palmerston into the skiff he untied the rope and set the craft adrift to catch the outgoing flow of tide. He watched for a while as the skiff floated with the tide through the ships at anchor and out towards the Pacific before returning to Kitty's parlour.

Pouring himself a drink he sat beside Kitty's bed and looked at her, spread eagled, legs bent at the knee and spread impossibly wide, a smile on her drugged face and oblivious to Palmerston's encroachment. He knew that if Palmerston survived his boat trip he would come after him but that didn't bother him. He knew also that if Kitty ever found out she would make life as difficult as possible for him but that didn't matter either.

He finished his drink, threw the bag of gold across his shoulder and left for Argyll. The fresh well water there would clear his head. As he walked he made a mental note to wash the barrel of his revolver as well.

CHAPTER TWENTY THREE

P iper's Australian Argyll, the dream, seemed to be slipping away. As the population of Cooktown exploded, he was forced to give up good land close to town for housing. It was proving too dangerous to farm further up the river on the rich alluvial flats. Every day, stock was being rustled by natives and townsfolk who were hungry for fresh food. Stock on the goldfields fared even worse. It would require a compliment of soldiers to guard the stock and successfully farm the region.

Still, a remarkably wealthy man, Piper made a calculated decision to put farming on hold and concentrate on local business ventures. He would keep his land holdings and lease them to new arrivals and would run only a small herd on the few acres near Argyll homestead. Mei's clever and cunning business mind would benefit their business interests.

On his next visit to Brisbane to collect Mei, baby Diego and Cookie, he also purchased of one of the grand mansions near Mei's house. Both were leased to members of the Legislature while the Campbells returned to Cooktown and Argyll.

'So, what do you think?' Piper asked Mei as he showed her around the completed Argyll homestead.

'Certainly is grand,' she replied. 'It must be the best homestead in Cooktown.'

'That's a fact,' he said proudly, as he walked her and Cookie through the polished timber hallways. 'Cookie can take the small house out back and Diego can live here with us.'

Mei entered the room overlooking the township. It had been set up as an office, complete with leather chairs and polished oak desk and tables. 'I like this room. We can run our businesses from here.'

'That's the idea,' he said as he hugged her. 'Who knows, maybe farming this country was never meant to be. I know one thing, our supply wagons, trade stores and hotels will return much more than cattle would.'

Her eyes lit up. 'We have another hotel?'

'You bet; bought it last week. It'll have the best liquor and best food available in Australia, you mark my words. You know there are now better than thirty hotels here but none like ours, most of them are simple fronts for whorehouses and contraband from the East,' he said.

After settling in, they strolled to town to take in the sights. Buildings were growing out of the ground, it seemed, and what used to be dozens of pedestrians had grown to hundreds, even thousands. Ships of every kind jammed the small harbour while the upper-reaches of the river were nearly choked with Chinese junks. The sound of poorly tuned pianos bounced from each hotel door as dozens of ladies of the night squealed with either delight or discontent as they plied their trade.

Mei took it all in as they walked. 'I'm sure that you have made the right decision, Piper,' she said. 'Just about any business you could put a name to would prosper here.'

Returning back up Charlotte Street they detoured towards Chinatown. 'This is where the money is to be made,' she said to Piper. 'There are twice as many people with just as many needs here and you'll find that their products will be in demand by Europeans as well as Chinese.'

Piper nodded. 'What did you have in mind?' he asked cautiously.

'Oh, I don't know. Perhaps an import business bringing fine materials from the East, perhaps another restaurant,' she replied.

'No whorehouses?'

'Business is business, Piper, you know that. If

349

everyone wants longhorn cattle, do you run shorthorn, just because you personally don't like longhorns?'

'Big difference between cattle and whores.'

'Similar difference between rich and poor, I guess. Just a matter of which one you want,' she said. 'I see no reason to leave out the most lucrative element of business simply because we may not agree with that type of business.'

Piper was quietly spoken. 'I don't know, Mei. Can't we just leave that to Ah Chee and Kitty?'

Mei stopped, turned to Piper and gazed into his eyes. 'This is a Gold town, probably the biggest in the world at the moment. Diggers are winning thousands of ounces of gold; it's up to us to relieve them of that gold if we wish to survive this place. Now, what do diggers want?' She asked

Piper shrugged. 'More gold?'

'Well yes, but what are their needs?' She corrected. 'Once they have the gold they need food, drink and the fleeting company of a woman. Their needs come in that order of priority and that order of monetary return to the provider. We have the ability to supply all three, in fact, we probably have the ability to control all three. The other businesses are merely bits and pieces to stabilize the platform.'

Piper couldn't help being impressed with her logic and business acumen. He knew that she had the ability to topple the big players and take control, but he was bothered by the thought of her running a whorehouse again.

'Okay, you win,' he said. 'Let's go over some ideas in the morning and see what we can come up with.'

She smiled before reaching up and kissing him quickly. 'I'll see Ah Chee in the morning to get his opinion.'

He didn't answer. Why she couldn't just see him in the morning puzzled him. Why did she have to call on Ah Chee? He knew that he would need to keep a close check on what she became involved in, especially with Ah Chee. Although it worried him, he decided to put it out of his mind, for the time being at least.

In the morning they went to N'kawa's grave. Mei knelt and placed flowers on the grave while Piper looked on. As they left he noticed a tear in her eye and was pleased that her memories of his brother were fond. 'Miss him, don't you?' he said.

'Yes, I miss him,' she replied as she dabbed a handkerchief on her eyes.

After inspecting the site of their new hotel they made their way to Ah Chee's hotel and settled into the comfortable window cubicle. It wasn't long before Ah Chee invited himself to join them.

'Ah, my most honoured customers have returned,' he said as he bowed before them.

'Hello Ah Chee,' Mei greeted warmly. 'It's good to be back. I see that you have more girls than before, I hope that the meals are still good.'

Ah Chee grinned slyly. 'Meals are excellent, even though you have the best cook to yourself. Oh yes, we have more girls, they learn well here before going to the goldfields.'

Feigning surprise, Mei sought confirmation. 'Hotel on the fields, my goodness, you are spreading your wings. How many hotels are there out there now?'

'Twice as many as here in Cooktown,' he replied. 'I have plenty girls working there from a dozen hotels.'

Piper was fast developing a dislike for this man whose eyes sparkled when speaking of the girls and hotels. He knew that their working conditions would be all but intolerable, half of them would succumb to some disease or another and none of them would leave the fields with the money promised them.

Ah Chee sat beside Mei and commenced dialogue in Chinese.

'Hold on a bit there, Ah Chee,' Piper interrupted. 'Let's keep the conversation on a level where we can all say our piece, not just the two of you.'

'Ah, sorry,' Ah Chee apologized. 'Maybe Mei can teach you to speak Chinese some day.'

You arrogant little bastard, Piper thought. Leaving the table, Ah Chee again addressed Mei in Chinese before casting Piper a sly glance.

'What did he say?' Piper asked.

Mei started her meal before answering. 'He wants me to call at his Chinatown office tomorrow to go over some figures. He says that there is room for another import export agent, that's all.'

The only warmth in the atmosphere at Argyll homestead was the smiling Diego as Cookie played with him on the rug. He was growing fast and had been weaned from breast milk which meant that he spent almost all of his time in Cookie's loving care. Piper often gave silent thanks that Diego had not inherited the broad nose and typical facial features of the Merkin. His eyes, although slightly slanted seemed to somehow fit well with his fine features and coffee coloured skin. In fact, Piper thought, baby Diego would pass as the son of any of the West Indian people he'd once worked with on the ships.

Mei had told Piper that it wasn't necessary for him to keep apologising each night for his inability to consummate their marriage but he knew that she was becoming more and more disappointed. He decided against introducing the bedroom acrobatics displayed by Kitty for fear of ridicule. He had secretly spoken to Doctor Stewart who could offer little advice. Time would be the corrector was all he could come up with.

Against Piper's wishes, Mei soon set up a second office next to Ah Chee's in Chinatown, often spending all day and half the night there. Although he disagreed, Mei did seem to thrive on the long hours and was more at home there with Chinese clothing and Chinese surrounds. Any questioning of her business affairs led to heated debate followed by long periods of silence between them. Piper decided that it was far better to show an interest and compliment her, rather than question her activities, the household was happier for it.

'How's that Import/Export thing going Mei?' he ventured one evening as they sat on the verandah taking in the fresh sea breeze.

'Really good,' she answered enthusiastically. 'The Chinese duck eggs have gone much better than I thought and we've just been granted a license to export the remains of dead Chinese back to Hong Kong, that will be a very good money-spinner.'

'Don't the eggs go off on the trip?' he asked.

'Mmm, not all, some,' she replied casually.

'Are those sealed clay pots out the back Chinese remains?'

'That's right,' she replied. 'Not all dead Chinese will make it back to Hong Kong, only those with families who can afford it. The Chinese here are very pleased that we're doing that to help them and they pay well for the service.'

'You haven't entered the ladies for hire market yet then?' he asked bravely, knowing that such a question could cause an argument.

'No, actually I get along with Ah Chee's girls very well and often sit and chat with them. Most of them are nice girls and said they'd come to work at our hotel if we asked them.'

'Well, I think that we can leave that one alone, don't you think?'

'Up to you,' she replied without any commitment. 'Its cooler tonight, we'll sleep well.'

As the weeks passed, Piper noticed that more and more clay pots were being consigned from the sheds at Argyll. The imported cases of duck eggs came and went, most of them by-passing the Customs checkpoint being moved directly to Argyll from the arriving junks under the cover of darkness. Piper knew that the activity was partly illegal but decided to turn a blind eye; after all, he was a shareholder in her business activities too. As far as he was concerned, excise avoidance, although illegal, hardly rated on the list of things to avoid at all costs, in fact, he was sure that a bottle of fine scotch would suffice to avoid any unpleasantries if they were ever questioned.

Rising early one morning he went to the shed and selected two eggs. They were unusually heavy. Turning to leave, he bumped his elbow on an urn, causing him to drop one of the eggs. Cursing, he bent to scoop up the egg but instead found black treacle oozing from the cracked ceramic shell.

'Bastard!' he hissed. 'Bastard, bastard, bastard!'

Words failed him as he watched the raw opium spread across the floor. Selecting another egg he marched back inside and met Cookie in the kitchen. 'There you go Cookie, boil these up for breakfast, reckon Mei will have one with me.'

'Okay,' she smiled, taking the eggs to the saucepan.

Mei was nursing Diego at the table when Cookie arrived with the boiled eggs and fresh-baked bread.

'Aha, this looks mighty fine, let's see what them Chinese ducks have done for us,' Piper said as he took one of the hot eggs.

Mei almost dropped Diego as she quickly passed him to a confused Cookie. 'No, don't eat the duck eggs, those ones in the shed have gone off, they have to be thrown away,' she said urgently, almost grabbing the egg from Piper's hand.

'Nah, they're fine,' Piper said, retrieving the egg and slicing the top off with his knife before she could stop him.

Hot opium poured from the ceramic container as Piper dropped it onto his plate. Cookie rattled something in Chinese and rushed Diego from the dining room. Piper took the other egg and smashed it open on Mei's plate. 'Look a little pale, my dear. Feeling alright today?' he asked sarcastically.

Mei buried her face in her hands for a moment before answering. 'Alright, its opium, very expensive opium but it's needed here by the Chinese.'

'It's also very illegal opium that could land us both in jail, Mei,' he said angrily. 'The clay urns, what about them, what little secret do they hide?'

'They hold the remains of Chinese and just a small amount of gold,' she answered defiantly.

'I knew it,' Piper exploded. 'Soon as that damned Ah Chee became involved you'd be dealing in contraband and flesh. Well that's it, Mei, get some coolies up here and get that shit off Argyll, right now!'

Mei leapt to her feet and glared at the fuming Piper across the table. 'Alright,' she spat. 'Alright, I'll do just that but I'll warn you now, if I can't have a free reign up here then I'll have it down there in Chinatown. You want me to work down there? Fine, that's what I'll do.'

'Go ahead, go on and get down there. See if I care,' Piper replied. 'Hell, you spend most of your time there anyway.'

'Well now I wonder why?' Mei said cruelly as she stormed from the room.

By the evening, all Chinese crates and urns had been transported to Chinatown. Piper was bitterly disappointed and enraged by Mei's involvement in smuggling. After checking on Cookie and Diego, he walked briskly to town and entered Palmer Kates. Kitty sauntered across the floor and pulled up a chair beside him. 'I hear Christie is back in town,' she said with a raised eyebrow.

'No, I hadn't heard that. Who cares, get me a bottle of that good Brandy you have stashed out back.'

'He tells me that he went sailing a while ago.' She added.

'Sailing and fishing; honourable pastimes, now how about that drink?'

'Sure,' Kitty answered with a cool look.

After a few shots of brandy his temper eased somewhat, enough for him to cross the street to Ah Chee's hotel and straight to the rear office where Ah Chee sat counting money.

'Ah, Piper, you surprised me. Though you might be a thief,' he laughed.

'Only one thief in this room my friend and I'm lookin' square at it. Where's Mei?' he demanded in an even voice.

'Oh, she's probably at Chinatown office.' Ah Chee replied as he bundled the money into a drawer.

'Reckon I only need to say this once. You or any of your crooked dealers get her tied up with contraband again and I will personally shoot the lot of you,' he said.

Ah Chee's face turned serious as he stood to face Piper. 'I only need say this one time as well. The contraband you speak of was Mei's dealing, not other Chinese, other Chinese not happy about Mei taking such a large share in the market but she has money to back her. Mei also cause much anger in Chinatown for paying Chinese whores too much money, other Chinese cannot compete and forced to sell best girls to Mei Ling. So, you not know all facts.'

'She's running whores again?' Piper asked.

'Of course, best whores and traded only to very high paying client, no digger or Chinese can afford. She even get Christie Palmerston to cross the street,' he replied.

'What? She's pimping for Palmerston? You sure about that?' Piper asked. 'The only good Chinese to Palmerston is a dead one.'

Ah Chee resumed his chair. 'Why I lie to you? As we speak, Palmerston is busy upstairs with Mei's girls. He only come to town after dark to avoid arrest and the only one who can always afford best girls.'

'You dumb son-of-a-Chinese-bitch; the gold he pays with comes from dead Chinese coolies!'

'Ah, so, but only way Chinese can recover gold, yes?'

Piper shook his head in disbelief. 'Damn, is there nothing you celestials won't do for money? You don't care, do you? As long as there's a quick buck in it for you. That's where Mei gets it, it's in her damn breeding,' he yelled angrily.

'Perhaps you should go to China and see why wealth is so important,' Ah Chee offered sincerely.

'Bullshit, I'm goin' up them damn stairs to find Mei,' Piper said as he stormed from the office, across the hotel floor towards the stairs.

Brushing the stairway minder aside he bounded up the stairs, ignoring the Chinese shouts behind him. Bursting into a room he disturbed his banker and a Chinese girl. Excusing himself he turned to the opposite door. The grinning face of Ah Chee presented itself before him. 'Mr. Campbell, the door at the end of the hallway, that's the one you want,' he said.

Reaching the door he flung it open to find Christie Palmerston sitting in a chair, a pistol levelled at Piper's chest.

'Please, come and join me,' Palmerston offered cordially. 'You certainly do make a ruckus when you come visiting. Oh, you don't mind if I play with this pistol for a while do you?'

Dumbfounded, Piper walked slowly into the room, closing the door behind him. Mei slowly rolled some towels as she glanced nervously at the two men facing each other. Palmerston, dressed only in a flowing Chinese silk gown, stood slowly and motioned for Piper to sit in the chair by the bed, which had obviously been used recently.

'Mei, be a sweetie and fetch my friend a drink, would you,' Palmerston called.

Piper's blood boiled as he moved his stare to Mei. 'So this is what it's come to. Not only are you pimping, you're screwing the clients yourself.'

'Not true, old man,' Palmerston said. 'This dear lady has friends in very appropriate places, out at sea for example. You see, after you so rudely cracked my skull, after I had agreed to ease off the Chinese I might add, her friends rescued me from the reef. Not only have I eased off killing the little chaps, I'm totally indebted to them, so when the highest class Chinese lady in Australia offers to ease my aches and pains with a superb Chinese massage, well, who am I to refuse?'

Mei moved to leave the room but was halted by Piper's voice. 'Stay here,' he demanded.

'I need to check on the girls, you stay here if you like,' she replied defiantly and left the room.

Palmerston was obviously enjoying his evening. 'Now then, I won't be as rude as you were because I now know that the barrel of a pistol being shoved up one's arse is most uncomfortable. I'm prepared to let the past remain there and stay on friendly terms with you, and your business partner, of course. In return for my generosity, I would expect that you would at least pass that bottle of Brandy and share it with me. Think about it, we can fight until one of us is dead, or we can enjoy what life has to offer in a civilised way.'

Piper walked to the table, poured two brandies and crossed the floor, handing one to Palmerston, who still held the pistol trained on Piper's chest. Returning to his chair, Piper froze as Palmerston raised the pistol, drew the hammer back and squeezed the trigger. The metallic sound of the hammer landing on an empty chamber echoed around the room, again, again and again as Palmerston laughed.

'Had no intention of shooting you my good man,' he finally managed. 'You see, we're business partners now, hell, I'm invited to Argyll this Sunday for dinner. Get used to the idea, Piper, now drink up, and let's talk about old times.'

Piper felt completely gutted as he sat there staring at the smiling Palmerston. Declining a second drink he departed the hotel and walked slowly home. He passed up an offer by the sad-faced Cookie for a late supper and sat on the verandah, alone in the dark, not bothering to swat the mosquitoes that swarmed his face and neck. His anger had been overtaken by total depression and despair.

What did he have? Wealth, position and community standing. He also had a beautiful Chinese wife, but she was whoring in town. He had a child by default, a black bastard created by rape, and he had Argyll. Really, he thought, what did he have really? The only thing that couldn't be taken from him were memories. Memories of growing up during the wild times of East Texas; memories of a fine family and memories of his adopted brother and companion N'kawa. None of that could be taken and he would trade everything he now owned to have those times back.

In the morning, it was clear that Mei had not returned to Argyll. Piper took breakfast alone before visiting Doctor Stewart. Diego developed a rash on his stomach and Cookie was concerned. It was clear that she loved the baby as her own and panicked whenever the slightest problem arose. She reminded Piper of Black Abraham's wife who had nurtured him through his childhood.

Piper insisted that he carry young Diego into the Doctors room. For the first time he felt comfortable with this little bundle that looked up at him with a smile as his tiny hand gripped his finger.

'Mr. Campbell,' the Doctor greeted. 'How can I help you today?'

After Cookie had explained the symptoms and displayed the rash, Doctor Stewart dismissed the complaint as very minor and prescribed a small amount of lotion to ease the itching. Cookie quickly beamed a smile, snatched baby Diego off the table and rushed off towards Argyll leaving Piper with the Doctor.

'You're lucky to have a nanny of that calibre,' Doctor Stewart said to Piper. 'I never met the wee child's father but from all accounts he's a dead ringer. It's a wonderful thing you've done by accepting him as your own.'

'Pardon?' Piper asked.

Doctor Stewart looked over his spectacles. 'You know, electing to bring someone else's child up as your own.'

'His father was a Merkin who raped Mei in a cave on the trail through the gate,' Piper said resolutely.

'Oh dear me,' the Doctor sighed as he leaned back in the chair. 'You don't know, do you?'

'Know what for Christ's sake?'

'When Mei arrived here after the attack, she was already well pregnant. The Merkin has no claim to that child, son,' he explained.

Piper was getting accustomed to falling through holes in his life at this stage. 'So, what you're saying is that Mei was pregnant before we left Palmerville. Is that what you're saying?'

'Yes, that's exactly what I'm saying. The child's father is your late step brother.'

Feeling a little weak, Piper took advantage of the couch as he fought to clear his mind. 'So baby Diego is the son of N'kawa. Now it all makes sense. The flowers on his grave, the necklace, the naming of the child and how Cookie knew to go to Brisbane … yes, it all makes sense now,' he mumbled.

'And your problem?' asked Doctor Stewart.

'Ah, well yeah, my problem,' Piper said as he stood to leave. 'I don't know; reckon I just solved my problems.'

Walking back to Argyll seemed to be taking too long so Piper broke into a jog. Bursting through the door he called to Cookie, who shuffled into the hall, a worried look etched into her face. Passing her, he entered Diego's room and lifted him from the cot. 'Didn't look like no damn Merkin. Come on little Diego, got something to show you,' he said, as he walked to the bedroom and took N'kawa's necklace from Mei's bedside drawer.

'This is yours, Diego. It belonged to your pa, my brother and the best damn friend I ever had; bit sneaky, but the best,' he laughed.

A concerned Cookie trotted behind as Piper strode with Diego in his arms to the cemetery. Kneeling beside the headstone he again chatted to the babe. 'Now I know you ain't up to readin' yet, Diego, but this here tells of your pa, the last of the Karankawa.'

Cookie wept openly as she knelt beside them. 'So sorry, Mr. Campbell, so sorry I cannot tell. What you do now? Please don't take baby from me,' she pleaded.

Piper reached his arm across to her and drew her close. Her gentle hand reached for baby Diego's forehead and lightly stroked it. She smiled through her tears as Diego smiled his recognition and love for this caring human he had bonded with almost since birth.

Control threatened to desert Piper as he sat there cradling Diego in one arm, the other arm on N'kawa's headstone. Cookie gently caressed his back before taking Diego from him. Pent up emotions poured from him as he sobbed until he could sob no more, all the while aware of the tiny fingers that gripped his thumb.

'Cookie,' he finally said, clearing his throat, 'I've got something else to show Diego, but I need your help.'

'I help,' she replied weakly.

'It will mean making the choice between your people and baby Diego. It will mean leaving your people. Are you willing to do that?' he asked.

'But why?' she replied.

'Because there is something else that Diego needs to see, and I intend showin' it to him. Hell, I don't know what this wee fella is to me, son or nephew but I do know one thing, he don't belong here and I know that if N'kawa had known that Mei was carrying his child I would have been told, and I know where the child would be right now. Don't you see, Cookie, this little chap here, Diego Campbell, is now the last of the Karankawa.'

The trade winds dictated a night's sailing which suited Piper just fine. The first class accommodation had improved somewhat since he was last aboard an ocean going clipper. Cookie gently rocked Diego to sleep. She could not bring herself to go on deck to watch the lights of Cooktown disappear. Piper left his cabin and went next door to check on Cookie and Diego. The sweet innocent face of the sleeping babe made him feel better than he'd felt for months. As the ship rolled slightly, filled her sails and headed towards the open seas. Piper comforted Cookie as the gentle, rolling motion of the clipper rocked the sleeping babe in his makeshift crib.

'I'll be up on deck,' he whispered to Cookie. 'Anything I can get you?'

'No,' she replied, shaking her head gently.

The cool night breeze combed his flowing hair as he stood motionless and alone on the foredeck, gazing to the heavens. He was not seeking answers, nor was he about to question himself about his actions. Weeks at sea lay ahead, an abundance of time for reflection and planning. But for now he would let the immediate past slide away behind him like so much foam in the ships wake, his concentration had to remain focused on the undisturbed water that lay ahead … the future. If he were to pray, that prayer would be for the peace of his family, especially N'kawa. He would pray for an end to genocide; he would pray that baby Diego would never witness those horrors; he would pray for forgiveness.

The great southern land had offered so much, but taken so much. Those who remained, the diggers, settlers, Chinese and soldiers would continue their expansion into the wilderness. The stakes would remain high, especially for the fearless Merkin, who would attempt to halt the expansion.

For Piper, uncertainty lay ahead. What had become of his father's Argyll in Texas? He would return there, but only briefly. His future lay further north, perhaps even outside his beloved Texas. Although his wealth would allow the setting up of another cattle ranch, he felt sure that his future lay in other pursuits, yet unknown.

Almost unconsciously, he fingered the beads around his neck. It was if the spirit of N'kawa was with him, guiding him in his thoughts. Piper felt sure that whatever lay ahead had already been mapped out by his unseen but ever present brother, N'kawa.

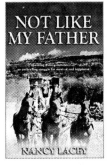

Best-selling titles by Kerry B. Collison

Readers are invited to visit our publishing websites at:
http://www.sidharta.com.au
http://www.publisher-guidelines.com/
http://temple-house.com/

Kerry B. Collison's home pages:
http://www.authorsden.com/visit/author.asp?AuthorID=2239
http://www.expat.or.id/sponsors/collison.html
http://clubs.yahoo.com/clubs/asianintelligencesresources
email: author@sidharta.com.au

Printed in the United States
116633LV00003B/9/A

9 781921 030437